Silent

MW01110384

Silent Blue Tears

Nancy Truax

Milo House Press
New York, New York

Cover by: Kim Schum
Manuscript Assistant: John Beanblossom

Printed in the United States of America

Author's Note

The events in this book represent my view of a woman's twenty year career in a police department as she struggles against an abusive marriage. I have taken creative license with some events and have changed most names for reasons too numerous to mention. Where newspaper articles appear, I have changed the names in the article to match the actors in the story. Those names are italicized.

My blessings to all who pass by these pages. My prayer is that you learn from what you're about to read.

The Soldier

Fear stands guard at his designated Post,
As a well trained Soldier,
Protecting his Host.
His uniform, pressed and gray,
Highlights shinny medals,
So evenly upon his heart they lay.
These polished awards pinned to his Soul,
Paint his inner being
With colors as dark as coal.
These medals he wishes he had never received;
But now they're attached,
Like new-born they cleave.
They suckle from him all nourishment they need,
And leave his craft empty,
He can't even bleed.
So now this fine Soldier assigned to this Post,
Has grown tired and worn,
Nothing left to boast.

Nancy J. Truax

Her Life

Flickering images of that little girl standing in the
direct heat of the southwestern sun: soft brown fly-away
hair; a thrifty blue dress with white ricketing at the
bodice and hem, gathered at the waist and tied with a bow
in the back, its tail and her hair blowing in the warm
breeze, her feet brown with the play-dirt though sandals adorn
them. A mother's constant battle for tidiness. The wind
whispers the secrets of growing up, and she glows with
anticipation.

The woman fingers pink swelling on her arms and looks
bleakly at the desolation within her spirit-house. Now she
replays the heartbreaking scenes of her cold marriage.
Looking down she sees her feet are now brown from walking
in the filth of anger, and her blue dress is torn at the
bodice from the tight grip of relentless torment. But, the
wind.....

Life. Now she must adorn herself with the robe of White
Peace. After all...she's still surrounded by the
ceaseless beauties of the
earth.

Nancy J. Truax

Chapter 1

Dragon Slaying

Since I can remember, I've had a sense of adventure and risk that made me want to be part of a gigantic universe that cried out to Me, and I to it. It was all there for me - if I could just find it, experience it, test it, try it on and fit into it. Everything, everything was there for Me. Oh, it was there for others too, but I had a sense of belonging to it, and it to me. So natural was this feeling, that I assumed, without consciously thinking it, that everyone felt this way. Everyone knew they, as I , could share in whatever wonder, whatever action, whatever feeling existed, and then discard it if it didn't fit, or maximize it to our greatest pleasure, if it did. I was here to experience the world; I was here to swing as high as the swing set would let me, and bravely jump from my seat, at the highest point I dared.

There was nothing to limit me, except the limits I set. No fear could get in my way because, I learned early-on, how to fight my fears, how to counteract them. I was an optimistic, survivalist from day one. Most days it worked, but there were some days when this worked against me.

Four. Four seems to have been a year of curiosity for me. I wanted to try everything on. There was the time I came home from a treasure hunt in the woods bearing a nest of red fire ants all over my belly. Or the time I just had to know how it felt to be a piece of clothing going through the wringer of a 1960 washing machine. I stuck my left hand in the wringer and felt the rollers slide along my arm. It felt really cool until the rollers got stuck at my elbow, but continued to turn. I still bear the scar on my arm from that friction burn. Or the time I found it absolutely necessary to hang by my fingertips from a third-floor balcony, with nothing but cement below me. My mother found and rescued me, yet, I was not scared. Or the time I planned to sneak up on my brother and Ronny Belle, who were playing baseball in our yard. They didn't see me hiding behind a tree. When I stuck my head out to scare them, I was hit smack-dab in the face with a baseball traveling with the momentum supplied by the energy of a rugged, six year old boy. My whole face was bruised for a very long time. I do remember being too scared to look at myself in the mirror. Maybe that was a foreshadowing of my adult years. As I write this book, I am just now realizing the nakedness of this statement. True reflection is difficult since it reveals the real person. Truth makes one vulnerable, and it can be nasty. But that's okay, I guess, if you learn from it. That's what I think anyway.

On the very morning of my fourth birthday I awoke before the rest of my family. I couldn't wait to see what they got me for presents. My tummy was doing the "whoop" of a sudden-death roller coaster ride, as I envisioned the go-cart I hoped to get. Although my mom never gave big parties, or anything like that, she always made the day special. One Dowhan tradition was that the birthday person got to choose what to have for supper. We could go out to eat, if we wanted, or choose a special meal that Mom would cook. I laugh now when I remember choosing McDonalds, and how I thought it was so keen to eat there on my birthday. Big Mac, fries, and a shake!! Today was my day, and I was up early to meet the sun and all it could bring me.

I lazily shuffled into the living room where I turned on the black and white console t.v. that sat angled in the far corner. As my little fingers pulled the t.v. knob outward, my eyes, rather than focusing on the t.v. screen, focused on a bumpy, green, wine bottle sitting atop the television. My hand went directly from the knob to the neck of the green bottle. This was something that my parents usually kept in a 'high-up' place so that we couldn't reach it or get into it. I didn't really know what it was, but I did know that when they drank it they always had fun. It was a deep, see-through red, and looked like raspberry Kool-Aid. Knowing that this bottle was totally off limits, I unscrewed the cap with my left hand. I placed the black screw-cap on top of the black and white television console, and looked behind me, first to my left, then to my right, to see if I had been caught. I hadn't done anything yet, but I was gonna. No one around. No one had heard me. With my right hand still around the neck of the bottle, I put my left hand beneath the heavy craft for support, lifted the opening to my mouth and slowly tipped it, allowing one small gulp of the magical potion to fall onto my tongue and travel to the back of my throat. I gently replaced the bottle, and again looked behind me in either direction to see if I had been caught.

Once I had assured my safety, I allowed the mysterious flavors to register with my body. The drink tasted much different than anything I had tasted before and it made a kind of hot, fiery feeling on all the inside places it touched. I took a deep breath in and out and could feel the warm feeling as the air passed in either direction through my body. This is what a dragon must feel like!

I imagined I was a dragon breathing fire and protecting myself against the lovely maiden trying to conquer my cave by slaying me with her royal army. As I breathed in and out, I looked over each shoulder again. Seeing no one, and realizing the maiden was soon to be on her way, I squeezed between the t.v. and the wall, and crouched in the very corner that the television protected. This was MY dragon cave! I had to protect it against attack. I squatted down behind the t.v. so that no one would know that I was there. A few minutes passed and I slowly lifted my head so that my eyes were just above the top of the television. No maiden yet; I was still safe. I felt I had just enough time to reenergize my fires. I stood behind the t.v. and again brought the magic fire-mixture to my lips, and this time, took an even bigger gulp. I again breathed deeply in and out, this time throwing fire from my mouth and my nostrils. I quickly ducked and squatted down to avoid being seen by my foe.

I had to tip the bottle again and again in order to maintain my fires, and assure protection of my cave.

I thought that I heard the fair maiden turn the corner. She had with her at least a hundred armored soldiers prepared for battle. Every soldier had his own horse, and they carried the fair maiden in a white ornate carriage sitting atop some long poles. As they trampled toward me in unison, I stood up from within my cave, and breathed heavy fire on them. I had saved my life by burning them with my nostril fires.

Bodies strewn all about me, I celebrated with another gulp of my magical brew. I ducked into my cave and, as most dragons do, giggled uncontrollably at my huge victory. I had conquered the enemy and could now live safely for another hundred years in my wonderful, dark, cozy cave.

Ohh! Drat!! I spoke too soon. Again, footsteps. Footsteps and hoofsteps. Another army was coming! I must protect myself yet again, and perhaps after this I could be safe from peril for another 200 years. I bravely stood to face my enemy and quickly wrapped my heavy, long tail in front of me, to give me balance. Somehow, I was beginning to tip.

"Humph!" I breathed in enough air to make a good wind storm and hastily shot fire from my nostrils, mouth, and even my eyes. As I exhaled, I made a loud hissing sound, that sounded like a feral cat. Vanquish the enemy, I thought. Make them succumb. I will not be taken alive!!

This enemy was not as easy to destroy. They stood in front of me, I believe a bit weaker, yet not defeated. I breathed deeply in again, and this time with all my might, breathed hoards of fire in their direction, while at the same time hissing and screeching with all my might. Us dragons have an image to uphold. Exhausted, I collapsed into my cave expecting glorious death for my enemy. Ho, ho, ho, I thought. They will NEVER get me.

I heard another scurrying sound and jerked my head upward, quickly. It was enough to give a normal dragon whip lash, but I was the fiercest dragon. There would be no whiplash for me.

As I looked up, I suddenly realized that my latest enemy had been Mom and Dad. They gazed down at me with an expression

that suggested they thought I had gone mad. They were completely
perplexed as to why I was screaming like a cat, ducking behind the
t.v., and giggling uncontrollably. I smiled shyly as, at that point, I
couldn't exactly remember that I had ever acted this way! I stood
holding the neck of the bottle in my right hand (as I had intended to
have another victory gulp) and timidly raised it into view. Their
mouths dropped open in disbelief. Mom and Dad are very smart
people, but it didn't take a lot of brain power to figure out that I was
drunk.

My mom picked me up gently, carried me into the bathroom, cleaned
me up, and promptly put me back to bed....for the rest of the day!
My birthday had started on a high note, and ended on a very low,
low (hangover) note. Late in the day Ronny Belle came over to
see if I could play, and my mother had to tell him I was sick. I heard
him at the door and, screaming from my bed, tried to insist that I was
okay. I guess the yelling gave me a headache because I laid back
down and went to sleep. My parents never again left their wine out
where little hands could reach and make it part of *their* day, and part
of *their* fun.

Chapter 2

Dogs, Shirts, and Little Girls

The "shoulds" of appropriate femininity eluded me almost from birth. Perhaps the Gods of structure and social lines forgot to pay me a visit at conception, or maybe I was too busy experiencing *whatever* to listen or notice. Those things just weren't important to me. Better said, I didn't even realize these rules existed and when mom tried to teach them to me, I resisted, with all my might. Life was to be lived in whichever way or ways Joy could flourish, and then bounce out of me onto others.

My first struggle with feminine societal mores came at the age of four. I sat low in the front passenger seat of our old Chevy sedan with the blue and white plaid, vinyl seats. My little pug nose reached to about the bottom of the bright red steering wheel. I could only see out through the windshield if I looked straight up to the cloudless SanDiego sky.

"Mom, can I take my shirt off?"

"No honey"

"Why?" This was the first time she'd ever told me 'NO' to that question, and I thought for sure she'd made a mistake or I'd heard her wrong.

"Because" she responded absently, in a sing-song kind of way, as if that was enough and that's all I needed to know (and parents wonder why kids always answer 'cuz', as though that's all *they* need to say).

"But why?" I pleaded. "It's hot."

"Girls shouldn't take their shirt off."

"I always take my shirt off. Ronny Belle and Jimmy have their shirts off. See?"

"But they're boys."

"So. Fritzie never has to wear a shirt. She never has to wear any clothes."

Fritzi was our dog, a Doberman pincer. She had a silky black coat of short bristly hair and the sweetest disposition ever. I loved her so much that when I was about 7 or 8, I pretended to marry her in an elaborate wedding ceremony, in the basement of our house. Other times I would pretend that she was my lover and I had invited her to my house for dinner. I would set a beautiful table that consisted of a sheet, spread out on the basement floor, adorned with candles, flowers, and dishes. After carefully lighting the candles (I wasn't supposed to play with matches) I gave Fritzi her own dog dish, filled with some dry, Gravy Train, dog food and then placed my own china plate from mom's special hiding place, also filled with Gravy Train, opposite hers. We crunched our food in unison, Fritzi's beautiful brown eyes thanking me between chomps.

One day, Ronny Bell caught me eating the dog food, right out of the bag, and he told me I was gonna die cuz it was poisonous. I didn't believe him because I'd eaten it so many times before. I was cool-hand-Luke under the pressure of a serious tease. I was able to turn the tables and convince Ronny that he was missing out on a delicacy that most big people hadn't discovered. He timidly tried it, but being convinced that it was for dogs only, promptly spit it out.

"Fritzi is a dog, and dogs aren't supposed to wear clothes," she finally said.

Frustrated at having been told no, on top of not understanding what she was getting at, I said, "I'm a *person* though, and hot persons shouldn't wear shirts. I'm hot."

She looked at me with a glint of sadness, as though she knew the day would come that I would be forced to conform, and wished it didn't have to happen so soon.

"Okay," she said "go on, go play" and we smiled big at each other, as I expertly lifted my striped T over my dirty face and flung it in my mom's direction. Off I went.

I sprang out of the car and ran to where my brother, Jimmy, and our friend Ronny Belle were riding their bikes. At that moment I felt the youthful joy of total freedom, and was unaware that I had nearly been caught by a convention, yet to come.

Three years later, after a move to New England, I repeatedly found myself in trouble because of my lack of conformity. There was, however, one incident in particular that made me realize I was different than the others, and because of this, was considered by most to be 'inappropriately unique', whatever that means. Well, Mrs. Dempster thought so, anyway. She was my third grade teacher. I remember that she had lots of silvery, white, hair that she piled high, on top of her head. It was like the bee hive style except that rather than coifing the bun to the back of her head, she piled it right on top, like a tower. Sometimes she would place a shiny barrette in it, just above the middle of her forehead. It served no purpose really; just a decoration, I guess. Her face blended right into her hair because she didn't wear any make-up, and she had a pasty gray complexion, like she was sick or something.

I could tell she didn't like me too much because one day, I frantically raised my hand, and waved it wildly back and forth because I had to go to the bathroom. She told me that I had to wait, and she somehow seemed annoyed that I had asked. When I suddenly leaned to my left and threw up on the floor, she realized her mistake and said, "You should have told me you felt sick. Go, go to the bathroom. I'll have to get the janitor." She said this to me as if it were my fault I threw up on the floor.

Anyway, one night, my Mom returned from a parent-teacher conference with Mrs. Dempster to tell me that we needed to have a mother-daughter talk. This couldn't be good, I thought to myself; but I couldn't think of anything I might have done wrong that Mrs. Dempster should have to report to my mother. Mom took my hand and walked with me upstairs to my bedroom where we sat down on my bed. My bed was covered with a soft, multi-pastel-colored wool blanket and lots and lots of stuffed animals. Every night, before I went to bed, I had to take all the animals off so that I had room to sleep on it. We joined the animals, my mom beside me with her hand softly laying on my lap. I've always loved the way my Mom enhances a spiritual connection with the physical touch. It's always given me a full-up feeling inside, and taught me that in order to have a true and lasting relationship of any kind, you really can't have one without the other. With her hand on my lap and her loving eyes caressing mine, we were joined.

"Honey," she said, "Mrs. Dempster feels that you are too much of a tom-boy. She watches you rough housing on the playground with the boys, and doesn't feel that it's right for a little girl to behave that way. She's seen you play pig-pile with the boys and seen you come out for recess and immediately begin a game of chase with them. She's also seen you grab onto them and throw them onto the ground and she's concerned because you're not acting like a lady."

Again, like the time when I was four, and my mom wouldn't let me take my shirt off, I was utterly confused. This could only be the words of a person who didn't understand me, or who wanted to get me in trouble. I was crushed and hurt that my very own teacher would take something that was playful and fun to me, and turn it into something bad, or wrong. I just did not understand.

"But, Mom," I said, "It's a game! We were all just playing. And besides, I can run faster than them."

"But honey, Mrs. Dempster doesn't agree with you. She thinks you should behave more like a little girl. Like a lady."

"But, Mom. Boys play those games. Why can't I play those games? It's more fun than the games the girls play, like bouncing the ball back and forth and stuff. Sometimes all the girls do is talk."

"Honey," she said, "I love you, and I think I understand how you feel. But you must try to see it your teacher's way. Mrs. Dempster sees you, a beautiful little girl, playing chase games with the boys, and it makes you appear too rugged, like you are a boy. Please, honey. I know you don't understand, but, please do as I ask. Don't be so wild on the playground. Okay? Please tell me okay."

I looked down at my toes and saw my tears dripping onto the top of my feet, and made that promise to my mother by just kind of shaking my shoulders up and down. I couldn't say the word. It was just too horrible. Why should I get in trouble for acting the same way other kids acted? When my mother left the room I slouched on my bed and cried. I cried because Mrs. Dempster had rejected the essence of *me* just because I wanted to play like the other kids. How could I ever face her again? How could I ever go back to school knowing the bad things she had said about me to my mom? I cried some more, and I never forgot.

How, you ask, does a spunky little girl with this deep desire to touch and feel everything good, find herself at forty, taking Prozac for depression, and welbutrin for anxiety? That is part of what this story is about. Did it need to happen? Could it have been avoided? Most would say no, but being the positive-thinker that I am, I say yes. My condition is the result of a blind society. It is blind by it's own choosing, but doesn't even realize it. Let me explain. I believe society doesn't realize that it's blind; it thinks it is seeing, seeing clearly at that. Neither does society realize that it has chosen this illusion, because it is incapable of brutally, honest, self-evaluation.

Most of us walk through life with nary a thought about fitting-in, so, there's not too much to consider. Those who don't fit, struggle against this rigid, precast mold their whole lives. Society tries to melt these "miss-fits" down so that they can be re-poured, re-shaped, and re-cast. You see, it's too expensive, time consuming, and exhausting for a whole society to change. It's easier to keep the rules the same, and make individuals conform, than to alter a societal philosophy and way of life.

Society is right about one thing, though. We all need to grow up. When I turned ten, I didn't want to take my shirt off or eat dog food anymore. By the time I turned eighteen, with college plans in place, I knew I was going to be a police officer. I wanted to represent a strain of society that was different, and show the world that it's okay to stand-out, to be *appropriately* unique.

I plunged into my future a young, strong, competent and self assured woman. As I slowly exit the filmy passage of that police era, and begin a new journey, emptied of my youth and strength, and knowing that society has questioned my competency to the point of robbing me of my self-assurance, I think of others like me, and hope they, too, have the courage to stand up to their future, as well as their convictions.

Chapter 3

On the Job

Some days were good, some days were bad. For the first ten years or so, I thought I was having mostly good days. It wasn't until years later that I realized my peers and coworkers didn't have the same opinion. I was delusional. No, I was still the optimist who had become delusional. How I had been blind to it, I don't know. But I was. I think I was mentally focused on just getting through each work day; proving to each and every police officer that I belonged and I could handle not only the job, but whatever nonsense they threw in my direction. I honestly believed that there would be a definitive point in time when I would be· officially declared good enough to be part of the team. I would be able to physically mark that day on my calendar. Instead I learned that they were only allowing me to play the game, albeit reluctantly, and I would never be part of the team. Never. Even after eighteen years of hard work and dedication I wasn't considered part of the team. I had hit my glass ceiling. As Detective Jen Sives said, "You mean to tell me that you can work your ass off, give them everything you have, and they still won't promote you?" I had given her a tearful affirmation and hoped she would leave my office. I needed to be alone. At that moment, I felt like digging a hole, crumpling myself into a round ball, and crawling in. It would be okay if someone came along and shoveled dirt on top of me. I was humiliated and embarrassed that I had believed in them, that I had believed in myself. I thought that they respected me, even admired me for the stamina I obviously had.

It wasn't until August 11, 1998 that I realized that they couldn't even *see* the difficulties I had met, withstood, and overcome during my career. But I've gotten ahead of myself here. Let's go back.

In the spring of 1981 I nervously looked forward, staring out a dirty window, surrounded with black bars, while some old guy pulled and twisted my fingers, clumsily pressed them into the black ink, and then rolled them, one at a time, onto the official police fingerprint card. It's standard procedure to fingerprint all prospective police officers, and I was used to it at this point. I had already applied and tested at a variety of New England police agencies, and Portsmouth, New Hampshire Police Department was just another stop along the way.

"What would make you want to do this anyway?", the old

guy boomed at me. I thought it was a rather odd question since it was 1981, and women were allowed to vote. It seemed more of a judgment, than a question, but I let the feeling go.

"It's just something I've always wanted to do," I explained. I shrugged my shoulders hoping that that would suffice.

"You're kind of small, aren't you?" he asked.

"Yes I am," I responded. I had been quite proud of the fact that I was small (in height anyway...we won't discuss my weight) but sturdy. Capable, I felt, of handling most dicey situations, and eager to test my conviction.

That was all he said to me. He didn't seem impressed with my answers, but I was sure that everyone, once they got to know me, would come around to my way of thinking. I didn't realize that I was about to enter another dimension of the Twilight Zone; I suppose part of it's magic was that 'The Zone' kept me blinded to it's existence for about eighteen years. Or, perhaps it was I who refused to see what was right in front of me; I refused to openly recognize that I was being treated like shit. More appropriately, I should say that I was at the bottom of the pecking order my entire career, no matter how much seniority or rank I gained; but, on those bad days, when I could acknowledge my "ranking", I believed I could "fix" that problem by adhering to the Protestant work ethic. I can't really explain myself except to say that I don't think that there was any thought or understanding on my part that I had entered a culture that vehemently did not want me; well, not *me* per se. If I had a penis it would have been just fine, but I didn't; and I didn't know enough to go buy one. When I look back on how naive I was, I feel so inapt. Oh well, such is life.

The rest of the testing process was like all the others. I had already taken the written test and scored an 89%. This was not great by my standards, but considering the fact that I was still completing my bachelors degree, and juggling two or three part time jobs, I was okay with it. The physical agility test included a simple mile and a half run, some stretching and jumping. No big deal at all.

The polygraph test was something else altogether! Lest you think I am a puritan, I must tell you that Lt. Winters asked me some questions I didn't exactly feel comfortable answering. Oh sure, I could answer most questions without hesitation or explanation; have you ever had sex with an animal?, or do you see things in the dark others don't see?, or even have you ever had sex with another woman? I was quite confident with those responses (no, no, and no, in case you were wondering); but then he had to ask me that damnable drug question.

If you've never been polygraphed before, it's quite an intimidating process, especially if you have something to feel guilty about. First there's the attitude of the examiner. They're usually somewhat stiff so as to appear rigid, pure, and confrontational. This is so that the person being questioned is put a bit on edge before the questions even begin. Well, let's just say that Lt. Winters did his job. The antiquated machine is enough to remind you of the Frankenstein movie wherein the mad scientist tries to bring a monster to life. I sat on a hard black chair and was ordered to keep my feet flat on the floor, stare straight ahead at the dirty wall in front of me, and respond to each question with a simple 'yes' or 'no'. I was told to remain perfectly still, as any unofficial movement could nullify the test, or create a false negative (whatever that is). Wrapped around my body and attached to the machine was a coiled wire that would measure some unknown body function (I never did learn this particular science) and a tweezer-like metal thing was clipped to one of my fingertips and hooked into the machine. The clip reminded me of a roach clip. "Have you ever done drugs?" the Lt. asked.

"No," I responded, with my rear pushed to the back of the chair, feet flat on the floor, eyes straight ahead staring at the filthy wall. Inside my body was screaming "YES! Of course you've tried some drugs. You're lying. Tell him now, tell him now".

When we were finished, Winters had me take a seat in the hallway while he reviewed the examination results. The hallway was tinny and dim, the chair made of wood by the Shaker Community, and I was sweating bullets. I felt drained and unsure for the first time during my job hunt. I didn't know what to do, but, as I sat there my mind worked me over like a professional boxer. I think I would call it a knock out.

"Come on in, Nancy" he said. "I just have one question for you."

I nodded, expecting the worst.

"What part of this exam do you think you had a problem with?"

Not knowing that this was a ploy, and having been sufficiently exhausted by my own undoing, I said, "the drug question". I hung my head and knew I didn't have the job. That was it. Finis. C'est tout.

Winters cocked his head to the right and seemed to grin. Maybe it was my imagination.

"Well", he said, "before we go any further you'll have to tell me about it. If you can do that, maybe we can make this problem go away."

I was surprised and more than willing to make all confessions necessary. I proceeded to tell him my limited experience with the drug community. I was in college, after all, and had certainly been present during the consumption of any kind of drug you can imagine. Everything from mushrooms ("shrooms"), marijuana, acid, and cocaine. The only drug I hadn't been in the presence of (that I knew) was heroin. I had actually tried marijuana and cocaine. The tales are sleazy and tawdry, and perhaps I will tell them later. Suffice it to say that from the day of that polygraph to the present, I have not used any illegal drug.

Winters accepted my story without displaying one way or another whether I had violated a sacred ethical code, and would therefore be summarily escorted out the back door of the police station. Poker faced, he again told me to have a seat in the hallway. Again with the black, Shaker chair and fake wood paneling on the walls.

I had already been at the station for a very long time, two hours at least, and was now perspiring in a very unfeminine way and could smell my own nervousness

I was just beginning to wonder if Winters had forgotten about me, when he approached from a back stairway and told me to follow him. He brought me down one flight of stairs, gave me a different (but similar) black, Shaker chair, and told me to have a seat. Again with the "have a seat". I noticed more activity on this floor. Several people walked by giving me the "once over", but no one said anything. The chair had arms on it, so I occupied myself by tapping my fingers on the wood. My tummy was doing flip-flops so I didn't dare ask any questions. Things seemed to have suddenly taken on a more serious tone. I certainly understood why, but didn't know what they were about to do.

An office door squealed open, ripping me from concentration on my current plight. It was one of those old doors you might have seen on "The Barney Miller Show", or even at Rob Petry's office on "The Mary Tyler Moore Show". Most of the top half of the door was a smoked, bumpy glass with black lettering on it that said, "Interview Room". The door had been directly behind me. Before standing I peeked around the corner and looked in. The room was filled with old men. Well, okay. Not filled, and they really weren't that old. I was only 21 at the time and they seemed old. I surmised by the epithet on the door that I was about to be interviewed. Brilliant, I know. It's truly amazing what a college education can do for you.

There was one of those long cafeteria-type tables set up, and four men, all but one wearing suits, facing me. The other guy was wearing a police uniform bearing stars on the lapel. Lt. Winters brought the chair in from the hallway, and placed it directly in front of the table, facing the men. Oh joy! I had a fleeting humorous thought about the chair. I was wishing they would allow me to stand because my rear end had become numb and tingly as it had lost circulation from sitting like the Shakers. I was beginning to lose my concentration and become a bit punchy, and struggled to refocus.

"Have a seat Nancy", one of the voices said.

I sat. They introduced themselves. I was so nervous I don't have a clear recollection as to who was in the "Interview Room" on that day, but I know for sure that Director Hanes was present; he was in charge of Detectives at the time. I think that Don Samuels and Jimmy Smith were there. I can't remember whether or not Marshall Remick (the Chief of police at that time) was there, but think that he was. Like the window on the door, my mind is now foggy about who the players were that day. I do remember the atmosphere being formal and serious, and there was no horsing around at this point. That was okay with me. I really wanted this job and would do just about anything they asked of me if it meant I could be a police officer.

With Winters standing behind me, they individually asked me about my drug history. They wanted me to tell them about each and every time I had used marijuana or cocaine. They grilled me as to where I was, who I was with, and whether I had addresses for those persons. With good reason, they needed to be assured that this had been a "phase" (a poor one at that) in my life that would not be revisited. I gladly made the necessary commitment to them and simply hoped for the best. There was nothing else I could do; and, I was glad that the truth had come out. I wouldn't have wanted it any other way.

"Okay," Hanes said, "have a seat in the hall and we'll be right with you."

Lt. Winters gently tugged on the chair as I stood. He placed it in the hallway and I sat without being told. I had the routine down by this time. Tired, but mentally aware. Ha! I resumed my former game of 'finger tapping on Shaker wood'. Every now and then I tapped my foot in sync with my fingers; by now there was no thought or enthusiasm to the game. As I tapped, my thoughts slipped back in time to my youthful days in California. I had clear and happy memories of a small three year old girl, in a blue dress that tied in the back . My feet were bare and dirty, as was my face. I was always outside where the sun was warm and inviting. One particular day while wearing my favorite dress, I was swinging back and forth while my mother occupied herself outside by hanging clothes out to dry. Fritzi was running around the swing set as I pumped to and fro.

"Mom", I said, "am I having a happy childhood?"

"Sure you are," she said.

Why had I asked that question? I must have heard the adults talking about "happy childhoods" and wanted to know if I was having one. It was one of those moments you always remember. It flickers before you as an old movie clip, but it is real, so real. It pops up at the weirdest times, like now. Maybe I thought of it because God wanted me to think about whether or not this was what I really wanted. This job, I mean. But I didn't bring my memory full circle, so as to analyze the reason for having it. I am only doing that now in retrospect. Back then, I just had the flickering memory and was able to smile because of it's pure simplicity. Life is a little more complicated at 21 than at 4; little did I realize just how complex it was about to become and the incestuous roles that would be played by the people I had just met, and others I had yet to meet.

I knew they were inside the interview room talking about me, but I avoided wondering what they could be saying or what they might decide. I wasn't exactly proud of myself. Regardless of their decision, I would understand. If I didn't get the job, I would keep plugging away. "Persistence, dedication, and hard work will always win" my dad would say.

Several people walked by without saying a word. Doors opened and closed; bathroom doors, office doors, exit doors. I could hear the hum of numerous conversations taking place but couldn't hear any one, specific conversation. It was as though I were invisible in a very public place. I felt very detached, and I should have taken this as an omen , but I didn't.

"Nancy, come on back in," a suit said.

I had been day dreaming and hadn't heard the door open so I jumped when he called my name. Swift! That's the way to make a good impression, I thought. So far, so good. My God, I should just turn around and go home right now! What could I possibly do next to impress these people? So far I've been asked why the hell I'm even there, been accused of being small, lied to a future boss, then confessed (twice over) a whole host of illegal activity. Why shouldn't they give me the job?

Knowing I wasn't the perfect candidate *(understatement)*, I timidly approached the group. This time they left the chair in the hallway, but it had become like a security blanket to me and my thoughts again focused on the qualities of that chair, in a more positive light than before. It was, after all, hand made by a group of dedicated, hard working people who enjoyed the simplicities of life.

"......offer you the job," someone said.

I hadn't heard the whole sentence but was sure he must have said he couldn't offer me the job. I smiled and started to say something mature like, 'I understand. Thank you for your time', but as my lips parted to express my simple thought I heard,

"When can you start?"

"Start? Oh," I said, "I hadn't thought that far ahead, but I suppose I could start right away."

"How does December 26th sound?"

"Perfect," I said.

And that was that. I was just as surprised as anyone else that I got the job, but happier than a bat in a dark cave with plenty of perches to hang upside down on, and lots of mosquitoes to eat. Who could have known? Even though I had been offhandedly told that I would be the first woman police officer ever hired in Portsmouth, it didn't dawn on me that this would be a problem. Why should it be? As I said earlier, women had the vote. We were an integral part of the sexual revolution in the 60's (it takes two to tango and all), and we could wear jeans in public, see-through shirts with no bra , bell bottoms, hip huggers, mini skirts, maxi skirts, flower power, and jean jackets with studs. We could be the CEO of a major corporation, work construction, or stay at home. We had the best of all worlds. No problem.

As I floated out the side door of the police station, Sergeant Place ran out behind me and yelled, "Oh. Hey Nancy. You'd probably better get a hair cut."

"I was planning on it," I said.

"And I'm assuming you have a driver's license?"

"Yes," I yelled. I got in my little green Datsun and drove home.

And I was home.

Portsmouth is a small town of about 25, 000, located on the Seacoast of New Hampshire. The salt air breathes of American History, freedom, and small town politics promulgated, managed and infested by the 'good-old-boy' system. The downtown area bustles with activity from antique, artist, and new age shops, upscale and down scale restaurants, and pubs. The harbor is outlined with a beautiful boardwalk that is attached to red brick structures that are now businesses, shops, restaurants, and expensive condominiums. The harbor docks visiting tall ships and cruise ships, old wrecks hauling scrap metal, salt, and of course its' signature tug boats. Something for everyone, it seems, including me.

When I first visited Portsmouth I knew I had come upon something refreshing and different. It was a feeling of home and final destination. I had found what I didn't know I was looking for, and I'm sure I remember breathing a deep sigh of relief as this knowledge swept over me. To this day, my feelings for Portsmouth have not diminished.

Chapter 4

Breaking In

Before my first day on the job, I had been told by Captain James Cooper (soon to be Director of the entire patrol division, and who loved to be affectionately called "THE DI-REC-TOR", or "Captain Free") that I had a reputation of being a "know it all". I was told that my best bet was to show up to work, but keep my mouth shut; the guys, after all, don't like people who think they're smarter than them. I shook my head in agreement but "Pooishly" muddled over this new characterization of me. I wondered how this reputation came about since I was not from Portsmouth, and had only recently relocated to a nearby town, from another State completely. I didn't know anyone, and no one knew me. Although I was puzzled, I realized that too much contemplation on the issue would find me, like Pooh, stuck in a doorway, unable to get in or out, and on the road to nowhere, the honey just out of reach. I decided to let it go, but filed it "in the vault", as Elaine would say.

I was to work a midnight shift my first week, and then begin my eight week tenure at the police academy the following week. This was a simple plan, or so it seemed. I soon realized that 'they' didn't know what to do with me. 'They' had no formal training program at the time, but believed they needed to develop one just for me, or any other woman that might be hired in the future. The simple fact of the matter is, police agencies should have field training programs for all new police officers. That should have been standard practice at the time, but it wasn't. I'm happy to say that it is now.

I was partnered with a different officer each night of the first week, and received no formal training. That wasn't the worst part. The worst part was entering the police building each night and watching, as they watched me, without saying a word. Sometimes I would approach a doorway to go to one room or another, and an officer would side step in front of me to block my passage. "Excuse me" I would say, and then I'd brush by. They never moved, but I didn't go around either. I figured they'd have to get used to me one way or another but their collective smirks and chuckles hinted that it wasn't going to be easy. As much as I put on a brave face, deep inside I was scared to death. No one spoke to me unless it was absolutely necessary, and then sometimes when it was necessary, they didn't talk to me.

I responded to my first burglar alarm that week. I was the greenest of any green officer there ever was. Although I had finished college, I was not street smart, and I knew it. I was anxious to learn, but no one was teaching. We approached the building with stealth and caution; no lights or siren and we turned the headlights off before reaching the building. My partner dropped me off at the front door and told me he would check the back. I stood at the front door... no, I stood directly *in front* of the front door and peeped into the window it afforded. I brilliantly planted my face against the window like a three year old kid looking in a fish tank. No signs of illegal entry. My partner returned to the front of the building with the cruiser and I hopped in feeling success because I had just responded to my first burglar alarm.

"Never stand directly in front of a door, especially a door with a window," he said. That was all he said that night. As a matter of fact, I can say with a great deal of confidence that those were the only words he said to me during my entire first year. I had learned something new, but I wished someone had clued me in *before* I provided a healthy target for any prospective bad guy.

I had been issued all kinds of equipment that I didn't know how to use, or which situations to use them in. I was given a 38 revolver (we later graduated to a 357 revolver, and soon afterward to a 9MM Sig Sauer), a 12" billy club, a 24" billy club, a flashlight, handcuffs, a knife, a radio, something called a 'claw', and so on. I remember exiting the passenger side of my cruiser one night with the flashlight in my back pocket, and both billy clubs in my left hand. Now, what in heavens name was I going to do with both clubs? Two other officers had responded to the call with us and after we "cleared" the area (which means we had checked for signs of illegal entry, and there were none) we met in a circle to the side of the building; actually, *they* met, and I stood there. They glared at me, surely thinking I was an idiot. I was still holding both clubs, a flashlight, and had the claw in my back pocket. I must have looked like a little kid trying to play cops and robbers.

"Hey," said officer Middlston, "what is up with these college kids anyway?"

"Who knows," Hurst said, playing into his rehearsed scenario.

"They never make it. They've tried before, but they just don't have what it takes to make it on this job."

I was fly in their web and I knew that my lousy bit didn't have any speaking parts, but I was supposed to appear nervous and uncomfortable as "the guys" dutifully berated me. I looked to the side, then down, hoping this game would soon end.

"We don't need officers here with a college degree. They

think they know it all, but they have no practical experience or common sense," Middlston expounded.

The light dawned. This is where the "know-it-all" image had come from. The word must have gotten around that I was a college graduate, which in police logic means that I think I know everything. I learned a valuable survival lesson at that moment. Sometimes the best way to solve a puzzle is to just sit back and wait for the answer without saying a word. If you're surrounded by conflict, as I was, the solution will often just drop into your lap because people love to talk. You know that saying, 'let 'em eat cake'? Well, now I say, 'let 'em talk'.

"Remember the guy who just left? He had a bachelors degree and he was outta here within a year. Yeah. He couldn't handle it so he took off for the FBI."

"Yup," my partner said, "and remember that black guy we hired a few years back?"

"Yeah," Middlston said. "That's another issue altogether. What a cowardly nigger he was! Glad we finally pushed him out."

"Had to," Dale said. "He was shaking in his boots at every call he went to."

"Had to set him up."

I missed which one made that statement, but the message was clear. I wasn't wanted, and logic and reason were not applicable to this game. At whatever time "they", the brotherhood, deemed appropriate, I too would be out of a job. I felt like an African American woman in the middle of a KKK rally. I had entered a time machine and been transported back in time; back to a time when the ignorance of the white race created extreme hardships for anyone that was different or unique.

I learned later that one of the many reasons the alleged "brotherhood" so detested my hiring, was because I have to pee differently than they. Yup. When they feel the call of nature they can simply pull up to a donut shop, find a bathroom, and go. A simple matter of manipulating their zipper downward, and retrieving whatever package they might locate (if, indeed, they can find it), and pissing into the urinal. I, they reasoned, would probably want to pee in the comfort of the police station no matter which beat I was assigned. This would cause me to be out of position for a major call. To add to the problem, I (as I explained earlier) don't have a penis that pulls out, so I would have to remove my entire gun belt in order to get my pants down. For those of you who aren't familiar with police equipment, in order to get the gunbelt off you have to first remove a series of at least four 'keepers'or snaps that are placed evenly around the waist, and then the outer belt can be unbuckled and removed. It's usually easier if you remove the weapon from the holster first and place it carefully on the sink, or floor.   This makes the belt lighter and easier to control when removing and putting back on.   Beneath the heavy gunbelt is another belt, which also has to be unbuckled in order to get the pants down or off.   Then, as everyone knows, the pants must be slipped down to about the knees and we must, God forbid, *sit* on the toilet seat while we pee.   This, they reasoned, is an officer safety issue.   What if she is on the toilet when that 'hot' call comes in?   She won't be of any use to us....not that she is anyway.   Not only will she be way off her beat, but she'll have her pants around her ankles too.   Someone could be badly hurt or even killed because of her, a *female* officer.

I'm not kidding.   That was their logic at the time.   It didn't dawn on me until much later that most of my co-workers were in the habit of taking a nightly constitution in the PPD toilet.   This, of course didn't happen until they first located their favorite reading materials to take with them, which usually consisted of Playboy or Hustler (kept in various places in the police building).   After finishing the academy and being assigned a permanent field training officer, I was often purposely prevented or delayed from using the bathroom.   There were times I had to go so badly I was afraid I would burst; this, in turn, caused a series of bladder infections that took a long time to finally clear up.   As my mother used to say, 'if you want to play with the boys, you have to expect these things'.   But did I really?

Memories of that first week are deeply etched into my memory, but they are in a random order now, due to the passage of time.   One of my first nights I had to work with a guy named Lance Peters.   He's about 6'5" and as evil as he is smart and just as cunning.   He was suspended once for intentionally destroying someone else's property while on duty.   Years later he resigned from the Department under questionable circumstances, but that's a story for later.   Being alone in a cruiser with him, during an especially cold Christmas season is one of the creepiest feelings I've ever had.

He was the only officer that talked openly with me, and it made me suspicious.   He was being too nice; filling me in on all the dirt, and speaking poorly of the other officers.   Of course this had all been prefaced with the standard spiel: "What's said in the cruiser, stays in the cruiser."   Bull shit.   I've yet to meet another profession or group that thrives so heartily on gossip.

They've always got something or someone to talk about; and, if they're out of fresh material they make it up.   It's so ironic that the people endowed with the power to help and protect us are also the ones who use these opportunities to spread rumors and gossip.   What they fail to understand is that negative words (whether they're true or false) can cause personal damage.

Anyway, that night we had traveled to the end of Market St. Extention for no other reason than to assure that we covered our entire beat. In 1981, Market St. Extention was actually a dead-end road that stopped just beyond Granite St. Now Market St. extends all the way through, to Woodbury Ave. The weather of late had been colder than other winters with a lot more snow fall and ice accumulation. Peters turned the cruiser into a frozen and slippery side street, and then attempted to back out, and turn around. He got the cruiser stuck between two small trees that were connected by a path of pure ice. The nose of the cruiser was jammed into a semisolid, and crusty snow bank, while the bumpers on both sides were wedged between the trees. I didn't think much of it until we had been sitting there for quite some time, rocking back and forth on the ice, spinning our tires, and Peters said, "We've gotta get outta here before someone thinks we've been having sex."

"Now, call me crazy, but where the hell did that comment come from?" I thought. Stupidly, I smiled and shook my head as if to say, 'tsk, tsk'. I didn't know what else to do. At that moment I wished I really was a 'know-it-all', because I would have known the proper response to a statement of that caliber. Within seconds Peters gunned the engine while it was in reverse, and we spun back onto the street where the car almost did a complete three hundred and sixty degree turn. Peters chuckled, obviously feeling pumped up from the thrill of his adventure. I breathed a heavy sigh of relief and let the incident pass.

At about 2 a.m., while driving down Court St., we came upon a woman lying on her back, in the middle of the road. Peters threw the blue lights on, shoved the car in park, and stepped toward the woman. I leaned on the icy road and put my left cheek about one inch from the woman's face; thankfully, I could feel her breath whisking my cheek. I could also smell the rancid odor of cigarettes and alcohol; her whole body smelled of it.

"I know who she is," Peters said.

I looked at her lower body and noticed that her pants were unbuttoned and unzipped and her shirt was untucked and partially unbuttoned.

"She probably came from the Starlight Club," he said. "She hangs out there all the time, and I'm pretty sure she lives up there." Peters stood above me and pointed to a third floor apartment, accessed by a metal stairway meant to serve as a fire escape. "She's got a roommate. Why don't you just carry her up and get her safely inside?"

It wasn't a request, it was a test. One of many that I would experience over and over again throughout my entire career. There were never enough tests, no matter how many I passed, so I was never able to completely prove myself; only, I didn't realize this fact for many years. Oh, bother.

The woman, whose name was Janice, was 5'7" tall and weighed about 140 lb.. I am 5'2" and (okay, okay) weigh 120 pounds. This was far from an even deal, but I was being sized up by my partner so I didn't have much choice. The way these guys gab, if I failed this test, I would be quick prey for the "set-up" guys. Maybe if I did it without Peter's help, not that he was going to help anyway, the word would get out that I had done well, and I could be on the road to being respected. Fat, fucking chance.

I placed one knee on the snow covered pavement while strategically planting my other foot solidly on the ground. I grabbed onto Janices' hands and pulled her forward as I stood, and at the same time leaned backward with all my weight. As she reached my height I stepped forward and allowed her waist to bend over my shoulder. This left her head and arms dangling down my backside, with her buttocks and legs hanging to my front. I stepped slowly in order to test my balance with this new burden. She was a heavy one, but I was pretty sure I could make it.

I gently placed my left foot onto the first step while wrapping my right arm securely around her thighs just below her buttocks. The metal steps were completely covered with ice and quite treacherous. After placing my foot on the stair, I gently rotated my toe from left to right; my idea was to create just enough friction to melt the ice and prevent a fall. It seemed to work so I leaned on that foot, and used my leg muscles to push straight up and place my right foot onto the next step. I followed the same process with my right foot so that I was able to then raise my left foot onto the next, higher step. I followed this pattern until I had climbed the entire three flights. As I climbed, her hands would occasionally slap against my backside, or her boots would get tangled between my knees, but I went slow enough to avoid any hazard.

When I reached the last step I felt emotionally and physically as though I had just finished a marathon, or a rock climbing expedition. I stepped to my left in order to knock on the door and speak with her roommate, and was astonished to see that there was no door!! I had climbed all the way up, and there wasn't a door. I was just beginning to get real pissed of because I realized that Peters had known this all along. I had seen his smirk before, and had a clear vision of how he must look now.

I heard some rattling to my left. There was a loud bang, like a hammer hitting wood, and then a sliding sound. An older woman had opened the fire escape window, and was asking if she could help me. At that moment I thought about how foolish I must look, a short police officer in full uniform, standing outside a third story window, on a fire escape, with a woman hanging over her shoulder.

"Well," I said, "I thought you might be interested in helping your roommate," I tried to sound playful, as though this was no big deal, but don't know if I succeeded because I was very much out-of-breath.

She looked at me as if she were trying with all her might to make sense of the situation. Her brow furrowed and her eyes squinted as she tipped her head and looked straight at me.

"This is your roommate," I said, "Janice?"

Another pause, and then the awakening, "Ohhhh!" she exclaimed. "What the hell happened to her?" She was slurring her words and had my nostrils not been overloaded with Janice's odors, I was sure I'd be able to smell alcohol on the roommate also.

"I'm not quite sure, but would you mind if I popped her inside that window? She's awful heavy. We found her passed out on Court St., down below. My partner says she lives here. Is that right?"

"Sure, let me help you."

I stepped backward to allow my burden's feet to reach the window first. The roommate leaned forward and grabbed onto Janice's feet while I held onto the major portion of her body, and slowly stepped forward. Just inside and under the window was a couch which we conveniently laid Janice on. She stirred a little bit, but not enough to take notice of the adventure she had just weathered. I stepped into the apartment also, ducking my head and nearly missing a fall onto Janice. I think my legs were a bit weak from the climb.

The apartment was far from being top of the line, but I suppose it provide a roof for two very hard working people who found their money was better invested in alcohol, and maybe drugs. In addition to being heavily cluttered, it was dirty and dusty too. Some kind of animal hair was clinging to the rugs and furniture, and in the far left corner of the room I could see a pile of poop that hadn't yet hardened. It was either a big cat or a small dog, I decided.

My not-so-keen eye for style told me that the apartment had possibilities; the old, uneven brick from the early 1800's was exposed and provided beautifully rustic walls, and ceiling beams accented the fireplaces that were built in every room including the kitchen. Definite possibilities, but it would need a good cleaning or disinfecting.

I asked for the roommate's name and she told me as she puttered around the apartment looking for a spare blanket. It was a common name like Cindy, or Ann so it didn't lock into my long term memory, 'the vault'. I made sure that Janice would be safe with her and told the roommate to keep a close eye on her. I was worried that we should have brought her to the hospital, rather than home, but I had already been told that my opinion didn't matter and I should just do as I was told. Before climbing out the window, I leaned close to Janice to make sure she was indeed breathing and was satisfied with a sudden heavy intake of breath. She would be okay.

I stepped slowly down the stairs and immediately envied my partner's strategic location; he was sitting cozily in the cruiser with the heat on and the radio blaring. As I stepped into the car, he put the transmission in drive and pressed on the gas before I had even closed the door. He looked straight ahead and kept driving. Not a word was spoken the rest of the night.

Had he expected me to ask for his help? Did he tell me to do this because he thought I would fail? He seemed mad at me, yet I had done what he asked. Well, I thought, maybe this was just part of my indoctrination. I guessed that my part was to sit back and say nothing, so that's exactly what I did. Besides, I was just happy to have a chance to warm my very cold hands and feet.

"Two oh two, to two oh five," the police radio blared.

We were 205 so I reached for the radio intending to respond. My hand was quickly pushed away with the admonition, "Don't touch anything in this car unless you're told by me that it's okay. Understand?" he boomed.

I shook my head up and down and sat back in the seat.

"Two oh five, go ahead," he said.

"10-78 in the Bridge Street Lot?"

"10-5. I'll be there in two minutes".

A 10-78 is a meeting, and 10-5 means okay.

I was excluded from the conversation between the guys. When the other cruiser arrived, my partner got out of our car and got into the passenger seat of the other cruiser. They sat laughing and joking and talking about God-knows-what for about 45 minutes. I stayed in my seat and not-so-patiently listened to the radio.

As I sat doing nothing, and I do mean nothing, another cruiser pulled into the lot. It was officer Lanko; a tall, rather overweight guy whose nickname was Murray from that show "The Odd Couple". Lanko looked and acted like Murray the policeman; you know, kinda dumb and happy, with food being of primary importance to him. Anyway, to my surprise, Lanko got out of his cruiser and sat in the driver's seat of my cruiser. This, I said to myself, is a set-up of some kind. With my side view mirror, I could see Peters and Middlston peering at me from their cruiser. They were talking and laughing as they looked, so I knew something was up. Lanko just sat there. He didn't say a thing; just stared at me. He made me feel very uncomfortable, as though I were a newly discovered germ, forming in a petry dish at the Center for Disease

Control. I hoped that if I turned my gaze away from him he'd catch the hint and leave me alone, maybe even go away.

Within seconds I heard the driver's door slam, and big fat Murray got out of my cruiser and waddled to his own. Then it started; pop, pop, bang, bang, bang. I could feel a bunch of small explosions at my feet and couldn't fathom what might be happening. I looked down and saw bright flashes of light synchronized with the bangs. I pulled my door handle in an attempt to exit the car, but quickly learned that Murray had locked my door from the controls on the driver's side. I reached over, unlocked all doors with the driver's control button, and jumped out, while the book of firecrackers continued to pop and burst on the floor of the cruiser.

To my right I saw Murray circling the lot and grinning from ear to ear. Peters and Middlston were bent forward in hysterical laughter. I stood outside until the popping had ceased and my partner had settled down enough to reenter his own cruiser, our cruiser. I got in and we drove off. I didn't say a word, even though I had a serious burn on the inside of my right calf from one of those suckers hoping up the leg of my pants. I couldn't wait to see what was next.

As Murray and the guys were busy getting their kicks at my expense, a tragic scene was unfolding on the other side of town. Doug was rushing to take his girlfriend, Susan, home after keeping her out past her curfew. Doug, a senior in high school, a football star, excellent student, and well loved by his peers, was madly in love with Susan. They had been dating for a year and a half, and she represented, for Doug, everything he hoped to find in a relationship.

Susan, aside from being attractive, tall, thin, with chocolate brown hair and blue, eyes, was ambitious and talented. Not only did she and Doug have their entire future together mapped out, Susan had already been selected to attend the Rhode Island School of Design for a five year program studying architecture. She had done so well in her high school classes that concentrated in math, art, and architecture, that she knew a job in this field would be the best way to secure her future. The fact that she could bring in a substantial income doing something she loved, intrigued her also.

Doug, although bright and talented, wasn't as sure of his own future. He knew he would go to college, but was still having a difficult time deciding on a profession. In many ways he felt like he was floundering compared to Susan, but this difference in their personalities created no tension between them. Doug made up for it with his daring and adventurous style. Susan loved this about Doug because he used it to remind her that life can be, and should be fun; it doesn't always have to be serious. One doesn't always have to be planning and arranging for tomorrow. Some days it was just okay to experience what life gave you.

That's what tonight had been all about. Doug convinced Susan that there could be nothing as daringly, exhilarating as a motorcycle ride to their favorite beach spot, in the middle of winter. They took the coast road, Rt. 1A, in Rye and pulled onto their cliff, overlooking the ocean. They loved it because the waves splashed so viscously against the cliff, they were often sprayed with a mist of ocean foam as they sat. This is the place they came to sit, next to one another, on a blanket, and softly touch and feel one another. They talked about their dreams for their future. It was as though this was the place that gave them the power to achieve their dreams; it provided the fuel for their future successes.

Properly helmeted, and wrapped in heavy layers of clothing, Doug expertly wrapped his Honda 550 through the windy roads. These motorcycle rides were part of their ritual. They had at one time made an agreement that they would never again go to the ocean unless they were on a motorcycle. It was as though the open ride ceremoniously solidified what ever they had agreed to while sitting on their cliff. It was an especially cold night, and the force of the wind playing against them bit any exposed skin.

Not realizing that he was going too fast, Doug approached a corner on Sagamore Ave., by the Moose Club. He became gripped with fear as he realized that the rear wheel of the bike had slipped on some ice, was skidding to his left, and sliding out from under him. Doug tried to right the motorcycle by shifting his weight. With the sudden shifting of his weight, Susan realized that they were in trouble.

The rear wheel was no longer in a straight line with the front wheel, but was almost on it's side. Susan felt as though she was going to fall off the right side of the cycle, onto the moving pavement. In a natural reflex reaction, she put her right foot out to keep from tipping over, as if she were on a bicycle, and as her foot hit
the pavement, it served as an anchor that allowed herself to be torn in half, at the crotch, and then thrown from the motorcycle. She landed softly in the white snow, as though God was there to catch her.

As Susan was lifted from the bike, Doug was falling to the ground. The motorcycle was on top of him as though *it* had decided that it wanted to ride him. When Doug came to a stop, he was several feet further down the road, unconscious, but breathing.
Four police units were dispatched to the scene, as well as 2 ambulances, and some fire trucks. As the new-guy-on-the-job, I was placed at a traffic post, while the other units conducted the bulk of the investigation. It was clear by all counts, that although Doug would be seriously injured, he was going to be okay. Susan bled-out at the scene. She had been torn. Ripped straight up her middle, from her

crotch into her stomach from the forceful momentum of the pavement against the foot she used for balance. There had been no hope for Susan.

After the street was cleared of the accident scene, I was assigned the task of guarding the body at the funeral home until the medical examiner could perform an autopsy. I followed her body from the scene, to the funeral parlor, in order to maintain proper chain of custody.

Susan was brought into the cellar, through the bulk head door and placed on a firm slab, in a room that held several other bodies. One of the duty officers came, and placed a sheet over her to keep her eyes from glaring at me in the darkness. He located a chair and placed it next to Susan so that I was close by; as if she would get up and walk away.

Against the stone walls were shelves that could have held books, but instead were laden with two, newborn babies wrapped in plastic. One little baby couldn't have been more than a few days old. When I took a closer look, I thought I could see that one side of it's head seemed to be caved-in, or distorted in some way. I couldn't be exactly sure what I was looking at because the plastic created such a bizarre charicature of death, that I refused to satisfy this morbid curiosity by looking more closely. I walked directly to my chair and sat down, taking the guard position, thinking that I would just stay right there. I didn't need to do any more exploring. I would sit right here and try to keep my mind on happier thoughts.

Just as I sat, I heard a noise. It sounded as though something had dropped. I fleetingly wondered if there was someone in the room with me. I started to stand up, to peek around the corner when I heard another noise. This time it sounded like a voice. I could make it out. It *was* a voice. There was somebody else in here with me.

I drew my revolver and took a defensive position around a corner. As I stepped forward to begin my search of the building, I heard the voice again. This time I heard it as clear as day.

"Nancy, Nancy."

Someone was calling my name, but who and why, I did not know. At this point I grabbed my radio and called for back-up.

"Two oh two to dispatch," I said

"Ten, three, two." That basically means, 'go ahead, Nancy.'

"Send me back-up to Wards funeral Home. I've got people in the building, and no one should be in here."

I heard it again.

"Nancy, Nancy. Get me out from under the sheet. My leg hurts, my stomach hurts," It was clearer this time. But the words didn't fit. I couldn't place them and didn't know what was going on.

"Nancy, remove this goddam sheet. I need fresh air. I need to breath," it said.

The noise was coming from Susan. But, the voice I was hearing was a man's voice. Startled to the point of inaction, I tried to regain my composure. I heard sirens just outside my door. The radio crackled.

"Two, oh, one to two, oh, two. We're off at scene. Could you step outside so we can get a handle on your location?"

'Gladly,' I thought to myself.

Gun in hand, I crept quietly to the bulk head door and softly pushed it open. The shift from darkness to daylight caused a momentary blindness. When my vision cleared, I saw the entire midnight shift standing in a semicircle in front of me, laughing hysterically.

Knowing I couldn't ask why they were laughing, or what this was about, I stood facing them wondering what was so funny. It was at this point that I saw Tim Mentzki lift his police radio to his mouth. At the same time, behind me I could hear a male voice calling, "Nancy, Nancy."

That's when I knew. How stupid I had been! I trounced into the parlor, lifted Susan's sheet, and found a police radio neatly tucked between her legs. One of the men in blue had secretly placed the radio under the sheets of a dead body. I picked up the radio, placed it outside, and slammed the door. I returned to Susan where I apologized to her for the callousness of my coworkers.

Practical jokes were the theme during that first week. I took it all in stride because I firmly believed that their insecurities about me would eventually subside and we'd all be able to look back at this time period and have a hearty laugh. I would be laughing about their immaturity and ridiculous lack of acceptance, and so would they. In my dreams they would look back at this time and be filled with wonder as to how they could have been so ignorant or distrustful of me. As I said, it was in my dreams.

Chapter 5

The Academy

In January of 1982 the New Hampshire Police Academy was located in Portsmouth at Pease Air Force Base. This meant I had a very short drive from my parent's home in Rye; ten minutes at the most. It has since been relocated to a new facility in Concord, NH. which is more than an hour from Portsmouth. I really lucked out because the short distance made it so much easier on Friday's when we were allowed to break camp, or go home. Some of the students had a two or three hour drive ahead of them.

I had been given a list of items to pack, along with an itinerary for the first day. I spent the weekend prior to the first day fretting over exactly what, and how much to pack. Being a southern California girl, I had never gotten used to the cold New England winters and was afraid we'd be forced to do cadence for hours at a time in the frigid weather. Along with the required clothing and equipment, I packed plenty of cold weather gear. I brought long johns, hats, mittens, extra T-shirts to wear beneath my issued clothing, and thick socks to keep my feet warm. As it turned out, I needn't have worried so much. The temperature for the entire eight weeks was so extremely cold that the weather experts advised against anyone being outside for any length of time. Although we sometimes had to run or march from class to class, for the most part our Commandant was forced to keep us inside for the first time in academy history.

We were due at the base gym at seven a.m. sharp that first Monday. Anyone late would be turned away without question and no guarantee that they'd be given a slot at the next academy session. I pulled into the parking lot at 6:30 and nervously stepped toward the gym, leaving all my luggage in the car. I had to pass another series of physical agility tests before I could be allowed to continue the program further. Once those tests were given, anyone who failed would be sent away with little hope for another try. I was dressed in my gym clothes, some sweats, and my running shoes. I hadn't prepared myself as much as I had wanted to; working those midnights during my first week of duty was more draining than I expected.

I entered the gym and was immediately ordered to take a seat on the floor in the far right corner. I was the first candidate there, with four men from the academy who were also dressed for exercise training. Three of them were the short-militaristic type; you know, muscular, stocky, flat-top hair cut, tailored sleeves with tattoos on their bulging biceps. The fourth was taller, about 6'5" or so, medium build, and a softer look. It turned out that he was Trooper Jenson of the NH State Police and would be our assistant Commandant for this academy session. I kept my gaze away from them as I didn't want to antagonize them into making my life any more difficult than it was about to become. I didn't like the feeling of being there alone with them because I felt far too vulnerable. Exposed. I was relieved when others straggled in wearing the same peculiar expression that I must have had. Each candidate was gruffly ordered to take a seat and keep quiet. Slowly, a crowd began to form around me and in front of me. Like a herd of helpless sheep we sat and watched as the four men from the academy took several orange cones and placed them strategically about the gym. Then they brought out a couple of life-sized dolls and laid them on the floor near the cones. They paced back and forth yelling at us all the while. They were trying to pump themselves up for the long day ahead, and break us down. They didn't want any wimps as police officers.

"Okay you sorry bunch of losers! Get off your butts and stand in straight lines across the gym." This order didn't come until 8:30. I'd been sitting there for two hours, now I could finally stand. "Count off into four groups starting at this end," and he pointed to a heavy set guy to my left. There were about sixty of us.

Each of the four groups was assigned a different station where our physical abilities were tested. My group drew the mile and a half run first.

"Okay people, get this straight. You will run one point five miles, which is fifteen times around the outer portion of the gym. You will NOT cut any corners, and above all you will not puke on this floor. If you are so out of shape that you must throw up, do not, repeat, do not, puke on the floor. Puke in your shirt or swallow the goddam stuff. If you puke on the floor, you're OUT! The gym is small and crowded. It's going to get hot as a bastard in here so we'll see what you're made of." The guy making the speech tuned out to be the head-commandant, Crompton.

Just the suggestion of throwing up made my stomach flip. I had been in such a rush that morning I'd forgotten to eat breakfast, yet I had taken my daily multivitamin. I had already begun to feel the effects of the vitamin on an empty stomach, but had been trying to put it out of my mind. Now I had been foiled. They had pulled one over on me. They had gotten to me. Mind games. Oh bother, again. I knew I would be the one, and only one, to make their wish come true. Please, God, no!

The whistle blew and our group began the running test. The more laps we finished, the smaller, and hotter the gym felt. The other teammates seemed to be crowding and pushing me at each turn, and I'm sure they felt the same. My ankles weakened with each corner I turned. The heat, the stench of heavy, group, perspiration, the crowded conditions, and my extreme nervousness worked me over and eventually provided the one forbidden thing: vomit. Vomit that couldn't go on the floor. Oh shit! I folded my T-shirt upward to make a pocket and openly puked into my shirt, just as they had asked. I finished my run holding the pocket of vomit upward, to avoid spilling any on the floor.

Well, I gave them what they wanted. Not only did I give them puke in my shirt, but I was now a target for future humiliation in front of the group. And, sure enough, it happened.

"Well, well. What have we got here?" Crompton asked. "What's your name trooper?"

"Dowhan, sir".

"Well, Dow..**Han**. Would you like to go home now? Is this a bit much for a little girl like you?"

Everyone had stopped what they were doing and they were staring.

"Sir, NO SIR." I responded as I had been taught.

"Doesn't appear as though you have much stamina, Dow...**han**. You've got three more tests to complete today. You haven't even begun yet. **GO HOME!**"

"Sir, no sir. I would like to finish my tests, sir"

"How did she do on time?" Crompton asked the monitor.

"A bit above average," said Jenson, "well within the guidelines."

Crompton scowled as if he were disappointed, then turned toward me. "One more mistake, Dow...**han** and I'll make sure you don't pass! **Got** it?"

"Sir, yes sir," I meekly replied. I've always wanted to make it onto someone's "list of most favorite people"; it appears I had done just that. Things just couldn't get any better.

Crompton directed our group to the next station and left us with a guy dressed in camouflage gear, sporting a bald head and a hideous scowl. Hadn't his mother ever told him that his face could freeze like that? I wished I could ask him but I was sure he would miss the humor.

"Okay folks," he yelled, "We are about to test your strength with the dummy-pull. The dummy weighs 150 pounds, and each one of you must weave this dummy around the cones, across the line, and then straight back to the starting line without going around the cones. Have you got that?"

"Does it matter how we carry it?" someone dared to ask.

"This is a true to life situation. You carry that dummy any

way you need to, to get the job done. You can carry it on top of your head for all I care. Just get it from point A to point B in less than 30 seconds."

I saw some concerned glances from a couple of guys. I don't know if they were worried about me, or whether their concern for themselves was showing. No matter. I was pretty confident that I would get this one right. I'd had previous police agility tests that included this test. I'd say the one for Vermont State Police was the most difficult. Their test had the dummy seat belted inside a car positioned outside. The scenario was that the car had been in an accident which gave the driver a concussion. It was our job to free the 'driver' from the Seat belt, pull him out of the car, and far enough away to assure that if the car blew up the driver wouldn't get hurt. Pulling the dummy was extremely difficult because of the friction caused by the rough landscaping. Today, though, we were inside a gym with nicely polished floors. Once you got the dummy going, there should be no problem.

I stepped forward to go first. My temples were pounding from the stench still clinging to my shirt; I couldn't get away from it. I placed the dummy on it's back and positioned myself so that my feet were at its head and just before the starting line. I looked behind me to judge the exact location of the cones, then looked down at the dummy. I purposefully kept my gaze downward to avoid being a part of the nervous tension that electrified the gym. I didn't know when he would blow the whistle, but I stood and waited, taking deep breaths to help summon some inner strength. "You're strong enough", I said to myself. "Keep a tight grip and use your leg muscles, not your back."

The whistle shrieked. I leaned forward and grabbed the dummy under his armpits; one of my hands tightly gripped each pit. I pushed backward with all my strength, of course using my legs. The dummy followed. I kept my head turned backward to keep the cones in full view, and expertly navigated the dummy through all ten cones and passed the halfway mark. I whipped the dummy around and ran backward as quickly as I could. I crossed the finish line with a time of 17 seconds. All right!! Well under thirty seconds.

"That can't be right," I heard camouflage-man say. "Do it again."

"Me?" I asked.

"Yes **you!** Are you **deaf?** I said **DO IT AGAIN!**"

"Yes sir." This place was getting creepier and creepier by the minute.

I skillfully twirled the dummy back around, and resituated myself. I was not about to give this guy a chance to wash me out. No way.

The whistle blew and I flew through the course again. My anger propelled me even faster than the last time.

"Sixteen seconds. Hold on a minute. Step aside *recruit*. Let me have a look at that dummy."

He leaned over and pulled the dummy by its arms in an attempt to lift it to a standing position. He was able to pull the dummy's rump about one foot off the floor and then dropped it. His face turned red; he leaned over and tried again. This time he was able to lift it to a nearly standing position, but he dropped it again. "Just checking," he said as he turned his back to me and hollered to the next recruit to 'take the line'.

More of the same, I thought. I sat on the hard floor and rested while I had the chance. The fourteen others in my group had to take the test before we could move on to the next station. Two didn't pass. I felt bad for them because the pressure was now on. We were only allowed to flunk one of the tests; more than one and we were kicked out.

The last two tests were easy. We had to do a series of push-ups and sit-ups. I forget what the requirements were, but I've never found either of those exercises difficult so I, along with most of the group, breezed right through them. I think the idea was to do a certain number of each in one minute.

As each group finished, we were escorted to the bleachers where we had to wait for everyone else to finish. No talking was allowed. I don't think anyone wanted to talk. We were all very exhausted from our long and tiring morning. It was after one in the afternoon and we were ready for lunch.

"Okay people." Jenson was talking now. "I'm going to read a list of ten names. Those people will please step forward and face the rest of the group. Randy Kost, Jeffrey Small, Deborah Dean, Lionel Prism, Eric Trader, Joshua Smith, Walter Griswold, Michael Dumont, Lee Moger, and Scott Jefferson." The instructor waited impatiently for the chosen ten to present themselves in front. "Come on, come on," he yelled impatiently, "you're as slow as a bunch of old ladies. Get on up here."

The group scuffled forward, and I now realize that they must have known what was coming; that's why they weren't rushing and why they looked at the floor as they finally reached the front . "You ten," Jenson said with tone of disgust, or even contempt, "can go home. You have embarrassed yourselves and the agencies who hired you, by failing two or more tests. We don't want you, but maybe your **mama** does. Get outta here!" he bellowed.

I cringed with the brutal cruelty of his words.

"The rest of you will follow me in your cars to the chow hall. From there, we will unload our cars and set-up your living quarters for the next eight weeks. You will not speak at chow, and you will eat a healthy portion of food to rebuild your strength. We'll be working till the wee hours of the morning so you'll need your strength. Let's go!"

Chow was nothing special, but it filled my belly and subdued the acidy feeling the lone vitamin had caused. There were fifty of us left, and I wondered if we would lose any others. I sure hoped not as my logic suggested that the more recruits, the better I'd be able to hide or keep a low profile. I had been instructed by Captain Cooper and Officer Peters to keep my mouth shut unless I absolutely *had* to speak. They thought I should keep as low a profile as possible, otherwise I'd run the risk of becoming the class scape goat because of my size and my sex.

Crompton led us, caravan style, to our barracks parking lot where we were ordered to grab our belongings and line up.

"Okay kids. We've got more work ahead of us. I want you to take all your stuff onto the third floor, find the room with your name on it, dump your gear in the room, and then form four lines, 12 or 13 people deep, in the main hallway. You will run while you do this. You will not walk. **GO!**"

Like a pack of rats we squeezed ourselves through the thin doorway, and ran the three flights of stairs. The stairwell echoed with our collective huffing and puffing and the sound of tired, heavy feet hitting the cement steps. I was carrying a large suit case and a suit bag (with my police uniform in it). My hands were full and I felt as though I was going to drop everything in my arms. I imagined my suitcase flopping down the stairs, knocking and bouncing against my colleagues, as they tried to dodge it, and having it finally slam down the last stair. Man, that Crompton guy would be pissed. I reached the top step and scuffled to the various doors looking for my name. Finding it, I dropped my gear and joined the already forming lines. I was situated somewhere in the middle which, I felt, would be a perfect hiding spot. I was the shortest of everyone and could be easily missed in the center of the pack.

We all stood, wondering what could be next, but not really wanting to know. Even though it was only three o'clock, we were all ready for a nap or long rest of some sort.

"What clumsy idiot dropped this prissy mitten?" Crompton yelled.

I paid no attention, waiting for the sorry sap who dropped it to get his ass kicked.

"I said, whose mitten is this?" he barked, impatience oozing from his tone.

Nothing but silence. I picked my head up and could see Commandant Crompton standing in front madly waving a blue and yellow mitten in the air.

"This mitten wasn't here this morning........" My brain
started buzzing as I recognized the mitten as MINE. Oh man, oh
man, oh man alive!! It was my ass I had been waiting to get kicked.
My sore, tired, and female ass was about to get kicked by the guy
madly yelling as he waved my mitten. I couldn't lie. I couldn't not
tell him that it was mine because it was the second half of the only
pair of mittens I had brought, and there's nothing I hate more than
being cold, or letting any part of my body get cold. It's a full blown
phobia with me. A down right fear. I have to say, I fear the cold
more than I fear getting my ass kicked.

I slowly raised my hand and stood alone in the middle of the
crowd. My neighbors turned in my direction and then hung their
head in embarrassment for me. There was a slight parting of the
crowd, like the parting of the Red Sea.

"**Dow...han**, Get your sorry **ass** to the front of this group!"

I stepped forward and hoped for the best.

"Dow...han. What the hell is wrong with you? Can't you do
anything right? First you puke on yourself and make a god-awful
stench that the rest of us have to smell, and now you can't even hold
on to your own belongings. Is this how the whole eight weeks is
going to go? Should I kick you out now and save us all one big
hassle?"

"No sir," I said.

"No sir?" he mimicked.

"**SIR, NO SIR.**" I bravely retorted.

"I think I'd like to put this up for a vote. Who thinks
Dow...**han** should go?"

My knees shook as he looked hopefully at the crowd for a
positive response.

"No one? Is there no one who thinks she should go?" The
air in the room was stuffy and still. "Okay, Dow...han, take your
mitten and get back in line. I'm keeping my eye on you."

A new friend. How nice. Our relationship would flourish in
this setting for sure!

I made it through the rest of the day by becoming a robot.
Whatever we were told to do, I did without thought or question. At
one point we formulated a three story assembly line and passed all
sheets, blankets, pillows, pillowcases, from the 1st floor all the way to
the top. The bedding was stock piled in the middle of the main foyer
and then divvied up. Khaki uniforms were issued that were either too
big or too small. My shirt tails were so long that when I tucked them
into my pants the tails reached my knees. This, in turn, made it feel
as though I was wearing diapers because the shirt made so much
extra padding in the seat of my pants, they were too small at the hips.

Rooms were cleaned, beds were made, and suitcases unpacked. I was put in a room with two other women. One, Linda Kempton, was a police officer from Goffstown, NH, and Leslie was from Laconia. We learned to lean on one another when times got tough. We were the only women in this academy class and we were determined to graduate. We had all been given the inside scoop that the State doesn't like to graduate women police officers, so Academy Commandants put extra pressure on the women, hoping to push them out. This is especially true if there is only one woman in the class.

Leslie was more weepy than Linda and I, but if the truth be known, she was only expressing what the rest of us were feeling. Linda and I spent a lot of time convincing Leslie not to quit, and explaining the whole concept of mental warfare to her. She wasn't used to being ridiculed and yelled at; nor was she used to the long and tiring hours. Leslie, being wiser than Linda and I, left police work after a few years, moved away, and went to law school. Good for her.

Many exciting and memorable things happened during those eight weeks that will provide a lot of mirth in my elder years as I sit outside my seacoast home, rocking back and forth in the heavy, humid climate. I'll be at least 90 years old, still wearing shorts (although I'll have had to buy them just a bit longer than the short, shorts I wear now); but some portion of the back of my legs will definitely be sticking to the seat of the old cane rocking chair I've used for half a century now. The sea breeze will whisp my straw-like gray hair from side to side and into my eyes as I try to read the latest romance novel wherein love gets all twisted around. My shirt will be sleeveless or short sleeved, and my brown and sun wrinkled arms will glow with the pride of age. I won't wear make up because I never want my lipstick to seep down the age cracks of my lips, to give the impression of a clown, or an old lady trying to look younger. I will be fulfilled and happy and fun because I have lived a life filled with lessons and wonder. In my book, you can't get any better than that.

One of my favorite memories will be of my second week in the academy while sitting with the recruits at noon chow. We sat rigidly listening to the tapping of our plastic utensils on the cardboard plates, mixed with the clinking noise made by our Commandant's food ware. The Commandant and the instructors always sat at the head table and were afforded accommodations considered much better than ours. It was like the King and the paupers. We were lowly, oh, so, lowly. A few knowing glances were shared as we individually tried to reenergize ourselves from the flogging routine of wake-up at four a.m., rigorous calisthenics, shower and change, breakfast, and back to the classroom. There was little time, if any, to wonder how the hell we'd gotten ourselves into this situation. If that time did exist, it would have been during the afternoon meal. Well, just as I was getting used to a regular, mundane, routine which gave me a bit of that private time, I heard the scuffle of a 'better' chair, made of real wood unlike our cold metal chairs with rubber knobs on the bottom, being pushed backward by a human buttocks. Then I heard the tapping of footsteps around the room and behind me. No one in the room dared to look in the direction of the noise. Per usual, like the Jews being led to the gas chambers, we looked down at our plates hoping that nothing terrible was going to happen; we learned that looking at plates doesn't make the bad things go away; it just makes you look more closely at your food remnants and wonder who could have cooked the shit you were eating.

BANG!! The Commandant had walked around the room to the front of his luncheon table and pounded his gavel behind him.

"I've decided that you've had enough time to eat and we should begin a new exercise," he said. This meant nothing to any of us, and, simply put, we were afraid of the unknown.

"Put your food aside. **NO MORE EATING!**" he bellowed. **"JACKSON, PUUUT, THAT FORRRRK DOOOWWWN!"** he screamed. This was by far the loudest I had ever heard him yell because he was standing directly behind me. Close enough for me to spit on...stop thinking like that.

"Bean, get your bonny ass up here!" he instructed.

Little Sean Bean, I'll never forget him. He was being sponsored by the Nashua police department and I think he was littler than me. He was certainly skinny. And short. He was just plain little. He drove a Cadillac, a BIG Cadillac. The Commandant and his elite entourage were forever ridiculing him about his "classy, stuck-up car".

"Start talking Bean. Tell us all about you and your big fucking Cadillac. You are required to give a lecture in front of your class and I've decided that now is a good learning platform. Talk for five minutes about anything you want. If you stop talking you will receive demerits. GOT THAT RECRUIT?" Crompton screamed this directly into Shawn's ear.

"Sir, yes sir." Shawn shifted his weight from spit shined boot, to spit shined boot as he faced his colleagues. His brow furrowed and moistened. His chin trembled slightly causing his upper lip to twitch in an ackward way giving him an almost-Elvis look, perhaps a smaller version of Elvis. I could tell he was a bit uncomfortable, but didn't expect what happened next.

His right knee began to shake just enough to cause his tan khaki pants to flutter, creating a closer Presley mirage. The only difference was that Shawn's right foot stayed flat on the floor. He didn't raise his heel and step on the ball of his foot in preparation for swinging his knee about. All he needed was a microphone. This was kind of a nice distraction from the norm, I thought.

"Please, oh please tell me that Elvis is **NOT** in the fucking ROOM!" Commandant bellowed. The Commandant had noticed too. "Get on with the show, Bean".

Then I realized. I saw. The dawn broke. Shawn's color was pasty-white and he obviously had stage fright. This whole scene was torturing him beyond his capable limit. He had already been seriously reprimanded today by having to do extra push-ups and laps during morning · calisthenics. This current harassment was punishment for slipping, falling and tripping two other recruits, during the run.

That wasn't so tough, but afterward he suffered a barrage of insults from the athletic director and the commandant because they considered him to be a complete failure. But then, they said that to *everyone*. Anyway, one asshole had stood directly in front of Bean, face to face, nose to nose, screaming God-knows-what at him for what seemed an eternity. Another jerk stood directly behind him, leaving just a hair of space between he and Bean. This tactic was meant to physically box the recruit in, and force him to receive the insults.

I decided that Shawn had been worn down enough for one day, and knew that on any other day, he wouldn't have reacted this way. It was also the latter part of the week and everyone was tired of the lousy routine and thinking about home. I looked around the room to see if anyone else had noticed Shawn's predicament. Their expressions told me yes. I didn't think Shawn could withstand any more insults that day. I signaled my brothers and sisters to follow my lead.

I pushed my hard metal chair backward, tipping it over as I did so. It made a slight "whomp" sound as it thudded onto the dinning room rug. I took one step forward and stood next to Shawn; I looked directly at him and began moving my upper lip as if I was imitating Elvis also. I looked straight ahead and shook my right leg slightly; enough so that it looked like it was quivering, and I lifted my knee upward. As I began to sing (squawk is more like it), "You ain't nothin'....." a third recruit pushed his seat back, stepped to the front of the room, and now the two of us, embracing Shawn, arm in arm, swayed back and forth and continued with, "but a hound dog". Shawn suddenly smiled and grinned from ear to ear. By the end of the song, the whole 58th Academy Class was standing together, arm in arm, proudly singing "You Ain't Nothin' but a Hound Dog", over and over again for the required five minutes.

Shawn and I suffered a penalty of 500 push-ups each, which

took us a good part of the rest of the day to finish. As we did the push-ups we were called lovely names and accused of being lovers because I had come to his aid. What a trip!

Anyway, when I'm 90, I'll ponder that story and smile, I know it.

Hours bled into days and days into weeks. We had survived, and were preparing to graduate. Our Commandant seemed friendlier now and life was a little more relaxed. The morning before graduation, a local psychologist was offering an optional class about the unique stress that police work causes in relationships. All recruits and their significant others were invited to attend. I was engaged to a guy named Carl Beech at the time and thought this would be worthwhile. Carl and I both attended.

As we entered the lecture hall together I felt truly accomplished and fulfilled. I was proud to be a police officer, and was anxious to put all my training into practice. I couldn't begin soon enough.

The Doctor began his lecture by telling us that police officers have the highest divorce rate of any other profession, and having that information, we should prepare ourselves and our spouses for the difficult road ahead. Of course, he suggested that communication was the key and we did some role playing to bone-up on that skill. Neither Linda nor Leslie attended the meeting, so I was the only female officer in the group; the rest of the women present were wives of the police officers that had attended the academy. My Deputy Chief, Samuels, attended the meeting also. It was an informal lecture; we had each grabbed a metal chair and placed it so as to form a circle. This set-up allowed for open communication amongst all participants. I smiled as different people gave input to the discussion, and supported others as they expressed their concerns. To tell you the truth, I wasn't too worried about this divorce issue because I firmly believed in marriage and all it represents. Then a woman's voice came crashing across the room at me.

"What ever gave you the right to be a police officer?" she asked as she leered at me. "How do *we* (meaning the wives) know what you're doing with our husbands during those late night hours? I don't feel comfortable knowing that you will be in a cruiser with my husband," she accused. At this point I went into a mild state of shock and can't remember the rest of her tirade.

I slumped down in my seat and looked to Deputy Samuels to educate Mrs. Clements about the progress women have made in this world, or maybe even stick up for me and the City of Portsmouth. He said nothing. I could tell by the dumbfounded look on his face that he didn't dare say anything. I didn't feel it was my place to say anything either, so I didn't. No one said a word. They just looked from Mrs. Clements to me and then at her husband, Ed.

As I sat like a stunned guppy, I recalled a Friday afternoon that ended one of our academy weeks. We all ran to our cars hoping for a quick escape and maybe a relaxing weekend at home. I got in my car and noticed that Eddy Clements was having trouble with his car. He looked frustrated, so, because I lived near by, I drove over to see if I could lend him a hand. He had an older car that was refusing to start due to the cold weather. We monkied with it for about fifteen minutes with no luck. He suggested he had some tools at his house that might help to get the car started, so I offered him a ride home. He lived right on base so it wouldn't be any inconvenience to me, and even if it were, I would have done it anyway because, by this time, everyone else had scattered.

I drove him to his house and he invited me in while he retrieved his tools and some jumper cables. His wife and kids were home and I met them all. I sat on their modest living room couch and subconsciously fiddled with an ashtray on their coffee table while Eddy's wife and I talked. I could tell she was feeling me out, but didn't give it much thought as my own thought-life trailed off in another direction...my free weekend. Ed's family seemed very nice, cordial, and appreciative that I was able to help him out.

Needless to say, her outburst at this meeting surprised me because we had a very nice first introduction. In retrospect, she must have disliked the fact that I helped her husband that night, and resented it even more that he had invited me into their home. It's times like this that I wonder why and how my thought process could be so different from others. It wasn't until this very outburst I began to see that other people didn't necessarily respect my decision to join the force because they were either threatened by it, or, for reasons only they can enumerate, they simply didn't agree with it. I didn't, however, apply this realization to all people or women in general. I figured this was an irrational outburst by an insecure woman who had issues with her marriage. It was only a guess and I had no way of knowing. I didn't understand then, that she perceived me as violating some long standing ground rules, and that I would be labeled and resented for that, much like the woman who had to wear the *Scarlet Letter*. I didn't think that I was breaking new ground. I had been brought up to believe that anyone can accomplish anything as long as they try; or if you fail, but you tried, at least you tried. If you don't try, you run the risk of regretting that decision. Life is too short for regrets.

Anyway, I didn't get the whole worldly picture, so I let the incident pass without comment but, like the devastation I felt from Mrs. Dempster in the third grade, I never forgot.

By now, a pattern was emerging that followed me throughout

my career. That is, because I was considered a big-mouth, know-it-all, and I so desperately wanted to shed that label, I suffered quietly, all the while maintaining a mask of cheer and positive thoughts. The quiet suffering is the pattern I'm speaking of. But, let's remember, I was doing it for a specific reason. I believed that soon, within a year or two, the discrimination would end and I could do my job, just like everyone else, and other women would be better off for it.

Chapter 6

Dating

Patterns are woven into cloth.
Cloth is used to make garments.
Habit patterns are woven into people.
People make relationships.
The quality of our relationships define our humanity.
Therefore, our individual or collective patterns, habits, customs,
define our ability to love ourselves and others. What kind of garment are
you wearing?

On the day she met him, she had to admit that there were some strange and mystical sparks that flew; and, to this day, she wishes she hadn't been tuned-in to them, or noticed them because perhaps she could have escaped this whole thing, this mess. As a matter of fact, on the very moment she saw him, she felt the tension he exuded, that thereafter, like a perfect lazer, beamed into her deepest parts, and created a physical pain in the center of her belly, unlike any other she could remember. If she were ever to describe this feeling to anyone, which is highly unlikely because she has learned to hold these secrets close, she would probably say that it felt like an old fashioned hand-drill was stubbornly, but silently burrowing a deep, deep cavern into her very self. The only purpose of this hole, if indeed an inanimate thing can form its own purpose, is to supply the holding entity with a home for it's inevitable darkness. Her body, from the day of their first meeting, began the process of accepting this entry, and she has never fully recuperated.
She often asks herself how one can possibly get rid of something inside of you that you never wanted there in the first place.

She has learned to hide the darkness that his anger caused by pretending, to all her family and friends, that everything is okay; she pretends that she and Vince only experience occasional outbursts, not unlike other couples. She has many excuses for hiding the truth, but she knows that none of them outweigh the importance of confronting and acknowledging the overall damage this relationship has caused to everyone around them. Even knowing this, she feels stuck in time; stuck in a poorly thought-out decision; unable to change because she has forgotten how to move. He has taken this ability away from her, and it will not be restored until she is free of him; but, she cannot be free of him because she has forgotten how to move, or where to start if she wanted to move.

They met at work at a time when Nancy was already engaged to another guy named Tom. Tom was the cliché of tall, dark, and handsome; he was also controlling and believed that he should be able to determine his future wife's profession (amongst other things). He was openly embarrassed by her current career choice, but, this didn't bother her at first. Nancy was willing to quit her existing job in order to make Tom happy. In very short order Nancy gave Tom the money for a down payment on a house that was in his name only. She thought this an odd detail, but pushed it out of her mind, and they proceeded with wedding plans. The house was on a corner, one acre, lot and was quite large for a new couple, just starting out. It had three large bedrooms, a kitchen, sun room, living room, and a finished basement.

Their new home, located in Manchester, NH, was over an hour away from Nancy's home of Rye, NH, so Nancy only saw him on her days off. These were special times between them; they made the most of their days together and looked forward to a happy future.

On one particular occasion, Tom had insisted on taking her to lunch at one of their favorite spots called "The Vault". Nancy hesitated because she was aware that they were short on money, and didn't have a lot of extra cash that week. Tom insisted, by telling her that this was something he wanted to do for her, and she should order whatever she wanted, and he would settle for a sandwich. It didn't take much convincing because the menu contained her favorite meal, Alaskan King Crab Legs served with drawn butter. Besides, Tom seemed genuinely happy to do this for her.

The date went well. They had a lot of polite conversation during their meal and Nancy was most happy with the companionship he gave her. When Tom paid the tab, Nancy noticed that he had just barely enough cash to cover the bill, so she offered to leave the tip. He accepted and she felt even more content, feeling like she was a real a part of his life, and was sharing in it. She left the tip on the table, grabbed her doggy bag (left-over crab legs), and held Tom's hand as they walked to their very old, and very blue, Datsun B210. It had a black stripe going down either side. Life was simple, but good.

The ride home that day proved fatal to their relationship. As some psychologists will tell you, she experienced a 'significant emotional event', strong enough to change her life course; but, not quite strong enough to teach her a lesson. They rode along the highway making small talk when Tom lovingly asked her if she had enjoyed her meal.

"Well," she said, "the crab legs were a bit dry. I've had better," and she was just about to add that it had still been a wonderful meal because they had been together and she enjoyed his company . The earth suddenly and unexpectedly, shook and rotated, causing a complete reversal of his attitude. He glared at her with angry eyes, grabbed the doggy bag that had been securely placed between them, rolled down his dirty, B210 window, and threw the doggy bag onto the road from the moving car. All the while, and afterward, he angrily lectured her on the attribute of gratitude. He told her that whenever she was given a gift, she should never say anything negative about it, or admit that it displeased her. She should accept it quietly and without question.

He fumed further about his experience with the gift giving process as a child. He told her how embarrassed he had been when his sisters were given a gift at either Christmas or their birthdays, and then complained that it wasn't what they wanted. He found this embarrassing and unacceptable and he would not allow his future wife, wearing his one carrot diamond, to behave so selfishly.

Nancy's confusion caused her to become dizzy with fear. She had never seen Tom act this way and couldn't imagine what caused the eruption. As a child she used to have what are commonly called "night terrors", wherein, as she slept, she dreamt that her life was spinning so out of control that she woke up screaming and could not be calmed for quite some time. When Tom berated her, her body reacted as if she was having another "night terror"; her body trembled, and her mind became a bit jumbled in its thinking. Her body had its first physical reaction to an emotional event.

She attempted to calm herself by stating her case; she told him that she thought a lunch date was a bit different from a gift, and that she thought they were well enough along in their relationship that she could be honest with him. He disagreed and that was that...literally. Nancy ended the relationship soon afterward. She didn't end it because he yelled at her. She ended it because he made her experience something that she hadn't felt since she was about ten or eleven years old, and this terrified her.

One day when she returned to "their" house to move her belongings out, he attempted to seduce her by saying that, although he wouldn't allow his wife to be a police officer, he would allow his girlfriend to be one. Having said this he placed his arms around her waist and bent down to kiss her. Disgusted, Nancy pushed him away and walked out of the house, leaving all her belongings behind. A lesson learned; or so she thought.

If Nancy were going to be completely honest she would tell you that she had, by the time she broke up with Tom, already developed another love interest, to whom she was drawn like a magnet. Her affair with Vince had intensified the very week of her wedding shower (for her expected marriage to Tom). She felt no need to broadcast the affair because she figured most people would figure it out eventually; and, why make the situation miserable for herself sooner than was necessary? Time would reveal everything soon enough.

Her break-up with Tom was solidified when one of her coworkers asked her to house-sit for him while he and his wife traveled to Washington, DC. Knowing that her own wedding was looming, and feeling the need to have some moments to herself, she accepted the opportunity and told her fiancée, Tom, that she needed this week to be alone and consider her options. Tom didn't like this idea, and insisted on having the phone number of the house she was staying at. She refused his request and guiltily packed a bag, and moved into her coworker's home.

Being in a strange place made her feel the distance between she and Tom. It gave her the perspective she thought she needed. And it was here, in this house, that she and Vince eventually agreed that she would not marry Tom.

It was in this house that Vince taught her the "Trust Game". She had just finished making two liverwurst and cheese sandwiches, which they ate while sitting on the living room floor, when Vince produced a small rubber ball saying, "Let's play the 'Trust Game."

"What's that?" she asked.

"First we lay down, parallel to each other, with two feet of space between us; head to head, foot to foot."

They did this, all the while looking into each other's eyes, Nancy wondering and anticipating what could be next.
"Now", he said, "I'm going to place this ball between us. We both close our eyes as we bring our hands close to our own body. We count to three together, then we see who can grab the ball first. You have to keep your eyes closed the whole time."

This sounded simple and easy enough and Nancy played along. Eight or nine times she went through the process of trying to grab the ball first, but failed. At each attempt she felt the sudden and quick whisp of his hand skimming hers as he grabbed the ball between them. She didn't mind losing at first because she enjoyed his touch against her hand. It reminded her of an hour earlier when his hands had surveyed her entire body in such a sensual way, that the mere feel of the whisp of air passing between their skin was enough to excite her all over again. She felt her insides preparing for him, though they were fully clothed and playing this silly game. Refocus, concentrate on the game. Why does he keep winning?

He placed the ball between them again and ordered that they close their eyes. "Okay, on the count of three..one.."

Nancy decided she needed to win *one* game at least, so she opened her eyes in order to get a quick location on the ball. When she opened her eyes she saw that he was laying there with his eyes wide open with his left hand hovering two inches above the ball. At that moment they both laughed at how easily Nancy had been fooled into losing ten or twelve games in a row. Vince commented that he wondered how long it would take her to figure it out.

If Nancy had only known that the "Trust Game" was a real-life foreboding of how her relationship with this man would manifest, perhaps her life would have turned out differently. Little did she know that for many years she would blindly trust him, and he would hurt her in every way possible...emotionally, physically, spiritually. After each hurt she would rebuild a sense of trust for him, close her eyes, so to speak, and he would again hurt her. Each time he hurt her he would quietly laugh, as he contentedly took another piece of her away from her self. If she only knew what he had done with all those pieces he'd taken away from her. Have they been hidden in a secret place for her to find later like a long lost treasure? Or, have they been magically absorbed into the atmosphere that surrounds her? Will she ever be like she used to be, or will she forever remain a cracked and segmented human being with no true sense of grounding to anyone or anything? She feels no pity for herself, nor does she want others to feel sorry for her; she just
wonders.

Nancy and Vince dated for only two weeks before they got married. Maybe it was a month; but so much of her life back then is a blur that she doesn't remember a lot of things. The things she does remember are segmented, and out of order. There's no real sequence to the memory of her life back then ; and there's no real order to her memory of recent events either.
It's almost like her memory has purposely skewed everything so that she can't see the real picture; so that she doesn't shock herself with the facts of her own life.

There is no doubt that Nancy had a lot going on in her life at this time. Between breaking up with Tom at their own wedding shower, and being madly in love with Vince and wanting
desperately not to lose this one chance for love eternal (ha, ha), and not wanting the world to know about her love escapades, she was doing a lot of juggling.

Nancy was also trying to fit-in at a job where most didn't fully accept her. There were many people who refused to even work with her, and most of her coworkers will tell you (even today) that they did not want her there, period. Why? Because she was a woman. She was the first woman the agency had hired in their hundred year history; at least in the capacity for which she was hired. At this point in her life, which would be about September of 1982, she had lasted almost a full year at her job. She wanted to last longer, but pressure was mounting. The other employees had anticipated her exodus because of her engagement to Tom; her sudden change of course openly disappointed them. Some even suggested that she leave anyway. She didn't.

Anyway...back to the dating scene. In many ways, Nancy still blames herself because she is the one who actually initiated contact with Vince, hoping for courtship.

After working a midnight shift, Nancy was at her parent's home in Rye, laying comfortably in her parent's bed. The fact that she was in her parent's bed may seem odd, but hers bed was located in the attic which, although neatly decorated, could get very hot during the day time hours, which is when she needed to sleep. Her parent's room was on the second floor and provided an air conditioner.

She lay thinking about the shift she had just finished working, and pondered a new dilemma that had made itself known. She had been partnered with Scott Hurst, Vince's roommate, that night on the west side of town. After responding and clearing a burglar alarm that had activated at a local Rich's Department Store, he had pulled the cruiser to a nearby parking spot, put the car in park, and turned toward her with an unsure urgency she had never seen in him before.

"I would really like to go out with you, Nancy," he said. "We wouldn't have to go out around here. I have a lot of friends in Boston, I know Boston very well. We could go there."

"I don't know what to say," she said. When it rains, it pours, she thought, and how do I get out of this one?

"You don't have to answer right now. I just want you to know that I really like you. You have a great personality, and I see you're a strong person. You've put up with a lot of crap around here and I admire you for that. I promise you that we don't have to say a word to anyone. We could just try it out and see how it goes."

"That's very nice of you," she said. Nancy liked Scott; but not like this. Not like a person to date. More like a brother. Besides, as far as he knew, she was still engaged to Tom; and Nancy knew that she and Vince were very attracted to one another, *and* Scott and Vince shared an apartment together. This was trouble all the way around.

She laid in bed thinking about how to let Scott down gently, while at the same time letting Vince know that she was interested in him. A tricky task, at best.

She picked up the phone and dialed, 772-9191. It rang several times before, as Nancy hoped, Vince answered the phone. This was her first mistake. She didn't listen to her heart thumping wildly through her chest like a stampede of Mustang horses. She didn't listen to the vibration in her fingers telling her to hang up the phone. She was too single minded, too focused in her objective.

"Hello?"

"Vince?"

"Yes."

"This is Nancy Dowhan, from work."

"Yeah?"

"I have something I'd like to talk to you about. Do you think we could meet?"

"Sure. What is it?"

"I'd rather not talk about it over the phone. Besides, I'd like to see you in person. Is that okay?"

"Sure. I've got a ball game at 5 o'clock tonight. Can we meet after the game?"

"Okay, what time?"

"Let's say 7:30 at the Galley Hatch in Hampton. I'll meet you there."

"That's fine," she said, "Oh, don't tell your roommate that you're meeting me. This has something to do with him. Can you do that?"

"Sure," he said, and they both hung up the phone without another word.

She had never called him at home before, and knowing that Vince was a man of very few words, she felt the conversation went pretty well. Besides, she had gotten what she wanted...time alone with a man she wanted to be with.

Of course, Nancy didn't sleep well that day because she was very obviously excited about her first "date" with Vince. Maybe he didn't know it was a date, but he would figure it out. She set up the encounter, and the rest would fall into place; she knew it would. To this day Nancy can tell you what she wore to the Galley Hatch that night. She wore a pair of black, straight-legged, polyester (they were "in" at the time) dress pants that bore a very thin, about 1/4", baby blue belt, and a plain white top with a mock turtleneck. She wore the black pants because, as every woman on this planet knows, they are very slimming, and the white blouse helped to accent this.

This would be the first time that Vince would see her out of uniform, in real clothes, so everything had to be perfect. She believed herself to be a bit of a plain-Jane, with her pixie hair cut, brown hair, and brown eyes, and her five foot two stature. She never wore make-up either, simply because she didn't like the feel of it on her skin. Why would anyone want to put those extra layers of gunk on their face? She was only 22, so she could still think those things.

She checked and rechecked herself in the full length mirror and finally concluded that he would be satisfied.

Nancy arrived at the Galley Hatch first. She took a

seat at the bar and ordered a Dewers on the rocks, with a twist. She remembers that, because Vince had eventually commented that he didn't understand how people could drink whiskey straight like that. In later years, he would refuse to even sleep in the same room with her if she had had straight alcohol (not that it happened that often), even on nights when he had been drinking too. The alcohol smell, as well as Nancy, became offensive to him.   Years later she would yearn so, so, so much for just one thing. The thing she couldn't have. That thing was his love; or a sign or symbol of that love.

Does it mean anything that she can't remember what he wore to the Galley Hatch that night? She doesn't. She just remembers that they sat at the bar for a few minutes, then moved to a booth to eat. He drank draft beer. She was a bit on edge, and didn't know how he would receive the information she had for him.   Had she only imagined the messages he was sending her with his eyes? Had she misread them and was she about to make a fool of herself?   Again the thundering hooves, and the vibrating fingers. Perhaps she should discontinue this meeting while she was still ahead. Perhaps. But, she didn't.

"Vince, I'd like tell you something."

"Okay," he said.

The air was blank between them and she knew it was her turn to talk. She had never been one to beat around the bush before, but she was having a difficult time getting the words out now. She took a sip of her drink, a second Dewers on the rocks with a twist. As if to make her feel better, he mirrored her, and took a sip of his draft. All the while his gaze remained on her.

"Your roommate, Scott, has asked me on a date. I feel a bit awkward about it and I'm not really quite sure what to do."

"Really. Why?"

She fingered her glass trying desperately to think of some intelligent words. She returned his gaze while she fingered the lemon twist.

"Yes?" he asked.

"It's just that I would be interested in dating you. I'm not interested in Scott. I mean, besides, you're roommates and all. I just don't want to come between you two, so I thought if there were a chance, I'd come right out and ask you."

He didn't say anything; he just looked at her and smiled. She smiled back, and that is all that was said on that issue. Always a man of few words, except when he got angry. But, Nancy hadn't seen him angry yet. That would be later.

Although they were both scheduled to work that night, they agreed to go onto the Boulevard in Hampton in search of some fun. Hampton is a hopping spot in the summer, and it's right on the ocean. Lots of shops, restaurants, arcades, bands, and people. They played miniature golf that night and Nancy won. Pure luck. Vince sulked about it. Another sign.

Later they walked along the beach and Vince told her that he wanted to be married some day and have a son named 'Michael Vincent'. He had no reason for the name, he just liked the sound of it. At different times, they picked up the same pay phone and called out sick from work. Captain Cooper took both calls. He heard the rock and roll band that was playing in the background when Vince called. He heard the same band in the background when Nancy called in an hour later. Correct assumptions were made and rumors started.

Then they went to a dance club where Nancy dramatically told him that she didn't want to be another trophy for his trophy case. He had acted insulted when she suggested that he would ever treat her in such a way. Then they made love, for the first time, on Hampton Beach. Of course this is against the law, but that made it all the more exciting. Their only interruption was a golden retriever that kept trying to stick his nose into their personal adventure, in between moments of splashing in the summer waves. This memory is particularly surreal to Nancy because she remembers laying on her back in the sand, naked from the waist down, Vince between her parted legs providing the most pleasure she'd ever endured, and all the while a wet, sloppily panting dog was continuously running from the water's edge toward her and back to the water again. Each time the dog approached her he would stick his nose in her face, sneeze, and then run away again. Such an odd memory, yet undeniably there. As a friend of hers often says, 'You just can't make this stuff up.'

Vince drove her to his apartment that night and, after a healthy shower to rid themselves of the beach sand, they continued to make love, over and over again. Nancy knew that Scott must be in one of the bedrooms within the apartment, so she was sure to be as quiet as possible. She would deal with the rest of this problem later.

Another reason existed for Nancy's desire to be with Vince. This didn't come to the surface, even for Nancy, until years later. It was a powerfully, subconscious reason. She needed protection. Her work environment had become an arena of political and social webs that she was constantly trying to avoid or get out of. She was tired of it and hoped that by marrying a highly respected, and feared, member of the Department, attacks against her would diminish or dissipate.

Protection was a stupid reason, and she knew it; but, she'd have to admit it was there. After a full year on the job, she was tired of the daily testing, cajoling, and degradation. Keeping her 'mouth shut' was supposed to afford her some positive standing with the guys, but how much was she supposed to take, and for how long? Vince seemed the perfect answer.

After Nancy broke her engagement with Tom, she and Vince continued dating; and it wasn't long, two weeks to be exact, before Vince asked her to marry him. They had just finished making love in Vince's apartment when he asked her to move in with him. She said no, because (at the time) she didn't believe in living with someone unless they were married. Then he shocked her by saying, "let's get married, then."

"Okay," she said, and that was that. Once he said it, it was done. They made plans to travel to St. Thomas, and get married there.

Nancy was in romance heaven when, just two days before leaving on their trip, she and Vince went into Portsmouth for dinner. He took her to the upscale Library Restaurant, where they discussed their trip; they called it a trip, not a wedding, or a honeymoon. A vacation. As though they were ignoring what they planned to do there. It was like the Emperor and his new clothing. They avoided the obvious and thereby began yet another bad habit in their relationship.

If the dinner conversation didn't concern Nancy, the argument in the car, on the way home, should have triggered something. But no.

Nancy was driving that night because Vince's prized RX7 was in the shop.

"I don't think that's anything to worry about," Nancy replied. He had just finished saying that his car was going to be in the shop another week.

"Can't you get a friend to pick it up while we're gone?" she asked.

"No, dammit. I can't expect a friend to pay for it and pick it up."

"Pay for it in advance, or leave a signed check behind," she suggested.

"There's no reason it should take them this long to fix that car. They've really put me in a bind." The more Vince spoke, the more agitated he became. He was angry with the mechanic first, and now with Nancy for failing to see the magnitude of his problem.

"There are plenty of ways to work around this," she said as she slowed the car at the lighted intersection of Middle and Miller.

"I shouldn't have to work around it," he yelled.

"Well," she said logically, "if that's the biggest problem you have, you should consider yourself a lucky guy." And, as far as she could see, it *was* the largest problem he had.

At that, with the car stopped at the red light, he opened his door, and got out. He walked into a darkened side street, and left her sitting alone in the car.

'Now,' she thought, 'what am I supposed to do about this?' She blamed herself and wondered if she could have phrased it better, or not said it at all. He wanted support, not accountability.

Another missed signal.

She called him as soon as she woke the next morning.

"Hello?" he said.

Hmmm. Sounds okay; like he wants to talk to her. Maybe he's over it, whatever 'it' was.

"Hi," she said. "What's up?"

"You tell me."

"Are you okay?"

"Sure."

Emptiness in the airways.

"How'd you get home last night?"

"I walked."

"You walked all the way home? That's ten miles!"

"Yup."

"Are *we* okay?"

"Sure."

"Still going to St. Thomas together?"

"Sure."

"Good."

"Okay, we'll talk later," he said.

Click.

They didn't see each other again until the following day as they rode together to airport.

Patterns repeat, that's why they're called patterns. Complicated or simple, a pattern is a pattern.

Chapter 7

Patrol

From 1981 to 1986 I was assigned to the patrol division as a street cop. My first eight weeks were spent with my Field Training Officer, Shawn Beaumont, who later became Commander of the entire Patrol Division. Beaumont showed me the ropes; I should say, he showed me how Portsmouth Police Officers policed.

During my early years on the job, my confidence in the goodness of human nature never waned. My faith in the professionalism of my coworkers and bosses was the foundation of my prolonged stay with the PPD. It was the cornerstone of my longevity and diligence in the workplace. This faith in people applied equally to the folks I arrested. I believed then, as I believe now, that regardless of the situation encountered, yes even in arrest, others should be treated as we hope to be treated. That's what I tried to do. It wasn't until years later, just recently as a matter of fact, that my eyes were opened to the fact that many of my coworkers did not hold the same values. All these years I thought that even though the 'guys' often acted inappropriately rough and tough; treated the homeless person with disrespect, or ignored a tourist asking for directions, that these were only defense mechanisms used to mask their truer, softer feelings of compassion. But many of them really did have a very basic contempt for other human beings.

Even the media, at the time, referred to Portsmouth Police Officers as having the "thump-and-dump" mentality. This was the result of an aggressive policing style, enhanced by a notable lawsuit filed by Dale Daigle against the City of Portsmouth. Daigle, through his attorney Steve Jeffco, claimed that he had been badly beaten by a Portsmouth Police Officer (then Sergeant Parson), and left to die in the woods. Daigle said that the motive for the beating was his admitted theft of car parts at a local car business. He claimed that rather than being arrested, he was dragged into the nearby wood and beaten so severely that he almost died. Daigle openly blamed Sergeant Terry Parson for the beating; but had no evidence other than his own testimony. But, he was able to prove his case in civil court and was awarded quite a bit of money. Captain Terry Parson (he was promoted sometime during the cases' tenure) resigned under an ugly dark cloud, and to this day Parson claims that he is innocent. To top it all off, Daigle is now dead. He died of an overdose of some illegal drug, purchased with his new found riches, just a few years ago. Funny how some things turn out.

Whether or not we were responsible for the Daigle beating, we had been labeled; and, I soon came to know why.

My peers' collective contempt expressed itself in a variety of ways. I remember a time when one of the officers arrested a particularly drunk and feisty man for DWI. The officer's treatment of this prisoner was especially raunchy. I remember, too well, what happened to this old man.

After booking the prisoner, Officer Mentzki placed him in the old-style jail cell that our building accommodated. These cells didn't have the amenities of modern cells, with sliding doors and glass windows, soft bunks, and video cameras to keep an eye on the prisoner. But rather, they were surrounded by very thick, rusted, metal bars on all sides, including the ceiling. The bunk was only about two feet wide and made of the same rusted metal bars. It was like something you'd find in a dungeon. The toilet had no cover, and the water was brown. The cells were just four feet by five feet in size, and the floors were made of concrete that was never washed. The cells were so dirty they should have been declared a health hazard years earlier; but, considering the building was constructed in the mid 1800's we let it slide.

Mentzki stripped the prisoner, pushed him in the cell and slammed the door. You may be asking: Why did he strip the prisoner? Well, whenever a prisoner becomes out of control or somewhat violent, we advise him that if he doesn't calm down and control himself, we'll have to strip him and place him in the padded cell. This action gives more control to the arresting agency and further prevents the out-of-control prisoner from hurting himself with his own clothing.

It was at this point that officer Mentzki whipped out his penis and proceeded to pee inside the prisoner's shoe, laughing while he did it. Having heard the excessive noise, I stepped into the prison area and saw Mentzki, privates-in-hand, committing a most vulgar and illegal act. He smiled at me, a mouthful of yellow teeth showing below a twitching lip that bore a long, red, handlebar mustache. I turned around and walked out.

Next, Mentzki retrieved a Polaroid camera, took pictures of his prisoner as if the old man were his own Jewish experiment in Treblinka. Mentzki photocopied the pictures en masse and hung them up on telephone poles and grocery store windows throughout the entire town. It's possible the prisoner may not have discovered any of this, except that the cocky, genius, Mentzki, stuck a couple of the original Polaroid pictures in the old man's wallet, which he promptly discovered when he got home. This prisoner eventually sued the city of Portsmouth and won a substantial amount of money in settlement.

One of the officers involved, Jimmy Howe, commonly known as 'Quitter' because he always wore sagging socks that wouldn't stay up (sagging socks are often called "quitters"), was fired, and now works for the Kittery, ME police department. The other officer, Mentzki, was somehow sheltered from any ramifications for his involvement. He continued to work as a police officer for many years afterward, but eventually resigned. He delivers bread now.

On another occasion, while working a night shift, I became involved in a high speed chase that lasted about 20 minutes. In the early 80's the rules for police involvement in a highspeed chase were very different than they are today. Back then, it was understood that we were the good guys, and it was our job to catch the bad guy at all cost.

Now, of course, the rules are very different and most chases are heavily scrutinized, after the fact, by local politicians, including the chief of police. This is because we have learned that most chases originate out of the nonsense of minor infractions, and have a high probability of ending poorly for either the officer, the bad guy, or an innocent by bystander.

On this particular night I was partnered with my field training officer, Shawn Beaumont, and I was riding shotgun. One of the other beat cars had picked up a speeder and was attempting to stop it, but the driver was refusing to stop. The car had originally been picked up ten miles out of the heart of the downtown area, which was our patrol area. Though the car weaved in and out of many side streets, it eventually made its way to Middle St. and onto Maplewood Ave. It was at this point that Beaumont and I joined the chase. We pulled in as the third chase car in a string of six cruisers; the bad guy was driving a green Chevy blazer and was wanted for excess speed.

Blue lights and sirens dominated the town, and we hardly noticed as the array of blue lights seemingly multiplied as they reflected off the stream of windows lining the downtown area, or as the repeated "whoop, whoop" of the sirens bounced off the brick walls causing echo after echo. Suddenly, the suspect car, veered into the oncoming lane of Maplewood Ave. Cars approaching from the other direction, being driven by unprepared citizens or tourists, jerked to their right in order to avoid collision, and honked their horns in fear and frustration. The entire line of cruisers, like a group of second graders playing Follow-the-Leader, turned into the oncoming lane tailing the blazer as it jumped the sidewalk and just missed a row of parking meters.

Again, my cruiser jumped the sidewalk also. The second to last cruiser in the chase popped its left front tire, causing it to spin sideways, and come to a sudden stop. Unable to avoid the wreckage, the cruiser directly behind it slammed it's front end into the driver's side door. The chase moved on without them, and I would imagine that those officers stomped their feet and pouted because they couldn't see this chase to the end. They were out of the game.

The blazer took a sudden right turn onto Deer St., a quick left onto Russell St., and then another left onto Market St.   Twenty, speeding, smoking, black, rubber tires screeched, as those of us left in the chase followed relentlessly. Market St. came to an abrupt end, as did our chase. Our involvement, however, with the suspect was just beginning. It was at this point that guns were drawn by all officers, except the driver of the lead police car. This officer ran to the blazer in a crazed frenzy, opened the front passenger door, jumped into the front seat, and introduced his fists to the driver's face.   The introduction lasted quite some time. When this officer finished and jumped out of the car, the next officer, already impatiently waiting outside the door, jumped in. He also acquainted himself with the blazer driver; for that is all he was, a disobedient blazer driver. And so on, and so on, until each officer had taken their turn in the front seat. I knew what they were doing, but I didn't stop them.

My reasons were meager. Besides the fact that these were my peers, and it was strictly taboo to rat on them, I was beginning to realize that this was their culture. It was the only life they knew. It consisted of harassing prisoners, drinking on duty, sex on duty, extra marital affairs. It was as if this was a secret club
wherein membership was restricted, and only those held in the highest of esteem were privy to their immoral, and sometimes illegal antics. I had made the grade, but I wasn't so sure I was happy about it.

I knew then, as I know now that I was wrong to remain impotent. Years of infirm behavior can create lifelessness, or an apathy for living, which is what I battle now; but it is of my own doing. By the same token, I realize that I am responsible to learn from all this; and if I truly master the truths theses experiences hold, I can succeed, no, I can win this battle.

There were, however, many situations where we employed force justifiably.

One March midnight shift I slowly slid my Dustan into a narrow parking space at the station.   The police station, as I explained earlier, had been built in the 1800's, so parking spaces were very limited. I had been lucky to get one. I climbed the three flights of stairs to my locker room and changed into my uniform. At the time, the men's locker room was adjacent to mine, and sometimes the guys would exit their locker room to use the mirror in the hallway for last minute primping. The mirror was directly in front of my locker room door, so I could watch from the corner of my eye as they reviewed their handy work. If I needed privacy I could just close the door.

On this particular evening I was a bit astonished when Vince came out of the men's locker room with the waist of his work pants down below his butt. I watched as he made an elaborate production of first tucking his undershirt into his underwear, and then his crisp, blue uniform shirt was tucked over the underwear, and then his uniform pants were pulled strategically to his waist so as to maintain the perfection of his clothing line. He wasn't at all phased by the fact that I stood boldly watching him. Not that I wanted to, but because I was stunned at what he was doing, at the preciseness of his actions; I stood frozen. He knew I was there, and I think he liked knowing that. He slowly turned around, looked directly at me, and walked back into his locker room. "What the hell was that?" I thought to myself.

I purposely waited for most of the midnight guys to pass my door so that I could walk down the stairs alone. It didn't really seem to be getting any easier at work, but I vowed to keep on plugging. I was taught that it wasn't right to give up. My mom used to say "if you were only going to do half the job, you shouldn't have bothered at all."

As I walked the gauntlet toward my evening's mission, I considered the numerous rats rumored to be inside the walls of the old building . Every now and then I could hear some scratching in the walls which I assumed to be the rats; I was told they were the size of cats. I shivered as I pushed the idea out of my head.

Two officers from the evening shift passed by as though I were invisible; worse than that, it was if I never existed. How is that possible? Not a nod, a hello, even one of their famous smart-ass grins. They couldn't help but notice me considering the stairwell was less than three feet wide and there were three of us passing through the same opening.

Officer Beaumont hurriedly waved me to the exit door as soon as I entered the common area. There were three other officers chatting with the midnight Captain, Charlie Larose, but I had to skip the formality of roll call tonight and get right to the street. We had received a call of an unwanted subject at High Hanover Apartments. We had been told he was a bit 10-37 (nutty) and to use caution.

We blue lighted it to the area. High Hanover Apartments no longer exist because they were burnt down, and replaced with the High Hanover Parking Garage. At the time they were known to be low rent apartments in very poor shape. The owner was already trying to get the building off his hands and not having much luck; hence, the fire.

We creaked up the narrow stairs to an apartment on the

second floor. Shawn covered the front while I covered the back while we stood silently outside the apartment door and listened. We were both puzzled because the apartment was as quiet inside, as we were outside. There was no noise whatsoever. After waiting a full minute, I rapped loudly on the apartment door. Bang, bang, bang, with my flashlight, and then, "Police, is anyone in there?"

I stood to one side of the door while Shawn stood on the other. As the door opened, we were faced with a blonde, scraggly, haired, young, man with a light beard and mustache. He was sloppily dressed in a pair of old ratty shorts, and an seasoned white T-shirt that looked like it had been washed in bleach one time too many. It was covered with small holes that could be easily expanded by sticking the tip of a finger into it. Behind him, was a woman, in the same age group, dressed more neatly. Their living room held some very plain furniture which included a couch and glass-topped coffee table. It appeared to be neat and orderly.

"Did you call the police?" I asked.

"Yes I did. Why don't you come in?"

"Is the person you're complaining about inside the apartment?"

"No. No, he's gone. We don't know where he is, but we're pretty sure he's still in the building."

We stepped into the apartment and listened as the young man talked.

"His name is Brian," he said. "He's a friend of ours, and has been since high school. Over the last several years he seems to have changed. Gotten a bit bizarre."

"What do you mean, 'bizarre'?"

"Well, every now and then we let him come to our apartment and live with us till he can get back on his feet again. When he first moves in, his hair is usually, long, and he's usually got a beard or mustache, or both. He's heavy into the Bible and meditation."

"Okay." Beaumont said.

"Well, it seems he gets so heavy into it, he almost always reaches a point when he shaves his head. When he shaves his head, that's when we know he's going a little bit crazy."

"Crazy?" we said in unison.

"Yeah. He gets completely irrational. He believes he's God, or the supernatural, or something like that. I mean, I suppose we could put up with it except that at the point when he shaves his head, all he wants to do is preach and scream about hell and damnation."

"Do you think he needs to go to the hospital?" I asked.

"Probably."

"Is he on any medication?"

"Not that we know of."

"Does he do drugs?"

"Yes, but we're not really sure which ones."

My eyes floated to the bong standing neatly behind the couch, and back to the eyes of my complainant.

"Okay, well, sometimes he does acid, and he smokes pot, and I've seen him do a couple lines of coke."

"So what happened today that caused you to call? What did he do that made you nervous?"

"He came home today with a shaved head, and began ranting and raving at us. Quoting scripture and stuff. We asked him to leave, and he wouldn't go. He got all agitated and stuff."

"And you think he's still in the building?"

"Yes. I actually thought I heard him going up to the next floor, which is the top floor."

"Okay," I said. "We'll check throughout the building and see if we can't locate him and get him out of here. When we're done we'll stop by and let you know how we made out."

"Okay. Just be careful because he can get really wacko."

"Does he have any weapons?"

"Just a big, black Bible. Nothing else that we know of. But that doesn't mean anything right now. He's not thinking straight, so I suppose he could have something more lethal."

Weapons drawn, Beaumont and I stealthily crept our way up the last flight of stairs. It was a narrow stairwell, so Shawn stayed to one side, while I stayed to the other, yet strategically positioned several feet behind him. This allowed me to provide protection to our rear, while he covered the front.

As we reached the top, we were forced to turn a blind corner in order to see to the end of the hallway. Sure enough, standing at the very end of the skinny hallway, and directly in front of an open window, was a man about 25 years old, tall, thin, yet broad shouldered. His stance had his feet set about shoulder length apart, and he had his hands clasped behind his back, as though he was holding onto something.

"Show me your hands," Beaumont yelled.

Brian just stood there, statue-like.

"I'm ordering you to show me your hands. Put your hands in the air." Beaumont tried again.

The subject fidgeted with his hands a moment, as if they were stuck, and mechanically threw them in the air.

"Are you Brian?" Beaumont asked.

"Yes, I Am," he said, as if to mean, 'I AM THE I AM".

"Are those your friends in the apartment below?"

"A man like me has no friends. If you're asking if I know them...yes, I know them. The Lord didn't have friends either," he added.

"Did they ask you to leave their apartment?"

"Yes, they asked me to leave. I'm not leaving."

"You have to leave," Beaumont said. "That's why we're here."

"You don't understand," Brian said, "I can't leave."

"Why not?" Shawn asked.

"Because my Father told me to stay."

Knowing full-well what the answer was going to be, my weapon still pointed directly at him, I asked, "Who is your father?"

"God. God is my Father."

Shawn and I looked at one another, each a concerned, yet knowing look in our eyes. We had been around long enough to realize when our verbal skills would be useless. This was one of those times.

"Well," Beaumont tried again.

"And I said I can't. My Father has told me to stay, and I must obey my Father."

Without looking at me, and at the same time placing his weapon in the holster, Shawn ordered me to call for back-up. Shawn leapt toward Brian with his PR-24 swinging, in an attempt to make him comply.

My partner had given me no indication that he was going to make an aggressive move at that moment, and, although I was frustrated with his lack of communication to me (I would have advised we wait for the back up to *arrive* before engaging in a melee with a looney tune) I re-holstered my weapon, and stepped into the struggle in an attempt to help him.

Brian was on the ground now, but only because he had stumbled over a loose nail in the floor board. He fell on his hands, and we struggled to turn him over so we could handcuff him, but he had the strength of ten oxen. Nothing we did would pull his hands to the front, or turn him onto his stomach, so we could access to his hands.

He kept trying to buck me off of him, so I took my PR-24 and used it like a bar across his throat. I figured that would keep his head down for fear of strangling himself against it. Simultaneously, I could hear sirens in the background and I knew help was on it's way.

Just then, even though I was holding him down with all my might, and my partner controlled his feet, he sat straight up, and began to stand. As he did so, he thrust me toward the open window, where I grabbed onto either side, to create a wedge. Shawn was now at the other end of the hall way because Brian had flicked him off like a flea; I was on my own.

Now he focused his attentions on me. He pried my hands

open with ease, releasing my death grip, and began to steadily force me out the window. I tried to regain my grip, but found it impossible against his superhuman strength. From the corner of my eye, I could see Shawn charging toward us. By the time he reached Brian, I was dangling outside the window. Brian was prying my fingers from the sill as Shawn came at him like a bulldozer. Shawn shoved Brian forward, up against the window, giving him no room to move. It looked like I was going to be hanging here a while unless I fell the three stories. I wondered if I would survive the fall, and wished I wasn't wearing the extra 20 or so pounds that the gunbelt added. I thought this might make for a harder landing. On the other hand, how did that experiment go, where they drop a penny and a brick off the Empire State Building to see which lands first?

In all the commotion, I could hear a heard of footsteps coming up the apartment stairs. Four officers, and the on-duty Sergeant had come to the rescue. They must have seen me hanging outside, because the first place they ran to was the window. One officer grabbed my left arm with both hands, another my right, and the third gripped my torso from beneath my arm pits. At the count of three, and with a great big grunt, the three of them were able to pull me inside.

We immediately regained the focus of our mission, as it took five of us to control Brian and get him to the hospital. Five of us carried his one, thrashing, self down the three flights of stairs, each taking a portion of his body.

Brian was so wild in the cruiser that he had to be sat on by three officers to keep him from flailing and banging, and hurting himself, or even breaking something. Once in the hospital, after being harnessed at his hands, feet, and waist to a gurney, we discovered an open, four inch knife in his back pocket. That must be what he had been holding behind his back when we first arrived.

As it turned out, Brian was on PCP; a horse tranquilizer that some people use as a recreational drug. The power in PCP is it's ability to make the user feel invincible, and feel no pain. Two years later, Brian was found dead in a back alley in Boston. He had been stabbed.

Chapter 8

Married

After almost sixteen years of marriage, well, 15 years, six months, and five days to be exact, or, put another way, 5,661 days of marital bliss, or yet another way, 135,864 hours of incessant torture, or, 8,151,840 minutes of never knowing where she stood, how she stood, or even, if she stood in the relationship, or 489,610,400 seconds of connection to a man she did not know and who did not know her because he didn't have the tools to learn (he was missing something inside, an important link maybe).... after that amount of time, she found herself standing at the doorway to her daughter's bedroom listening to him explode about the dog while he slouched in a director's chair in front of their Gateway 2000 computer. It was like he was blowing up. No different than any other time he needed to express himself. He was like a professional baseball pitcher who had just one pitch. This could be a huge disadvantage to the team, just as Vince's limited thought process inhibited their marriage from moving forward. He had only one way to communicate. To yell and look down upon as if his opinion was the only considered opinion.

Anyway, he was yelling stuff like: "I hate that fucking dog and I don't think I should have to be responsible for picking up his shit, for feeding him, or for taking him to the vet when he is sick. We spend more goddam money on that dog than anything else. Did I have a choice about that dog? No. I seem to remember that you just brought him home and announced that he was staying. NOBODY ASKED ME. I think that dog is a shithead and I want him gone!"

Nancy responded to this lovely tirade by looking at him with an empty glance, turning her back, and walking away. It was as though further communication, if that's what you call it, was either not necessary, or considered futile by her. Her feelings emanated from her very self, like a late night mist over a calm and cooling lake, as he so eloquently threw his humbled opinion at her. Nancy became angry inside and consciously thought to herself that she really didn't care how he felt on the issue; and, the dog wasn't going anywhere. Fifteen plus years of this type of marriage can callous one like that.

Later, as she replayed the whole scenario, she wondered to herself why she had been so angry about his feelings (besides the fact that his method of delivery sucked; besides the fact that the way he talked to her was enough to make anyone feel smaller than the negative sum of her parts). It was his feelings, too, that made her angry. Very quickly the light bulb went on. How could she have forgotten? But she had.

It was all about Nimrod, a cat she had owned when she and Vince were first married. She had acquired Nimrod on the very day she left college for the last time, May of 1981. She had reentered her townhouse at Bryant College to be sure that she hadn't forgotten anything. Her little Datsun was packed and ready to travel home, into the adult world, the working world. As she stepped into her old college bedroom for the last time, there she was. A cute little tiger-kitten sitting all alone, on a naked mattress. How she got there, she didn't know. All Nancy's neighbors had already left for home and she was just about the last diehard to leave campus. Kitten was all alone; so, Nancy took her home to love her and named her Nimrod. Nimrod, in more common and slightly affectionate terms, means 'stupid little shit'. Nancy felt this an appropriate name considering the circumstances upon which she found her. If Nancy only knew that this too would be a foreshadowing of her own life. Years later she would feel like the epitome of the term 'nimrod', a living and breathing, 125 pound (or so..) nimrod.

Less than a month into their marriage they shared a wonderful apartment together in Hampton, NH overlooking a marsh and the Atlantic Ocean. It was perfectly located on the second floor of a larger, more modern home. It had a porch, overlooking the marsh and all the wildlife it contained; and it also overlooked the ocean. She loved sharing the early morning sunrise with a cup of coffee in one hand, a book in the other, and Nimrod at her feet, out on the deck. All of her favorite things. The only thing that could make it better was the softly sensual feel of a sea breeze whispering it's 'good morning' to her. That, and her dreams for a happy future with a true companion to whom she was now married.

For two people just starting out, they were doing okay. The apartment had a large kitchen. The size of the living room was enhanced by the large sliding windows which also faced the marsh and the ocean; in the winter, the fireplace just opposite the sliding door was often used to intensify an otherwise simple evening. Nancy enjoyed the smell of burning wood, and the bright light of the fire, against the frosted, white, and naked landscape of the marsh. The apartment had three bedrooms, only one of which was used. All in all, they had plenty of living space in one of the more picturesque areas of the entire country. During these early stages of her marriage, Nancy had seconds, even moments, wherein she felt the fullness of her bounty and thanked God for blessing her with so, so much. This was a physical feeling that could well-up within her, and felt as if her insides would actually explode with joy. During those moments, she pushed out all thoughts that reminded her of the truth. The evil truth.

Nimrod was a bone of contention. Vince bluntly told her on several occasions that he hated cats and didn't want this one, or any other one for that matter, in his home. She let the comments ride until, how odd, Vince finally exploded on the issue: "I hate that fucking cat. If you don't take care of it I'll kill the damn thing. All its good for is to be kicked around like a soccer ball. Does it make you feel good to know that I kicked it off the deck yesterday, just to see how far it would go? If no one will take it, have it put down, or I'll torture the goddam thing." End of discussion, if that's what you call it.

Early on, his feelings mattered to her; sometimes she feared that he would leave her if she didn't comply with his demands, and she loved him too much to lose him. Neither did she feel as though he considered her an equal partner, free to have her own feelings and express them. She felt stifled in this area and she hoped they would eventually learn to communicate better as a true couple. In the mean time, she was better off doing as he asked with Nimrod, even though this pained her immensely. She didn't know enough about these situations to understand that the memory of her actions would come back to haunt her at a later time. She was motivated by her youthful, blind love for him, her desire for his complete happiness, and her desire for their compatibility as a couple. Perhaps if she could make him happy, he would be less moody. Less hostile. Nicer to her.

We are all so much smarter in retrospect, aren't we? I suppose we wouldn't learn as much if we had the retrospect prior to making our major life decisions. Oh well. Just a thought.

In any case, for reasons only known to her, Nancy eventually brought Nimrod to a local vet to be destroyed. This cost her thirty dollars, and, as she paid the vet, she worried that Vince would be angry about the expense. He was a stickler when it came to finances. Just another subject they didn't agree on.

To this day she has a vivid memory of Nimrod jumping from her arms into the vet's arms not having any idea what was about to happen to her. When she thinks of this day, this moment, she feels terribly guilty and gets a huge knot in the pit of her stomach. Then she wishes she could turn back the clock of time and change her decision. She wishes she had never done this to Nimrod and knows that nothing like it could ever happen again.

It was this outburst from Vince that made Nancy realize that Weaver, the dog, was Nimrod's replacement. Weaver was pay-back for what Vince made her do to Nimrod sixteen years earlier. Deep down, Nancy had known that Vince would hate the dog, and by bringing him home without discussing it with him, she was basically telling him he didn't have a say in this matter. He didn't get to express his feelings on this issue because he had already used his allotment of opinions pertaining to household animals.

Perhaps bringing Weaver home was Nancy's way of doing "penance" for something she now knew was horribly wrong. It's funny how memories fade, but the feelings engrained in them become amplified over the years.

Well, Nancy thought, I think *you're* a shithead, and I want *you* gone. She didn't say it though, and the feeling only lasted for a millisecond. Feelings like that were far too exhausting for her nowadays. Vehemence was a trend of the past. "The dog isn't going anywhere," she said. And she walked out of the room leaving him to sulk.

Chapter 9

Opal Marie

Craig came through with his promises. On the first of October, 1987 my first child abuse case came in the form of a death certificate sitting on my desk. Never having seen a death certificate before, I looked it over quite closely. At first I was just trying to figure out what it was. It was one page. Just one page, which I suppose might be appropriate for an infant who only lived seven days. The information was scant. It included a date of birth, September 17, 1987, a name, Opal Marie Jefferson, the parents names, and their addresses. It was only when I saw the "Cause of Death" box that I realized what I was looking at. The box held the word "dehydration".

I didn't initially see much significance in this document and wondered what I supposed to do with it. Paper in hand, I turned around and took the two steps into Sgt. Brasso' office.

"Craig," I said, "what's the deal with this? What do you want me to do with it?"

"No big deal. I just need you to make a few phone calls on it. I got a call yesterday from the child's family doctor who thinks there was something hinkey with the autopsy."

"What do you mean? Did the medical examiner screw up?"

"No, no. Not that. It seems as though the ME and the family doctor are arguing over the significance of some details found in the post. Something to do with the saline solution in the baby's eyes. The pediatrician felt the saline level was high enough to indicate poisoning. The ME completely disagrees, but I thought you should look into it anyway. Don 't spend too much time on it though. I've got a few other cases for you to look into that are a little more important, and it's too late to save this one."

I must say this mystery intrigued me. How is it possible that anyone could purposely harm or kill a seven day old infant. It seemed to me the only possibility would be that she had died of an illness, not previously diagnosed.

The first thing I did was pick up the phone and schedule an appointment with a doctor Dixon Turner, Opal's pediatrician.

"Is Doctor Turner here please?" I asked the receptionist.

"Excuse me?" she asked.

She couldn't hear me because of the children haphazardly scattered about the waiting room playing loudly with match box cars, wooden puzzles, and fire trucks. The more miserable babies sat on their parent's lap while stories were read to them as they coughed, hacked, and played with the green stuff sliding to their top lip. Doctor's offices like this often frustrate me because they operate on the assembly line theory, as opposed to the old one-on-one family doctor concept. This particular association employed six doctors, each carrying appointments all day long, so at any given time there could be as many as fifty people in the waiting room. Today there were only about 25, so I considered myself lucky.

"Doctor Turner," I said, "I have an appointment to see him?"

"Yes, well we're closing our office for our noon break," she responded.

"Yes, I know. My name is Nancy Truax and I'm a detective for the Portsmouth Police Department. He made an appointment with me."

"Well hold on, let me check," she said this as though she didn't believe me. I pondered that I didn't know many people who would go to all the trouble of impersonating a police detective, just to get into a doctors office that's being over taken by the "Little People". I stood at the reception desk as it seemed the safest place to stand and awaited her return.

It wasn't until after 12:30 that I found myself sitting across from Doctor Turner.

"I'm so glad you came to speak with me," he said. "I've been concerned about Opal's death."

"You'll have to fill me in," I told him. "The only information I've got right now is the death certificate and a statement from my boss that you're a bit suspicious about her death.
Could you tell me why? And please, before you go into detail, remember that I'm not a doctor, so, explain things for me in a way that I can understand. Talk to me like I'm two."

Dr. Turner anxiously nodded his head up and down and said, "Well, for starters, and probably most significantly, is that the sodium level in Opal's eye fluid was at 189. A normal sodium level in the eye fluid should be anywhere from 135-140. On top of that, at 160 I've seen kids have seizures and die from cardiac arrest. A
sodium level of 189 is extremely high."

"Okay," I said. "Why wasn't this noted in the death certificate?"

"Well, what is noted is that she died from 'dehydration'. I've already spoken with Dr. Porter, the medical examiner. He believes that the high sodium level is a result of the dehydration. In other words, he thinks that a high sodium level is normal in a child who has died of dehydration. I believe he's wrong."

"Yes?" I asked wanting him to continue.

"I believe the high level of sodium *was already in her body*, and caused the dehydration."

"Isn't this like the preverbal question about the chicken and the egg?" I asked.

"Well, yes. Except in this case, if the egg came first, which would be the high sodium level, and the chicken came second, which is the dehydration, we have a homicide or an accidental death." He let this sink in for a moment. "In other words, I believe that the high level of saline is an active result of human action or inaction." More empty space. "Someone put sodium in that baby's body, probably through the formula."

"Tell me again why Doctor Porter doesn't agree with you."

"I can't tell you that. But, I will tell you that I've spoken with Doctor Flores at the Boston Children's Hospital. He too is concerned. He says he's never seen anything like this."

"What do you mean, *like this*?"

"This high sodium level. He's never seen a sodium level in the eye fluid this high in a dead baby. Even a baby who's died of dehydration. He's only ever seen it in cases where there had been prolonged breast feeding with the kids. This is obviously not the case with Opal. She was only seven days old when she died. Dr. Flores also reminded me that with diarrhea, which Opal had, there should be a lower sodium level."

"O.K." I said thinking to myself that this was getting far more complicated than I initially thought. But, I was hooked. I, like Dr. Turner wanted to find out what had happened to Opal Marie Jefferson.

"Have you got any medical records for her?" I asked.

"Sure, I've got them right here," he said. "Let me give it to you in a nut-shell. Opal was born on the 17th of September in Portsmouth Hospital. When she was born she weighed 5lbs, 15 oz. This is a low birth weight, but Opal seemed to be feeding well in the nursery. We subsequently noticed that Jane, the mother, didn't seem to be bonding well with Opal. Seeing this, we had the nurses work with them on this issue. This seemed to work. Opal was able to leave the hospital on the 20th weighing 6lbs, 2oz. The weight gain was a positive sign, and we believed she would do well. We never imagined that four days later Opal would be returning to the hospital, weighing 20 oz less than her birth weight, and not breathing.

The weight loss is another reason I'm so concerned about how this baby died. When Opal was brought to the hospital, we did a code, spent 15 minutes trying to resuscitate her while we massaged her heart, but there was nothing we could do."

"One more thing," he added, "one more thing bothered me about this whole situation. The mother didn't even bring the baby to the hospital herself. Opal was brought in by her aunt."

Back in the office I made a call to Dr. Porter in Concord. He was more than willing to speak with me, but felt my concerns were unjustified. He spent most of the conversation shrugging off Dr. Turner's theory. I didn't want to hear about that. One doctor insulting another wasn't what I wanted to hear. I wanted to hear him explain his own theory. His disposition was snotty, and it was clear to me that he was close-minded about this whole thing. I was able to squeak out of him that he had noticed some *residual* cells in the lungs. He told me that this meant that it's possible that the lungs never matured properly. Because of this, Opal may not have been breathing properly; if the child was not breathing properly, she wasn't eating properly.

"But," I said, "the baby seemed to be eating very well, according to Dr. Turner. In fact, didn't she have a full stomach when she died?"

"Well," he stammered, "maybe she wasn't processing her food properly and thereby was unable to absorb the minerals and liquid she needed to survive. Besides, I've seen children this age dehydrate in a matter of 4 to 5 hours. A child that's dehydrating is loosing liquid through her pores, by vomiting, and through diarrhea. This is how their body emits the liquid. If a parent isn't aware that this can happen, they may not catch it in time, no matter how much formula and water they give the child. It happens so quickly, that even if the child does make it to the hospital the likelihood of death is pretty high. This situation is just not as uncommon as the other doctors seem to think it is."

"Did you conduct any tests to determine whether Opal was absorbing her food properly?"

"Let me check my paperwork," he said. I heard the ruffling of papers over the phone and then a rather loud clearing of his voice. "Well, I believe I did conduct a test and it looks as though the child was absorbing food properly."

"What about the high sodium level in the child's eye fluids," I asked.

"Listen. No salt was added to the formula, or to the child's system. When a child dies, or any person dies, high sodium is a result of that person's death. You are barking up the wrong tree."

Deflated, I hung up the phone and wondered if Dr. Porter might be right. Maybe I *was* barking up the wrong tree and I should just close out the case as unfounded.

"What's the matter, Nancy?" Craig asked. He stepped forward placing his hand on my left shoulder and gave me a light kiss on the cheek. Goose bumps came alive on the back of my neck. I momentarily lost thought of Opal.

I knew this was wrong. I wondered if Craig knew this was wrong. If only things had been going better in my marriage, I wouldn't have found myself in this position. But, "if-only's" were just excuses. I realize that now, but I couldn't see it then.

"Well," I said, turning around to face my boss. He leaned down and placed his lips on mine and slowly slipped his tongue inside my mouth. I pulled away quickly, but not too quickly.

"What if someone sees us?" I asked.

"Don't worry," he said. "Everyone else is out of the office on investigations, so you and I are alone."

He pulled me out of my seat and into his arms and gave me a light kiss on my nose, then on my chin. He seemed to leave his lips there for some time, or maybe time had stopped, I don't know which. He lightly dragged his lips upward, to meet mine. I felt myself wanting him. My abdomen was pressing against his hip and I could feel him growing between his legs. I pushed harder against him, and felt it grow even more. It must be hot, I thought to myself. As hot as I am right now in that same female place. His head bent forward and his teeth grabbed onto my erect nipple that was
signaling readiness. He bit harder, through my blouse, harder onto my nipple, until my loins screamed for attention also.

"What's up Craig?" It was Captain Irons, one of Craig's closest allies.

I scurried like a detestable rat from behind the corner and returned to my desk, not having noticed that the front of my shirt was moist. I don't know if Irons knew what we had been doing. If he did, he didn't say anything.

A few days later I sat in Sheila's living room in front of the coffee table. Sheila was in her mid-30s, and kept a neat, but simple apartment. She surrounded herself with the trappings of conformity. Her kitchen refrigerator was plastered with elementary school calendars, lunch schedules, kids pictures, and a memo telling her that the next PTA meeting was coming up. The coffee table in front of me was scattered with magazines such as Good Housekeeping, Readers Digest, and Yankee. A Grandma Moses, farm painting hung perfectly over a love seat, while a small coocoo clock ticked softly in the background. I briefly considered that her bedroom probably contained a set of twin beds and ruffled curtains.

Mind you, I place no judgment on people for who they are and how they live, but under these circumstances, my surroundings seemed so practiced and unreal. As if the moment I left it would all be replaced with ashtrays and wine glasses. This was the home that Opal had died in, her aunt's home. A home screaming of appropriateness in child rearing and love. Yet, a home that housed the death of Opal Marie.

"So, Sheila," I said, "you are Jane's sister? Is that right?" Intelligent, I know. But, it was a way to start.

"Yes," she said.

"And you are Opal's aunt, correct?"

"Yes, that's right."

"Would you mind explaining what happened that day? I'm just trying to close up a few loose ends."

"The morning that it happened, Jane brought the baby over to my house at about 7 in the morning."

"How did the baby look then," I asked.

"Terrible. As a matter of fact, I told Jane that the baby looked sick and she should bring the baby to the emergency room."

"What do you mean, *looked sick*?"

"I don't know. She didn't look right. Maybe she was a little pale and she seemed a bit weak. Like, it was even too much of an effort for her to hold her little hands up, and it hurt her just to breathe."

"Okay," I said, "Is that when Jane brought Opal to the hospital?"

"Oh no. When I said that to her, she remembered that she had made a doctor's appointment for Opal that morning, but she had left her checkbook at home, in Farmington."

"Okay."

"She left the baby with me while she drove back to Farmington to get her checkbook."

"Why did she need her checkbook?"

"To pay the doctor. She didn't have any cash to pay the doctor, so she went home to get it."

"Do you know why, rather than taking Opal immediately to the hospital, which was just five minutes away, she decided to take a forty minute drive to get money? It doesn't make much sense to me. Especially if Opal was as sick as you say."

"Well," Sheila said, "I guess I never really thought about it. Jane is a new mother, you know. This is her first baby. Her husband was married once before, and he's got three other kids that are all grown. This is Jane's first. I think she was just nervous about being a mother, and I don't think she had that natural instinct about it."

"Okay. So, Jane left. Were you home alone with Opal?"

"No. My kids were home and I had to get them ready for school. They were due to catch a bus. At about 8 am, I packed my kids in the car, with Opal, and drove them to the bus stop."

"How was Opal acting at this point? Did she still look sick?"

"At that time, she looked a bit pale, but she was breathing and smiling. It seemed as though she was fine on the way to the bus stop. Her eyes were open, and she was smiling. Then sometime between 8:05 and 8:20 I looked at the baby and my stomach began to turn. A friend of mine, Faye, who was at the bus stop with her kids, came up to me and told me that she didn't think the baby was feeling very well and that I ought to get her to a hospital right away. She had a real urgency in her voice that really jolted me."

"Did you take her at this point?"

"Well, this is when things became very confusing for me. Julie and I jumped in my car and drove the baby to my house. I knew there was something wrong, and I have to tell you that Faye took control of the situation from here. I was so physically upset over what was going on, even though I wasn't consciously sure what was happening....I ran into the house, up the stairs, and threw up in the bathroom."

"You left Opal?"

"Yes, I did."

"Was Opal alone?"

"No. Faye was with Opal. Faye had placed Opal on the kitchen table and when I came downstairs, Faye was giving Opal CPR. I was no help because I basically lost control, I'm embarrassed to say. I went into the living room and began to spaz out. I was taken to the hospital with Opal because I had an anxiety attack."

"Who called 911?"

She thought for a moment and said, "Oh. Well, I guess I called 911 right before my attack. That was it. I called 911 and they put me on hold!! I couldn't believe it. I guess that's when I shut down and went into a panic. I do remember screaming into the phone that there was a brand new baby dying in my house and they needed to come right away."

Later, Faye and I spoke at police headquarters. She is a certified EMT who, I gathered, wished she were a doctor because she loved talking about the medical business. She's one of those EMT's who can find something wrong in the way other medical experts handle an emergency. She wasn't cocky in the way she expressed her ideas; it's just that she watched medical procedures with a keen eye and could report exactly what she saw.

Faye opined that Opal must have died of a diabetic coma; her training had taught her that dehydration can be a function of a diabetic coma. She backed up her theory with confirmation of Opal's skin color, her eyes, and her rate of breathing.

"Great," I thought. "Now I've got a baby who has died of dehydration, salt poisoning, or a diabetic coma." These interviews only seemed to be complicating the investigation rather than narrowing it to one causal factor.

"Tell me what happened at the bus stop," I said.

"Well, Sheila asked me to look in the car and check Opal's

skin color. When I looked in, the baby's skin was pale white, or even an ash white. It looked to me like she was in shock."

"What did you do?" I asked.

"I turned to Sheila and told her that there was something gravely wrong with Opal. We jumped in the car and drove back to Sheila's house and as Sheila drove, I turned around to check on the baby. At first she was still breathing, and I could see her cheeks moving, as if she were smiling. Then, I saw her skin color change. Her lips started quivering, and her eyes got glassy and dilated."

"Was the baby breathing when you got to Sheila's?"

"I'm not sure. As soon as we got there I heard Sheila scream that she was gonna be sick and she ran upstairs and threw up in the bathroom. Let me think about it. I think she was still breathing because I brought the baby inside and was sitting with her. It was when Sheila was still upstairs that I noticed that Opal's pupils were fixed. This is when I realized that Opal wasn't breathing. I tapped her feet, I called her name, Opal, Opal, and she didn't move. I blew in her face and there was no response. This is when I started CPR. Sheila called the ambulance."

"Was Opal breathing when the ambulance arrived?"

"No. I was still performing CPR. It was a good six minutes before the ambulance arrived, yet it seemed like forever. I assumed that I would go in the ambulance with Opal in order to continue working on her."

"What happened?"

"The ambulance crew made me turn the baby over to them and this is when CPR stopped, for the first time."

"How did Opal seem when you turned her over to the ambulance crew?"

"Her skin was still warm, so I figured that the CPR must have been helping her. The ambulance crew put a pocket mask on her. I noticed that it wasn't a pediatric mask, but an adult mask, which was obviously the wrong size for a seven day old baby."

"Are you saying the ambulance crew didn't have the right equipment?"

"No. They didn't. And, beyond that, there was no oxygen tubular which is the tube that connects the mask to the oxygen tank. They had to make a different kind of tube."

CPR had been stopped three times since the ambulance crew arrived.

"What happened next," I asked.

"Before the ambulance left, I asked them to take a bottle of formula for her in case she needed it later."

"Did they take the bottle?"

"No. They said they didn't want it, need it, and that I should keep it."

A glint of hope.

"Do you still have that bottle?" I asked.

"Oh no. I threw that away several days ago. Before the funeral, even."

I was disappointed as I realized that, before I had even found it, I had already lost the most valuable piece of evidence in a case where an infant was dead, we had three different theories on the cause of death, and an ambulance crew who didn't know the difference between an infant mask and an adult mask. Was this ambulance crew responsible, or a least a contributor to failing to maintain the delicate life of Opal Jefferson? This was a thought I could not abide. Would Opal have lived if the crew had been adequately prepared? With nothing left to go on, I realized that the time had now come to interview Jane and Sam, Opal's parents.

Jane and Sam had many things in common, aside from the death of their child. Neither had completed their high school education, they both worked at the Portsmouth Naval Shipyard, both were short and round, and they both wore that empty look of loss and despair. The kind of look you get when the thing you wanted most in the world has betrayed you. Like a lost child who has returned home to discover that her parents have moved away and will never be coming back.

Their story came haltingly as if they didn't care one way or another how the investigation turned out. The world had already taken away their most precious treasure.

Jane told me that the beginning of her pregnancy was normal, but toward the end her doctor became concerned that Opal was smaller than she should be. He thought the baby might be feeling stress, and ordered that Jane come see him every week for the last month, and twice during the last week. He ordered a sonogram for every visit. As it turned out, Jane delivered the baby that last week, just before the second visit. According to Jane, everything in the hospital was fine and she was released on the 20th. She made no mention of an inability to bond with Opal, or a low birth weight. This struck me as peculiar since the hospital staff remembered it so clearly.

When returning home from the hospital, Jane and Sam stopped at Osco Drug in the Demoula's shopping mall. It was here that they purchased a case of the same baby formula that Opal had been drinking in the hospital, Similac, ready-mix formula.

Jane said that nothing unusual happened with Opal until the 24th of September, the day before she died. She and Sam had brought the baby to Sheila so that they could run some errands.

"So you dropped her off together?" I asked.

"No," she said, "I drove the baby myself from our new house in Farmington. I dropped her off with Sheila, and then went to the shipyard to pick up Sam. We went to our appointment with the Service Federal Credit Union where we were signing papers on a re-mortgage. Once we finished that, we returned together to Sheila's and, we probably got there around 3:30 in the afternoon."

"How was Opal at that point?"

"She seemed fine. She was hungry and I fed her a bottle as soon as I got there. She drank the whole thing."

"Had she had any diarrhea while you were gone?"

"No. As a matter of fact she had her first bout of diarrhea after I fed her at Sheila's. I changed her diaper and she had just pooped all over the place. It was a mess."

From there Jane, Sam, and Opal went to the Toys R Us store in Newington. Inside the store Opal became so fussy that Sam had to take her out of the store to the car, and feed her the rest of the bottle. While out there, Opal continued to be fussy. Sam changed her diaper again, and it was filled with diarrhea. It had made such a mess that the poop traveled up the back of her diaper into her little shirt. Sam had to wash Opal completely down with baby-wipes, and give her clean clothes to wear.

Sam retrieved Jane, and suggested that they go home right away because Opal seemed to be in pain. Throughout the course of that evening, Opal continued to have diarrhea and even push water from her bowels. She went through so many articles of clothing that night that Sam thought he was going to run out of clothes, so he hand washed a couple little outfits for the morning.

By 11 o'clock that night, Jane and Sam had been pacing back and forth persistently with Opal. She was screaming and crying uncontrollably. It seemed to Jane that there would be seconds or moments when Opal would crunch forward, and up, as if her tummy were cramping, release a painful howl, and then squeeze out some form of liquid from her bowels.

At about 11 PM Jane finally called the nurses station at the Portsmouth Hospital complaining only that Opal was not burping. She didn't say anything to the nurse about the diarrhea, cramping, or screaming. The nurse told her not to worry. She should try laying Opal on her stomach, maybe she would pass gas on her own.

Up until midnight, Opal had eaten properly and eagerly. From midnight on she began to take only tiny sips of her milk. Then she would cramp up, and after crying for quite a bit, she would again pass large amounts of diarrhea and fluid. Then be quiet for a moment or two. This was the routine for the rest of the evening; to the point where Sam and Jane had to take turns staying with Opal because she was in such agony.

By 5 am, mom and dad were both frustrated and tired. They had been up all night with her. Jane called Dr. Tremont from Pediatric Associates and explained the situation to him.

"Is the baby cold?" he asked.

"Yes. Her feet are cold."

"I can't hear you," he said. "All I can hear is the baby screaming. Can you go to another phone so that I can hear you?"

"I don't have another phone, but I'll have my husband take her into the next room."

When she returned to the line she said, "Yes, her feet are cold."

"Is she spitting up?"

"No, but she's had diarrhea all night long. She just won't stop."

"Well, let me see....it's 5. I'll tell you what. Why don't you just bring her into the office at 9 AM and we'll work on changing her baby formula."

Here, I thought, was another decision that may have cost Opal her life. What would have happened had the doctor told Jane to bring the baby right to the hospital? Would she have lived? Would they have been able to hook an IV up to her and fill her with the fluids she needed to sustain life? Did Dr. Tremont know that he had made the wrong decision? Did he know that he had told this mother to sit back and watch while her child died? Did he know that if he had told Jane to bring Opal to the hospital, right then, and right there, Opal would be a bright, happy, young 12 year old girl today? I wanted to tell him myself. I think that if Jane had any remaining life in her she too would have liked to tell him this.

That morning, bright and early, Jane brought Opal to her sister's house on Porpoise way. It was here that Jane remembers Sheila suggesting that she bring Opal to the ER right away. Panicky, Jane remembered that she had forgotten her checkbook at home and would need it for the scheduled 9 am appointment. She asked Sheila to watch the baby so she could make a quicker trip back and forth, to Farmington.

This whole situation seemed to me to be so surreal. So real, but not real. Did Jane somehow know that her baby was going to die, and panicking decide that she didn't want to be around when that happened? Did she wish to toss blame on her sister, Sheila? Why didn't she just bring Opal to the hospital? It was a lousy five minutes away. Knowing that Jane and Sam didn't have a lot of money, I also wondered whether they had been frugal and refused the hospital photographer the opportunity to take little Opal's picture when she was first born. She had only lived seven days. Had they taken any pictures of her themselves? So far I hadn't seen any. It was as though the only tangible evidence of her life was the death certificate. Perhaps that's why I'm telling this story. By telling, I am somehow helping Opal to live on and be remembered by those who knew her. It is as though she is a fable that must be recounted to generation after generation in hopes that we'll all learn something of humanity from her. Maybe this was the purpose of her momentarily bane existence.

By the time Jane returned from Farmington, Opal was dead.

We sat quietly, across from one another as if to say anything else would destroy their brief memory of her. Realizing that I needed to put my detective hat back on I said, "When was the last time that Opal ate that night?"

Jane lifted her eyes and said, "Well. It would have been before 11 o'clock, when I called the nurses station. She drank a full bottle. That was the last she ate."

"Do you still have the formula you bought for her?"

"No," Sam said. "We gave what was left of the formula to our neighbor, Mrs. Jordan. She knew a needy couple that could use it."

"Okay. Tell me again what kind of formula you bought."

"We bought Similac with iron, in the ready-mix can."

"How much was it?"

"$33."

"You're sure?"

"Yes. I specifically remember because I was shocked at the price."

"Okay. Tell me again how you prepared the formula."

"All we had to do was open the can, pour it in the bottle, and warm it up."

"You didn't have to add water to it?" I asked feeling as though I was unnecessarily repeating myself.

"No. It was the ready-mix kind in the green can. I bought one case of 24 cans and it cost me $33."

"Okay," I said, "I'm just checking. And you bought this at the Osco Drug store on Woodbury Ave. in Portsmouth?"

"That's right. On the day we left the hospital."

As a last thought I asked if either had diabetes in their family.

"Yes," Sam said. "I have family members with diabetes."

Feeling more ineffective than ever, I retrieved information from them as to Mrs. Jordan's phone number and address. I didn't think I'd use it, but took it anyway.

By now, about a month had passed since I had started the investigation. Craig was on my back to hurry up and close it out. It seemed to me I was doing my best, but the longer I worked this case, the broader the possibilities became, and the more repulsed I was to the idea that Opal had been killed by someone she knew.

On November 3rd, I decided that this would be the day that I would try to find Mrs. Jordan. I had put it off for too long, using the excuse that I had other cases to take care of. I didn't want to give her warning that I was on my way so I got in my unmarked and headed out. As I traveled Woodbury Ave. I intuitively took a right turn into the parking lot of the Demoula's plaza.

"Okay," I thought. "Not my idea, but I'll check it out. It was one of those ideas that seemed to fall out of the sky and into my head (Chicken Little?). Where those thoughts come from has always been a mystery to me.

As I stepped into Osco Drug I realized that my heart was thumping quite quickly against my chest. It was the "what-if" heart beat that happens right before a stressful, exciting moment. Like, when you're scratching a lottery ticket and you've got one more square to reveal, and you think to yourself, 'what-if this is the matching number and I win $10,000?' Or like, making love in a public place and you say to yourself, 'what-if someone catches us?' Or even worse, the 'what-if' that happens just before your car crashes and you think to yourself, 'what-if I die?' Right now my what-if question was, 'what-if my hunch is right?'

I walked to the formula section and slowly studied the various choices that all new moms had. Pink cans, blue cans, tall ones, short ones. Every size and color. The store had the formula arranged alphabetically and by color. I found the Similac at the far end, toward the back of the store. My heart was still beating, 'what-if? what-if?', it thumped. I leaned forward to check the price of one case of ready-mix Similac. The ready-mix cans were tall, probably at least a foot tall.

Yes, they were green. The price on the ready-mix case showed $11.18. This was $20 less than the $33 that Jane paid. I also noticed these particular cases of ready mix only contained six cans of baby formula. I was pretty sure that Jane had told me that her case contained 24 cans. Thinking that Jane must have purchased a bigger case of formula, I continued my search. I was horrified to the point of feeling a distinct tremor inside me, as though all the cells within me had just accidentally collided, as my eyes rested on a case of Similac that cost $33. They were green cans. This must be it. I picked up a can and shook it, as if by doing so it could tell me the secret of Opal's passing. I waved the can in front of my face like an autistic child.

It had been right in front of me the whole time. This case of formula was *concentrate*. Stamped all over the top, bottom, and side of the can were the words, "**ADD WATER**". What if this was the answer? What if Jane had picked up this case of formula, thinking it was ready-mix and fed it to her own daughter in the concentrate form? I put the can down and ran out of the store.

"Oh, yes," Mrs. Jordan said, "I still have that formula. I've put it in the back pantry to stay cool until I could get it to the people who need it. They go to my church, you know. I know they'll be very thankful for the formula. It's so expensive nowadays, you know?"

"Yes, Mrs. Jordan. May I see the case?"

"Why, of course," she said as she shuffled from the kitchen to the pantry. "Let me get it for you."

My heart pounded hard and fast, as I hoped I was wrong. I was hoping that Mrs. Jordan would return with several tall, green cans of ready-mix, Similac.

"Just one moment," she hollered from behind the panel door. "I hope you don't mind if I bring them to you one at a time. I'm not quite as strong as I used to be."

"Not at all, not at all," I hollered barely hearing my own voice above the 'what-if' thud of my heart.

She returned, a smile on her face. I could see as she walked toward me in her bathrobe and slippers, that she was carrying a short, green can, like Jane said. As she placed it in front of me, the only thing I could have possibly noticed, were the big, black, bold letters saying, "ADD WATER"

"Thank you Mrs. Jordan. I hope you don't mind, but I'll need to be taking the rest of the cans with me."

"Oh dear." she said. "But I've already promised them to the couple.

"I know. I'm sorry, but right now I must take them. They're police property because they're evidence."

"Oh? Evidence for what?"

"I'm sorry. I can't get into it right now, but I have no doubt that you'll know very soon."

It took her several minutes, but she was eventually able to pull the rest of the cans from their squirrelly hiding place in the pantry.

On the way back to the station the only thought, like a chant, playing repeatedly in my head was, "Life Sucks".

As soon as I returned to my office I placed a call to Ross Lab in Columbus, Ohio. This was the company that makes the Similac that was fed to Opal. I punched the numbers quickly. 614-227-3333.

"Yes, hi. This is Detective Truax of the Portsmouth New Hampshire police department. I'd like to speak with somebody who can answer some questions for me about your Similac."

"Sure. This is Dr. Tony Ardire. What would you like to know?"

"I'm working an interesting case, and I really have just one question for you. What would happen to a three day old baby who was fed an exclusive diet of Similac formula in the concentrate form?"

"This is very dangerous," he said. "That baby would get very sick and might even die. If the baby died, the ultimate cause would be dehydration and the baby would have a very high sodium level."

"What happens when a baby dehydrates?"

"Well, you never want to see a person, especially a baby, die of dehydration. It's actually a very painful death that comes in the form of cramping, diarrhea, vomiting and perspiration.. Basically what's happening is that every portion of the person's body that allows fluids to escape, will become involved in the process. Many times it can result in a brain seizure."

I was stunned. "I have a witness who was watching the baby just before she died. She described some twitching in the cheek, lip, and eye area in Opal just before she stopped breathing. Is that significant?"

"Only if you consider it significant that you have a witness whose eyes were on the baby as she had the brain seizure. You see, that twitching was probably the brain seizure taking place. The twitching is an uncontrollable action, and although it may appear as though the child is smiling, it is an involuntary muscle spasm."

"What causes the dehydration?"

"Many things. Lots of times it's due to kidney failure. The kidney becomes so overwhelmed with an abnormal abundance of minerals that it becomes dehydrated. That's why water must be added to the concentrate formula."

By the time I had hung up the phone, I had already mentally calculated that in the three and a half days that Opal was home with her parents, she had been fed nine cans of concentrate baby formula.

The hardest part was yet to come. I had finally discovered how Opal died. She had, indeed, been poisoned by her own parents. Now I just needed to know if it had been intentional or accidental. Maybe this was a case of Munchousen Syndrome by Proxy. Munchousen is a sad and distorted disease wherein a parent receives some form of gratification from causing the sickness of their own child, and then bringing it to the hospital, sometimes near death. All the while the parent will dote, coo, and fuss over the child in a most appropriate manner while the hospital staff comments about how lucky this child is to have such a caring parent. By now, I figured that it must be Munchousen, or some other, more diabolical, plot to get rid of Opal.

Jane and Sam held all the right credentials as suspects in this case. It was a second marriage for Sam who already had three grown children and hadn't been expecting to have a new baby in his life when he reached the age of 50. There was a 15 year age difference between Sam and Jane. Neither had a high school education so their deductive capacity was limited; and , neither one could read or write.

Since their marriage a year earlier, they had piled stress on top of stress by buying a house they couldn't afford, a new car, and becoming pregnant. Perhaps it was all too much for them. Maybe one or both of them saw this as the only way out.

At this point in my career, I still hadn't been accepted by my coworkers. I can say, though, that it wasn't for lack of trying. I had tried every way I could think of to fit in; from attending those choir practices (the ones I was invited to), to willingly assisting others when they needed help. Nothing really seemed to work. I was beginning to accept this as just a matter of course. I didn't always like it, like right now, but I thought I could live with it. Right now was a time when I knew that I was going to have to interview Sam and Jane and I wished more than anything I could ask one of the other detectives to sit in on the interview with me. No. I wished that I could ask and they would say yes. The other detectives always had a partner to work with so that when the tough times came around, they had someone to do their brainstorming with. Someone to laugh at their stupid ideas and someone to cheer when a solution popped out.

I didn't make the grade in this category. According to Detective Lanko, as he told me many times, I was just a woman doing a man's job and taking money out of their pockets. The cliché of 'barefoot and pregnant' applied to all women as far as Lanko was concerned. But, if I *was* going to have to be allowed to work here, and siphon from their money till, it might as well be working with children.

Tom Lanko actually said those words to me. The others verbally 'poo, pooed' him, but bolstered his claim by failing to recognize me as a legitimate contributor to the agency. I was in my own dark box. Like a calf who's boxed and crated, without being allowed to move, so that they can be fattened, killed and eaten as a delicacy of tender veal. All the while the calf is living it's life in this dark, stagnant, world, another separate and lovely world surrounds them. This is a world that can touch the calf, but the calf cannot touch it. It is a cruel and hopeless situation, and the only saving grace is that this cow does not know that it's true purpose in life is to die and be consumed by people who gave nary a thought to what a perfect symbol of cruelty this small piece of veal represents.

Perhaps these thoughts were far too dramatic for the situation, but the bottom line was that I did not want to interview

Jane and Sam on my own, but I knew I was going to have to.

I had brought the cans of formula into the interview room with me. They were sitting in a brown paper bag to the right of my feet. As I questioned them at length, and made them repeat the facts they had already told me, I became sure that their baby's death must have been accidental. They watched cautiously as I reached to the right, uncrumpled the bag, and started to pull something out of it. I pulled the first can out and placed it gently on the table that separated us. They looked at me with blank stares. No reaction. I reached to my right and pulled out a second can, placing it next to the first.

Again, no reaction except a quizzical look that told me they didn't understand what I was doing. When I placed the third can next to the second I asked, "Is this the same formula you bought at Osco Drug?"

"Yes. It looks like it."

"Is this the right size can?"

"Yes. That's exactly the right size can."

"If I were to tell you that these were the cans you had given to Mrs. Towel, would you agree with me?"

"Yes." Jane shook her head up and down.

"I went and got them yesterday. Mrs. Jordan still had them tucked away in her pantry." I pulled out the fourth can and placed it next to the third.

"Jane, Sam? Do you see what these cans say? On the top? On the bottom and on the side?"

"We see the letters."

"Can you read them?"

"No. Remember?"

"I remember. Would you like me to tell you what it says?"

They shook their heads up and down.

I looked them each in the eye and felt shame, sorrow, and anguish as I was forced to tell them the words, "It says, 'ADD WATER'".

First a look of shock at me, then they looked at one another whereupon Jane collapsed into her husband's arms generating a wail of pain I haven't heard since, nor do I ever want to hear again. This woman emitted the howl and grief of a mama bear protecting it's already dead cub against the vultures of nature. Her husband looked at me and I could see the shame, guilt, and avid disrespect for himself and the life he had lived. He was thinking about death too; only this time he was wishing it was he. He had given the woman he loved the thing she wanted most, and then killed it. Perhaps they had killed Opal together. But that didn't matter anymore. Not too much mattered to the Robinsons anymore.

Amongst all the commotion, the interview room door pulled

open, and I saw chief Bird standing there, a concerned look on his face.

"Nancy, is everything all right," he asked.

"No," I said, disgusted with the question.

"Do you need some help?"

"No," this time, repulsed by the tardy offer.

He closed the door and left me alone with the people whose life I had just destroyed.

Chapter 10

The Promotion

There came a time in 1989 when I knew I would finally be promoted to Sergeant. This was a big thing since I didn't feel as though I'd 'made it' as fast as the others or as fast as I was supposed to, even though I was working harder than most. I was feeling stymied. Pushed back. It's interesting to note that Officers Demo and Shladenhauffen were eventually promoted before me even though they came on the job after me. The PD's reason for doing this was my absence from duty during my first pregnancy. As a result of my 9 month absence (I left when I was 3 months pregnant and returned when Mike was 3 months old), I lost about 9 months of seniority, which allowed officers who came on after me to jump ahead with total time served. This, of course, didn't seem right and I researched the matter to see if it was legal, but was stone-walled by the City Attorney, Bob Sullivan. I was also blocked at the state level as I was probably the first, or one of the first, women in NH law enforcement to remain employed as a police officer while having a baby, and there were no laws protecting my earned seniority.

Anyway, there were two openings for Seargent, and three candidates. One was on-the-line (Patrol Division), and the other was in Detectives. For the life of me I can't remember who the third candidate was, but I do remember that Joe Ellis and I were vying for top-spot. This is especially interesting because Ellis came on the job about a year after me, and even after being out for so long with my pregnancy, Ellis was still behind me in seniority. He was a bit unnerved about this as he had been counting on jumping ahead of me in seniority along with the other two; he told me that he hoped I would hurry up and have another baby so that he could make that leap. When he said that, I knew he'd be forever nipping at my heels unless I could buck him off.

This promotional event happened several years after that comment, when Joe and I were both working in general investigations. Joe worked the tedious job of handling the evidence, while I worked investigations such as burglaries, rapes, assaults, etc. We both liked our perspective jobs, but the promotions would be to Patrol and Detectives (handling evidence), which meant one would stay in detectives, and one would not. I had no desire to go back to the line, but since Joe already had the evidence job, it was assumed that he would get the detective slot. Joe, however, was kind enough to tell me that he'd be willing to go to the line, and I could take "his" job. He left me with this impression for over a week. Then he came to me and said he had changed his mind, that he had decided he should stay put. I was surprised since he had seemed so sure about his offer.

"Okay," I said, "but I'm going to have to compete with you for that slot."

"Sure," he said, "may the best man win."

The inflection in his voice told me that, as far as he was concerned, I had no chance. He already had the job, and I was foolish to try to win it from him. Joe is not a mean guy, but he can be very condescending.

In my mind, there were two possibilities as to why he changed his mind. He may have talked with his wife who insisted that he stay in detectives in order to avoid rotating shifts and working the weekends. Or, Commander Smith may have asked Joe to stay put and further promised that if he were to interview for the evidence job, he would definitely get it. By now I had learned that these behind-door offers occurred often. This is part of the old-boys-network that I have never been included in, but learned so much about. Sometimes I felt as though I should be looking for the sign that said, "No Girls Allowed! Do the secret knock .

I solidly prepared for that interview because I was determined to get the detective position. I learned ahead of time who was going to be on the oral panel; this helped because there was going to be a civilian on the board, who was a stranger to me. I researched this person through a local business magazine, and by doing this I was able to learn his likes and dislikes which further enabled me to shape some of my interview answers so his interest peeked. I even found a picture of him, and spent a lot of time studying it and talking to it, as if he were interviewing me. This may sound funny, but it helped to make me far more comfortable in his presence. By the time the interview date came, I felt that I knew him.

During those weeks between the time the interviews were announced, and the time of the actual interview, tensions were
running very high at the police department, especially between Joe and I. I tried as hard as I could not to contribute to it, but found it difficult because of his smug attitude about the whole thing. He and others assumed that he was going to be receiving the promotion in the detective division, and I would be going back on the line. As a matter of fact, there was a lot of talk about what my future would be like as a Sergeant in the Patrol Division. I think people like Commander Beaumont and then Captain Brasso were trying to prepare me for this eventuality. I understood where they were coming from, but refused to be taken in by their view point.

My lawyer has charged me with being a bit of an opportunist, and in retrospect, he may be right. I never intended for it to happen, it just did. I took advantage of the situation when it presented itself to me. What situation?

One day I was walking the hallway in the PD and happened to bump into Commissioner Len Daisy, who I knew would be sitting on the oral board. Commissioner Daisy is a fairly wealthy man who owns a lot of property in the Portsmouth Area, and is well known for his real-estate prowess. At the time he was in his mid fifties and had already had two serious heart attacks, and had been forced to lose weight in order to curb his problem. He wasn't a tall guy, probably about 5'8", with a paunch, and that kind of sandy blonde hair that never turns gray. I acknowledged his presence saying, "Hi Commissioner. How are you?" We ended up chatting about one issue or another. He seemed to be in a good mood, so I thought I would broach the subject of the promotion with him. I wanted to feel him out and see what his take on the whole situation was.

"Interviews are coming up," I said.

"Yes, they are," he said, "I'll be seeing you there."

"Sure. You know, one promotion will be to detective division and one will be on the line."

"Yes. I'd heard that."

"The one in detectives is going to be for the position that Joe is currently holding, and he along with everyone else are assuming that he'll get that job."

"Yes?"

"The other opening, the one on the line, will involve rotating schedules and work on the weekends. I'm just wondering why, if seniority has always counted in the past, it wouldn't count in this situation."

"How will Joe feel about being moved out of detectives?"

"Well, I'm sure he won't like it, but, I've already told him that I'm going to be competing fiercely for the position, because I feel I deserve it as much as he does, even though he's been doing the job for the last year."

"Just because of your seniority?" he asked.

"Not just that. I've put in a lot more hard time here than Joe has. Besides, when we were first notified of the interviews he told me that he wanted to go to the line. Suddenly he changed his mind. I don't know if it was personal, or if maybe Smith had a talk with him. You know, made some promises?"

"It's interesting stuff. Good food for thought."

"Who else will be on the board?"

"Myself, Barker, Chief, Irons, and Jim Schultz, who is an administrator for the hospital." And so, the conversation went on about other mundane matters. I had planted a seed, and that's all I wanted to do. I had been looking for someone other that the usual good-ole-boys to listen and hear me out.   I had tried to have discussions with Capt. Brasso and Commander Beaumont as to why I should be able to stay in detectives, but I was told they had already made up their mind. So what was the interview for? It seemed to me that if they could make deals behind closed doors, why couldn't I? Well, anyway, I hadn't really made a deal. All Daisy had done was listen. I didn't realize till later that I had just one-upped Joe Ellis.

August 11, 1990 was the big day. I wore a pleated blue skirt that hung below my knees (mostly because I was too short for it's length), and a matching jacket. I accented the outfit with a pure, white, collared, blouse that buttoned in the back, natural colored stockings, and black pumps with a very short heel. I was later told that I looked like a nun in that outfit. Not the effect I wanted, but several years too late to change that. I was pumped up, and nervous.

I waited my turn in Cindy Place's office; she was the Chief's secretary. Cindy smoked too many Virginia Slims, wore too much perfume, too much make-up, and too much hair spray. She's a powerful person with the inside scoop on everything.   Cindy suggested I take my coat off for the interview in order to present a more feminine side of myself. I left my jacket on. It didn't seem to me that femininity had anything to do with one's ability or inability to get the job done.   It's funny how, back in those days, I always felt so sure of myself when I went in for those interviews. I must say though, that as I write this, I feel embarrassed that I was so sure of myself. Embarrassed that I didn't see their point of view on the subject of *me*.

I was fully prepared for the interview and successfully answered all questions they threw in my direction, thanks to Vince.

Vince had taught me how to give a good interview. One of the tricks is to develop responses to any number of questions you may think are pertinent. Make your responses lengthy and detailed; but while giving your answers during the interview, only give partial answers, yet dangle the subject of a possible question when you finish your response. This will almost always cause the interviewer to subconsciously pick up on that dangling idea, and they will ask a follow-up question on that particular subject. Of course, you've already prepared a detailed answer to their anticipated follow-up question, because you are the one who wanted them to ask it. It gives the appearance of being able to respond spur-of-the-moment. Either that, or it's obvious to them that you've prepared fully for the interview. Either way, it works to your advantage.

Things worked just as we planned. It was as though I had chosen the questions for the board. Well, most of them, anyway. I had a few not-so-appropriate questions asked of me. I'd like to share just one, for now. Commissioner Barker prefaced his question my saying very intelligently, "I have a question for you."

"That's what I'm here for," I said.

"What will you do, if given the detective position, you receive a call in the middle of the night that a serious crime has happened, and your expertise is needed. How are you going to handle that considering you have two children?"

"Oh, I don't think that question is quite appropriate, Commissioner," one of the board members said. All five heads looked from one to another, and it was obvious to me that only two of them understood the reason why it was improper (illegal). The others were stumped. In order to ease the confusing tension in the room, I spoke up and said, "I understand that it's not an appropriate question, but I'm more than happy to answer it for the board." Nobody said anything; they just nodded their heads up and down.

I continued, "I've been a police officer here for over eight years now, and in that time I've worked patrol, juvenile, and detectives. All three divisions required that at some time or another I be called in, late night, for an emergency. I already have a couple baby-sitters lined up, and I have for quite some time because this is one of those careers where a parent can't go without it. So, to answer your question, this is something I've already had to face in my career, and I've handled it."

When the interview initially ended, I was pleased with my presentation. I went to my cubical to continue working on cases as though this were no big deal. Joe took his interview after me, so I waited, curious as to how he was doing. I had been told previously (by Brasso) that he didn't give good oral interviews, so I was banking on that, hoping that my interview would so out-shine his that the scales would be tipped in my favor. About an hour of time passed wherein I did busy-work. I made a couple of calls on cases, and checked the court log to see if I had any cases coming for court. Suddenly I saw Chief Bird, walking at a very fast pace, almost running, down the hallway, down the steps, through the old double doors and into the detective division. He brushed right by me wearing a comical grin. Bird loves two things, pissing people off, and controversy. He was happy about something. He went into Smith's office and slammed the door.

Something unexpected was going on. Must be they've decided to give me Joe's job and they're not quite sure what to do about it. I would imagine that behind those closed doors, they were fretfully discussing how the commission had decided to give me Joe's job, and they had no idea how they were going to tell Joe. They definitely felt a need to develop a strategy because they'd made a promise to Joe that they couldn't keep.

Per usual, they chose the least confrontational way of letting Joe know. They let him find out at the same time as everyone else, during the formal announcement. They didn't even have the balls to let him down easily, or give him a heads-up.

Joe, myself, and the third candidate stood formally in front of the board. This was an awful ritual for every promotion. We line up like dogs in a show, and they tell us who won and who lost.

"As Chair of the Police Commission, it is with pride that I am able to announce the following promotions: Detective Nancy Truax, effective today, is our new Sergeant in Evidence, and Detective Joe Ellis, now Sergeant Ellis, will be transferred to Patrol. To further formalize this process, Sergeant Truax will maintain seniority over Sergeant Ellis." I later learned that this last statement was a thrust into Joe's heart. When he finally did speak with me again, he told me that if they were going to take his job away from him, and give it to me, the least they could have done was to give him seniority over me. I find this logic incredulous considering I had been at the police department longer than he; and, it's another example of how Ellis pompously felt he was far more deserving of the promotion, than I. I wouldn't be stretching it too much if I were to imagine that Joe thought it was a joke that I had even gotten promoted. But the truth is that I had worked in more divisions than he, including the juvenile division wherein I handled some of the most difficult child abuse cases. I had made numerous felony arrests, and presented as many, or more cases to the Grand Jury.

Mark Twain once said, "A lie can travel half way around the world while the truth is putting on its shoes." Rumors were then, and still are, an integral thread in the fabric of the Police Department. The culture is such that, employees seem to thrive on talking badly against one another.   What most people fail to realize is that everyone at some point becomes a victim of this gossip. The result is a rather queer phenomenon wherein employees walk around feeling most superior to their peers, all the while they are being talked about negatively by someone else. This is a perplexing circumstance, and leads to a rather antagonistic environment. At the same time, no one seems to understand why they are not respected for the work they have done, or are doing.   I eventually figured this to be the reason for Joe (and other's) off-kilter view of me. My problems at home were beginning to leak out to the general public and this gave my colleagues room to talk.

Just recently, before taking a five week trip to write this book, I had received information from a colleague that Mildred Peas, the Chief's (current) Administrative Assistant was making negative comment (I won't be specific about what was said) about the very fact that I was taking five weeks off for "personal" reasons. She wanted

to know who the hell I thought I was; she had latched onto this small
piece of information as fuel for lunch room banter. I found
it interesting that she could say these things even though she wasn't
present in the meeting when I requested the leave, nor did she realize
that we'd been asked to use our annual leave (rather than save it up
for a later pay-off) as it is more cost effective for the agency this way.
Further, I've never worked with Peas in my life. There's never been a
time in my career when Peas and I have worked in the same division.
Why would she, a civilian secretary, feel a need to be negatively
opinionated about the fact that I was simply using some benefits that
I had earned? The only response to this could be that others were
filling her head with bogus information as to who I am, and what I'm
about. The end result causes friction between myself and someone I
barely know for reasons foreign to me.

Another example on the Mildred Peas front is that one day,
several years ago, when I was acting in the capacity of Sergeant in
Patrol, I had approached her (a detective secretary at the time) to
make arrangements to use an unmarked car for a directed patrol
project. When I asked her for some help, she became angry with me
and told me that it wasn't her job to help me. I simply responded that
I was a Sergeant in patrol, trying to get a job done and thought that
she might have the resources that I needed. Her attitude toward me
was immediately hostile, and could only been the result of having
received faulty information from others.   As senseless as it is, it
creates palpable, intolerable tension. Words are powerful!

There was a time in my employ with the agency, when I had
become particularly close friends with Linda Channels, a secretary.
Certain officers would approach her, saying bad things about me. In
the same breath, they were coming up to me, bad-mouthing her.
Over a period of time, this resulted in the break-up of our friendship.
But, by employing this tactic, the officers were also insuring that
Linda and I weren't putting our heads together and talking about
them. It's a cowardly approach to social life in the work place.
Unfortunately, most who work there aren't in tune enough to realize
that this is what's going on. I call it the divide and conquer tactic.

Because of this pervasive culture, the result of my promotion
to Sergeant ahead of Joe Ellis, was that I was again blackballed for a
long time by most people within the department. Even though I had
been senior to Joe, had more job experience, and in my view I had
done at least as well as, if not better than, he in job performance, it
was still fodder for harassment. The perception was that I had taken
something from Joe that was rightfully his. Even though I didn't see
this as the truth. that's how others saw it, so that became the spin.
Once the spin takes hold, it becomes fact... history. There was
nothing for me to do but wade through the wake of resentment that

had arisen from this and continue my work in silence. It took at least two years to recover. It took at least that long before Joe Ellis would talk to me again; and just about as long for fellow officers to speak with me again. Since that time, though, I have been viewed as the manipulative, greedy, bitch who will do anything necessary to get what she wants. I have a very wise friend who once told me that when people have a negative opinion of you, the worst thing you can do is try to argue against that opinion because it only serves to solidify their belief in whatever it is they think you are. So, I didn't argue.

It's been amazing to me that my entire career has been fraught with controversy of one sort or another, as a direct or indirect result of the fact that I am a female. As you learned in earlier chapters, I wasn't wanted when I first came on, and had to go through quite a bit just to stay on the job, never mind get promoted. Then, at this stage of my career, when I was given a promotion that I had well deserved, it was tainted with a great deal of animosity from the department as a whole. I found it rather humorous when, later, on the day of the promotion, Captain Brasso pulled me into the interview room upstairs. He sat across from me and had the gall to say, "Congratulations, Nancy. We did it." He was trying to indicate that he had a hand in my getting the position I wanted and maintaining seniority over Joe. The funny thing is, I know for a fact that he formally advocated that Joe get promoted over me. Strange how some people like to take credit for something they had no hand in. I figured it must have been a power play on Craig's part.

It was at this point that Craig told me that commissioner Barker wanted to see me. Craig led me to the Chief's office where the entire board had reassembled. I again sat in the chair provided. "Yes?" I asked

"I need to tell you, Nancy, that I was displeased with your interview style," Barker boomed. I looked at each of them and they were smug.

"This was not the time or place to uplift yourself over another officer. You should not have said that you were better than he, just that you were the better candidate. Because of that, I was a dissenting vote, and I wanted you to know that (Joe Barker and Jimmy Smith drank together. Jimmy wanted Ellis, so Joe wanted Ellis. They probably had a toast on it).

"Yes sir," I said. "Anything else?"

"No. That sums it up."

I left the room mystified over the political antics of men. For the first time in my career I had approached a promotional situation in the same manner I'd seen my peers do it. My preinterview conversation with Daisy, and my interview style were simple attempts at leveling a playing field that had become progressively steeper for me, and smoother fo rthe men. But, what I didn't know them, was that research does show that aggressiveness by women in the work place will most often backfire, while men can use it to their success.

Chapter 11

Rocking Her Life Away

She pulled into the driveway of their home anxious to see her family. She was especially optimistic today as she'd been thinking, imagining, all day about making this a special evening at home. No real reason. She just wanted to make things nice around her. Marriage with Vince had been so difficult from the start; but she knew, just knew, that it would work out.

She'd stopped at the store and bought the ingredients for a pasta dinner with garlic bread. Simple, but made perfect by the two bottles of red wine she hoped would create a light and casual atmosphere. She anticipated a late night love-making session to help muffle his inner demons. Sometimes it seemed as though sex was like a drug to him. Love making was never tender and romantic, but rough, needy, careless, thoughtless, as though something inside needed to be tamed. Tamed or expelled. When he was done there was always the surety that he would fall back in exhaustion, and slip into a world she would never see because he didn't want her there. Nancy didn't mind that too much because she too had private places in her dreams and mind that she'd never let anyone see. They were places just for her.

As always happened, when she pulled into the driveway she felt the contented swell of completeness that a home symbolizes. She loved that they had bought an oversized cape and not just a regular sized cape. She loved that they had dormered out the back in order to make even more room, and then built a huge room over the garage. She was in love with the idea of having flower gardens and vegetable gardens that needed tending and looked forward to years of manicuring her yard and maybe making a rock garden some day.

The brevity of the moment passed as she stepped into her kitchen from the side door. She was still in her uniform and felt hot, sticky, and anxious to get into some more comfortable clothes. Her heavy black boots made her feet sweat, and this was especially annoying to her, but something she had grown to accept.

"Hello? Are you here?" she yelled. She slammed the door behind her and went immediately to the dining room where she removed her gun, unloaded it, and placed it in a wooden box, high up. "Hello?"

Must be upstairs, she thought. She piddled in the kitchen for a few moments. She put the groceries away and remembered that Vince must be picking Mike up at day care. Good, she thought.

That will give me time to organize dinner. First, though, off with these clothes. She turned the corner to the living room in order to make her way upstairs and was surprised to see Vince sitting there. To this day, she has never seen another person wearing an expression similar to the one Vince had on. More than anything else, that's what she noticed first. His expression. It telegraphed his mood; and she knew that it was blacker than black. It was a mood that originated from below, from the belly of some very, very bad thing. Bader than bad. He appeared to be in a trance, but aware that she was there. He was aware because he'd been waiting for her; but not in the same way she'd been waiting for him.

She stood in the hallway by the living room entrace, fully aware of her surroundings. There had been enough times like this that she had trained herself to be cognoscente of what was behind her, and in front of her. She mentally calculated her escape routes. The front door was immediately in front of her, but she'd have to pass the demon to get to it. The side door was behind her and to her left. This route was a bit akward, but provided a higher probability of escape. There was also the slider going out to the deck, but that was probably locked. Better stick with the sure thing.

She stood very still for a moment, not wanting to make any sudden movements. He was in the rocking chair they had bought together for the birth of their first baby, Michael Vincent. He rocked back and forth, back and forth looking at her as though he had made some horrible, final decision and was getting ready to carry it through. He was pumping himself up, revving up his engines because he was at the starting gate. Nancy was the rabbit, and Vince the hound.

She stepped fully under the archway and leaned against it for support. Still no words, but he hadn't leaped out yet. That was a good sign. Maybe there was something legitimately bothering him, she thought as she consciously pushed her intuition aside. She slid sideways to the couch and sat timidly on it's arm, all the while remaining focused on Vince. She had by now learned how to control the dizzy feeling that used to overtake her at moments like this. It was all a matter of will power and control.

"You stupid bitch," he said.

She didn't say anything. Just looked. Just wondered how this had happened to her, and what had ever happened to Vince to make him this way. So many thoughts. Twirling. Whirling. In and out.

"Cunt," he said, this time louder.

She looked him straight in the eye letting him know that she would stand her ground. The routine had been shamefully practiced over and over again. Each time Nancy tried a different tact. She used to argue back, but that seemed to make him angrier. She used to go about her chores, ignoring him. That pissed him off even more. The ploy that pissed him off the most was when she began singing. That infuriated him to the point of cruel rage. Leaving seemed to be only a temporary solution because when she returned, his anger usually multiplied. The whole thing was a mind-fuck, like the Rubix Cube, you might never get the right solution.

"How'd you crack up the car?" he demanded.

"Is Mike home?" she asked.

"Ugly bitch. Tell me what happened to the car."

"Vince, you're only doing this so that you can start a fight, and I'm not going to force your hand. Tell me why you're in this mood."

"I am so sick and tired of you. I hate you and I hate being here with you. One of these days I'm gonna burn this house down while you're sleeping in it."

None of this was news to her. He had said so many terrible things to her that she thought there might not be any bad word combinations left. He had used them all up. It was only sometimes that she believed he meant what he said.

"Vince. Something is wrong. Tell me what's going on. I do not want to fight with you."

Then he was up, and on her. One of the things she loved about him was his athleticism, his overall quickness and speed. When she married him she hadn't imagined that he would use it against her.

She tried to push him off her but was only partially successful. She gave herself just enough room to stand up. She was hoping to get to that mapped-out exit. He grabbed onto her hair and pushed and pulled until he got her into an adjoining room. She struggled against him, screamed and yelled. He straddled her at the waist as she lay on her back and spit in her face. He grabbed another clump of her hair and slammed her head repeatedly against the floor. She kicked the air with her feet in an attempt to throw him off balance. She twisted beneath his powerful legs and refused to give up.

The pounding lump on the back of her head breathed strength into her body as she somehow worked her way from under him. She ran to the side door, but he followed her, grabbed her by the uniform shirt collar, and shoved her against the corner of a kitchen cabinet. She tried to scream in pain, but the shove had knocked the wind out of her. She automatically brought her hand to her lower back where she felt the slippery thickness of her own blood trailing the crack of her butt. It was somehow soothing, but she didn't know why. Maybe because it defined for her the meaning of this relationship. Maybe it meant sacrifice. Maybe it didn't mean anything and she just thought it should mean something.

Nancy hated him for this. Hated him for not loving her, hated him because she didn't understand him, hated him because he wouldn't leave her, but mostly hated him because she never lost hope. Hope is a bad thing sometimes because it makes you cling onto things that maybe you should give up. It makes you stay in places you shouldn't stay. It whispers false credos of 'better things to come', 'hold on', 'I promise', 'trust me', 'wait and see'. There are times when we have no right to hope, but we do anyway. It's an instinct, a survival mechanism for the eternal optimist. She didn't believe that hope was wrong; but she believed it was wrong to always have hope.

Her expression changed from disbelief to rage. She sensed his pleasure with this, as though that's all he wanted the whole time, as if he didn't want to be alone with his dark and cruddy feelings.

She shoved him backward and left the house, disgusted that she had allowed herself to be twisted up by him. Disgusted that she didn't know why he was angry, but believed he didn't know either.

Most of all she was disgusted because she knew she would try again, because that is what she, and people like her, do. Each time she goes back to the starting gate for another lap around the track. Sometimes the next lap is a winner, and this makes her so happy she has to try again Sometimes the next lap is a loser, and this frustrates her and sends her to the starting gate so that she can attempt to have a successful, perhaps winning, race. When she loses
the race, she feels like a failure and this, in turn causes a knot in her stomach the size of Texas, so her first desire is to do anything she can to get rid of it. I know!!! Another Lap around the track, and this time she'll do it right. What a concept. What a tiring concept.

Of course, there's more to the cycle. There's the period between the actual failure and the return to the gate to consider. You see, some take defeat quietly and walk away. These people eventually return to the gate unnoticed and without announcement. They hang their head, kick their toes in the sand, and don't really say too much. When the starter pistol sounds, they haven't thought too much about the lap ahead of them other than to feel they probably won't succeed this time either. But, from their perspective, at least they showed up.

Others approach the gate with anticipation and expectation. Before the gun goes off, they've made themselves known to the crowd, and look forward to the victory cheers.

What all these people fail to understand is that they have made this race their life's burden. There's no way to be victorious in the race, because a partnership is not about winning and losing. The race shouldn't exist. It's not up to one partner to be the pleaser and the doer, and the other to levy judgment. It's about love and respect, one for the other. It's about caring, really caring, about your partner's life, you partner's wishes and secrets, shallow or intense.

It's not up to anyone to win the race. It's up to everyone to work together for success.

Officer Nancy J. Truax

Officer Truax plays in a Celebrity Basketball Game

Officer Truax pictured with fellow officers
Third row far left

**Posted in the Portsmouth Police Station during
Officer Truax's tenure**

Result of a High Speed Chase

Departmental photo taken circa 1996
Truax regrettably is not in the photo. Arrangements and
the shoot itself took place while she was on vacation.

Officer Truax with son Michael and daughter Matty posing with Department Administrators as she receives an award for Exceptional Service in the Court Office

Officer Truax donates her time to raise money for Cancer Victims

Officer Truax donates her time and energy to raise money for the Special Olympics

Chapter 12

Commissioner-Elect

I'd never considered myself an activist or feminist, but as time passed, the kinetic forces of my personal experiences seemed to be pulling me toward that which couldn't be avoided. With clear vision I could see the goal line of social reform and knew that it must be reached, because it is the rightful conclusion to the entire mess "I" had generated. But, is it really "I" who was responsible? I was in conflict over the situation, and was in the middle of a real-life nightmare and forced to see it to the end. I'd never experienced anything like this and at first questioned...'Why me?' The answer came as I was studying one day for a promotional exam (from sergeant to captain, which I didn't get, but did succeed in making a complete ass out of myself). I read this in a management book: "It is not for man to question what the meaning of life is, but rather to acknowledge that it is he who is being asked. In a word: man is being questioned by life, and his answer to life can only be found in his answer to his own life; and to life his only response can be responsibility." It was at that moment that I understood that no matter how difficult, controversial and alienating the process, it was my responsibility to lead this cause to its finish. Or, as my parents would say, finish what I started. Never do just half a job. They used to say that to me after I plopped my clean clothes on the stairs and left them to be taken up and put away later. Of course, 'later' didn't come until I'd been scolded, at least twice, for leaving them there. Although this situation was more serious, the same rule applied.

If one were to glance quickly at my career path with the Portsmouth Police, I suppose one might conclude that its been successful, but with the normal amount of bumps and bruises expected after so many years with an organization. Scratch the mucky layer of political filth from the surface of the viewing screen, and I think you might change your mind.

A most recent event is a good example of the continued oppression I've encountered over the years, and its happening only intensifies, and brings to the surface, my beliefs about women working in a predominately male vocation: "the playing field must be evened-out".

A staff meeting was held just prior to the beginning of the New Year. It was mandatory, so all persons with rank of Sergeant and above attended. Our Chief and Commanders were also present, and next to the Chief our newest, elected, Police Commissioner (scheduled to take office just after the beginning of the new year). It had been rumored that the new Commissioner was a real hands-on type of guy and his attendance at the meeting demonstrated this. He took interest in all the topics discussed and even asked a few questions. Before posing his question, he would ask the Chief's permission to speak. By all appearances he seemed knowledgeable, and professional. I knew nothing about him other than that he was a Commissioner-Elect, a retired FBI agent, and that he was (on the surface) conscientious about his work. He had been quoted in the Portsmouth Herald on November 8, 1995, right after the election, as saying, "My election as police commissioner in one of the oldest cities in the New World does honor to my immigrant parents. God Willing, I'll do my best. I will not rush in and break the china." By all accounts, he seemed sincere and committed; except that he rushed in and broke the china.

I was scheduled for an evening tour of duty after the meeting, so I asked another Sergeant (Foley) for a ride back to the Police Station. At the time, Foley was the boss of the Juvenile Division. He is a very kind-hearted person, and I find him very easy to talk to, so in the short ride to the station we gabbed about a variety of issues pertaining to work. At one point he said to me, "Nancy, we're gonna have to keep an eye on the new Commissioner, Kupruck. Have you heard about the comment he made in the dispatch center?"

"No," I said, "What are you talking about?"

"While he was in the dispatch center visiting, he made a derogatory comment about women. He said, 'The FBI was a great place to work until they lowered their standards and let all the broads in.' Linda heard him say it." Linda is a dispatcher.

My lower jaw dropped noticeably, I'm quite sure. "You're kidding me." I was immediately concerned about working for a man who considers women to be "broads", and looks down on them in terms of professional performance. What could this mean for myself and the other four women working for him? Clearly this is a man who will be responsible for task reviews, setting department policy, and thereby organizational direction. Does this comment represent a new direction for our agency? A thousand other thoughts ran through my head and an overall sick and sinking feeling overcame me. For the umpteenth time in fourteen years I felt deeply offended on all levels.

In the past there have been scads of people who have voiced this and similar opinions to me, but those people were never in a position of authority over me. They had no power to effect my career. This man did.

As soon as Foley dropped me off, I went into Commander Beaumont's office to voice my concerns. Beaumont told me that he had been told of this comment about two weeks prior and had immediately advised the Chief because he too was concerned. Beaumont told me that the Chief would deal with the issue by telling Kupruck about our sexual harassment policy, but Beaumont didn't know if this had been done yet. In retrospect it seemed suspicious to me that during the previous staff meeting the Chief touched on the sexual harassment policy, and told us all to review it and be sure that it was enforced. Just as Chief Bird was beginning this portion of the meeting, Commissioner-elect, Kupruck, excused himself stating he had another meeting to go to.

I had another glaring question. If the administration knew about this two weeks ago, why had nothing been done? Apparently no one had dared to confront Kupruck directly.

Over the next two days I weighed my options as to how to address this problem. I knew it was a weighty issue and that , no matter what I did, the burden would wind-up on my shoulders. It was immediately clear to me that no matter what I did, I would be a loser in the end. It was a lose-lose situation. I could either lose quietly by saying nothing and take the great risk of allowing myself and other women to be managed by a man who may consider women to be simple tokens of the profession, and no more. I have heard theorized by those with this opinion that we (women) are actually taking jobs away from healthy males, who are, by the way, better qualified to handle the position. I work with some people who have this theory. But you know that already.

Or, I could take the bumpier road, and confront the issue head-on and risk the political ruin of my own career. After all, I am aware that whistle blowers are never rewarded for their convictions. I had to choose and it wasn't easy. The decision was based on one question: Which action could I best live with? Which action would allow me to look in the mirror each day and say, 'I can respect myself for this decision. I have acted responsibly.' As Colin Powell said, "I cannot control other people's actions - only my own."

One thing pushed me over the decisional edge. I learned that Mr. Kupruck had made overt sexual comments in the Police building to a newspaper reporter. Not just one comment, but three. He commented to her about the shortness of her skirt and the shapeliness of her legs. He was not friends with her or even an acquaintance. The fact that he had done this showed me that he had a certain mind-set regarding women, and I needed to, at the very least, find out if these statements were actually made by him. Thinking logically, I recognized that the police grape-vine is very capable of distorting truth; so, my first mission was to determine if Mr. Kupruck did, in fact, make these statements.

When dealing with the beaurocratic, political system one has to consider all angles of any problem. My next question was: 'How should I approach this? In what arena will this be played out? Should I make this a public issue?' My initial thought was to present the issue at an open and public commissioners meeting that would be held in just two days. My reasons for wanting to go public were simple. I was legitimately scared about our (women) future with the agency and felt that if I didn't receive support from my own organization, the public would at least see the injustice of the situation. I have since learned that that thinking, aside from being naive, was wrong as wrong could be. Those thoughts were the very foundation of my strategy; we all know that if the foundation is off center or cracked the house will come tumbling down, and that is exactly what happened.

In any case, that was my first intended approach until I received a phone call from Commander Beaumont the following day.

"Nancy," he said, "I've just finished speaking with the Chief about the Kupruck affair." I noticed a bit of anxiety in his voice...or maybe it was just my imagination at play. "He is willing to give you an audience, in private, if you'd like."

'Oh Goody,' I thought. Not.

Now I was getting nervous and suspicious. What was the Chief afraid of? I knew what I was afraid of and I told the Commander.

"Shawn, I don't like the idea of going behind closed doors with those people. I'm afraid if I do that, this will get swept under the rug, and nothing will be done about it except that I will be labeled a trouble maker and I'll have no outside support. I don't know if I want to do that."

"I'll go in as a witness with you," he said.

"I don't know. Let me think about it." I said.

The understood implication here was that I could speak my peace behind closed doors or not at all. I would be blocked from comment in the public hearing. To be truthful, I wasn't willing to do that until the day of the meeting when I was formally advised by Beaumont that the Commission wouldn't allow me to address them publicly. If I were to raise my hand during the meeting, they would refuse to acknowledge me. Another no-win situation, and I had to make the best of it. My convictions were strong and I felt it was an important enough issue to make this compromise.

My meeting with the Chief was very short; less than five minutes in total. These few short minutes were of the most impacting of my entire career (up to that point). I asked that both Commander Beaumont and Sergeant Foley be present as witnesses. Commissioner Ricci was present, and I directed all my conversation toward him as he seemed to be taking the lead. He seemed interested in my plight.

I very politely thanked them for allowing me the time to address them and openly expressed my concerns about being behind closed doors with them. Then I very simply said, "It's come to my attention that Commissioner-elect Kupruck has made some offensive statements about women. I do not know if they're true, but I would like the matter looked into. I was told that while he was in the dispatch center, and in front of Linda Channels, Robert Johnson, and John Salvatore, he said something like: 'working for the FBI was great until they lowered their standards and let all the broads in.' If this is true, I'm putting you on notice that I am personally and professionally offended and legitimately concerned for my future here. If it is determined that he said these words, at the very least, I would like an apology."

Commissioner Ricci expressed concern by stating that they would be sure to look into the matter and, as a matter of fact, (upon hearing of my coming) had already spoken with the City Attorney as to a proper course of action. They were considering hiring an outside agency to investigate the legitimacy of the alleged statements. Then he said, 'And if he did say those things, we will be looking for greater sanctions than just an apology.'

He shook my hand and we dispersed. Less than five minutes. More like three and a half minutes. Three and a half POWERFUL minutes. Would I take them back? Even though I lost friends from this? Even though I have been alienated and set even further apart because of this? Even though I now realize that I was set up by certain political factions within the department to make my concerns known? Certain people (Shawn Beaumont, Chief Bird, Butch Ricci etc.) wanted Kupruck out of the commission seat, and had conveniently leaked this information to me knowing how I would react. Other political factions (local patrolman's union, Portsmouth Police Civilian Union, Tax Payers Association, Auxiliary Unit) *wanted* Kupruck in the seat. This made me the punching bag for all factions. Would I alter my decision? NOT ON YOUR LIFE!!! I have a responsibility to MY life.

Well, the department hired a private investigator to come in and interview all involved parties and witnesses. This is when I heard rumblings of dissatisfaction from even the ranking officers. I had stirred up a goopy mess and, because they weren't directly involved or offended, they felt it should have been left alone. You see, I am a ranking officer; I was the only female ranking officer and at the time, and was also President of the ranking officer's union. My own peers felt I had done the wrong thing, and in their not-so-subtle ways they told me so.

On December 1, I arrived for work just before 3 PM. On that particular day I had my daughter with me and planned to drop her at

my mom's house as soon as I had a free minute. As I stepped into
the office, my seven year old daughter at my side, I heard Captain
Cooper say loudly enough for me to hear, "I wish someone had
spoken with me before they jumped into the hot oil." He was loud
and sarcastic and I could feel my blood pressure rising. He was
obviously talking about me and the Kupruck Complaint, and by the
sound of his comment he had been present when Kupruck opened his
mouth. At the time he said this, I wasn't aware that he had, for a
fact, been there. He sounded pissed off and guilty.

With my peers around me, my daughter wide-eyed and
wondering, he was putting on the pressure. This further angered me
so I said, "Why is that, John? Because you don't want to get
involved?"

He gave me a semi-stunned look and said: "Bottom line, yes."

"This conversation has ended," I said and walked away with my
daughter. I walked away because I didn't feel Matty should hear the
things I really wanted to say. John could wait. It was at this point I
first realized my query had shaken a bees nest. I am so goddam naive
that I hadn't even considered that my fellow ranking officers
wouldn't support my decision to have the "broad" statement looked
into. What ever happened to 'all for one, and one for all', 'the thin
blue line' and all that crap? It's moments like this that remind me I
was never openly supported as a full-fledged police officer, and now
was no different.   It's like I get lulled to sleep, swooned by some
temporary trickiness, and just as I begin to feel part of the team, I'm
bopped on the head with enough force to remind me that I had been
day dreaming. It is they who are in power, and I am only a
consequence of an administration that had been forced to hire a
woman in order to receive federal monies, nothing more. Oh, believe
me, I never felt sorry for myself . Only amazed that I continued to
believe in myself enough to keep getting back up. They'd knock me
down, and I'd get back up. That was the cycle.

The Police Commission chose to hire an impartial
investigator, Michael L. Middleton, to look into the complaint. Little
did the commission know, that Kupruck was considered such a
favorite by most of the Portsmouth citizenry, that they would rally
City Hall to discredit the Commission for spending city dollars at a
rate of $200 an hour, on a "witch hunt". Newspaper articles publicly
admonished the Chief and Commission for this decision and put
them on the defensive.

The following accounts were taken directly from notes and
transcriptions of Michael L. Middleton's interviews with each person
he spoke with. The first witness interviewed was Commander Shawn
Beaumont, on December 4, 1995.   It should be noted that only one
interview was tape-recorded; Ted Kupruck's, and he was interviewed

last. For the others, Mr. Middleton took notes and detailed a summary of the interview.

> Beaumont spoke with Captain Cooper one morning at about 7:30 in the shift commander's office. Beaumont learned that the night before, Captain Cooper had been present in the dispatch center when Commissioner-elect Ted Kupruck made a comment that indicated that the FBI was either better, or more difficult before they let "broads" in. Dispatcher Linda Channel was present, and heard the comment. Cooper noticed that she rolled her eyes when Kupruck made the comment. Cooper told Beaumont that he was concerned over the potentially serious nature of the remark as it could effect the morale of the whole PD. Beaumont subsequently told Chief Bird about the problem as soon as he could .
>
> Beaumont told me (Middleton) that Truax came to see him on November 27, 1995, after having learned about the comment at a staff meeting. He accurately reported Truax's concerns. Beaumont reports that Truax told Commissioner Ricci, "If this was said, at the very least, the women of this department are due a public apology." Chairman Ricci agreed and responded, "at the very least, you are right."

Middleton interviewed Sergeant Tom Lanko next. Lanko, as I've already explained, has problems of his own when it comes to women in police work, so I found it rather ironic that he got caught in the middle of this.

> One evening in mid-November, 1995, Lanko recalled an incident that occurred while he was working on a grant for Domestic Violence. As he walked down the hall past the communications module, he observed commissioner-elect Kupruck, John Salvatore, and Captain John Cooper standing next to civilian dispatcher Robert Johnson. Lanko was unable to hear any of their conversation. About fifteen minutes later John Salvatore introduced Commissioner-elect Kupruck to Lanko. Lanko is quoted as saying, "I had high expectations for Kupruck as a police commissioner. My expectations became even

higher since Kupruck had taken the time to come
to the police department at night to see what was
going on."

After Kupruck left, Captain Cooper told
Lanko what Kupruck's said.   The crux of
Kuprucks statements were three fold: 1). Kupruck
wanted to institute a physical fitness program for
the PD, 2).   Kupruck was naive about union
issues, and 3). some comment about women in the
FBI.   On November 28 Lanko learned from
Commander Beaumont that Truax was filing a
formal complaint regarding remarks made by
Kupruck about women in law enforcement.

This is where the shit starts flying.   Even though Captain
Cooper was a primary witness to the incident, and was obviously
offended by it himself , confirmed by the fact that he told Lanko,
Beaumont, and the Chief about it and further was concerned enough
to question another witness, Linda Channels, as to her feelings on the
issue (to which she replied, "God. For once I kept my mouth shut),
and *those* persons were burdened enough to discuss at length,
amongst themselves, how to handle it, **_and_**, there had been an initial,
active attempt to keep this whole thing under wraps, it was publicly
stated, over and over again, that *I* had filed a formal complaint on the
matter. That is not what happened. I went to my boss, who already
knew about it and should have already taken action, but didn't, and
asked him to find out if it was true. I did not accuse
Kupruck. Then, I said, if it is true, I want an apology and some type
of assurity that this mysgogynistic attitude won't effect my career.

Lanko expounded that "the department is
very concerned and sensitive about issues relating
to women and minorities in police work. I am
worried that Chief Bird will not be viewed
accurately regarding this matter. Chief Bird has
been a leader in matters relating to women's
issues."

Reading Toms interview told me that he
would do nothing to risk his own neck and career.
Tom had kissed up to the Commissioner, the
Chief, women, and minorities; he was covering all
his bases.

John Salvatore, Captain of the Auxiliary division, was with Kupruck when the statement was made, and was therefore interviewed on December 6th. I will quote directly from Middleton's report,

> "I (Middleton) was aware that Salvatore had supported Kupruck in the police commission election and inquired regarding this. Salvatore said he is a member of the Taxpayers Association, and is the chairman of the candidate selection committee. He said the Taxpayers Assn. supported eleven candidates, of which Kupruck was just one. All candidates were invited to give a speech in front of the Taxpayers Association and Kupruck took advantage of the opportunity."

I must comment here that fibbers can sometimes be so transparent. Anyone who could read a newspaper was aware that the Taxpayer's Association fully supported Ted Kupruck for police commissioner, and lobbied heavily for his campaign. The APT (Association of Portsmouth Taxpayers) released a formal statement to the press on January 3rd supporting Kupruck and calling for the resignation of current commissioners Ricci and Blanchard.

The point here is that Salvatore lied. The Taxpayers Assn. did invite eleven candidates to speak at their meetings; but they only supported one, Ted Kupruck. What did Salvatore have to hide?

Back to Middleton's report:

> "Salvatore has known Kupruck for about ten years because he's a customer at his barber shop. Salvatore described himself as being friendly with Kupruck as a customer of his shop, and is a bit more friendly with Kupruck than other customers because of Kupruck's police ties. Salvatore said that he has never socialized with Kupruck, but once loaned him a charcoal grill."
>
> On the evening Kupruck visited (the Police Station), he and Salvatore had a conversation about the physical fitness room. Salvatore showed Kupruck the room (gym). .....Then the two men walked into the dispatch center where Salvatore introduced Kupruck to civilian dispatchers Johnson and Channels. He remembered there being a discussion about the changes in the dispatch area from the old station which was

followed by a general conversation of some sort. Salvatore did not remember any specifics [of course he didn't].

Then Captain Cooper came into the room and joined in the discussion. Salvatore said, "I can't be more specific about the subjects being discussed. It was just four guys batting the breeze." He recalled Captain Cooper saying that each of them was a little pudgy even though they were eating less while working more. Kupruck then asked if the department had a physical fitness program. Salvatore and the others replied no, and added that nothing was covered by the Portsmouth Police Department S.O.P.'s.

Salvatore said that Kupruck remarked, "Back a few years ago the FBI had hired two female agents. At the time, the FBI did have a physical fitness program and these two agents could not keep up with the program. I think he said they let them go and they sued the FBI and got their jobs back. This was the end of the physical fitness program for the FBI. And that was it."

Salvatore said that he didn't hear Kupruck make any comments that he felt were inappropriate.

I asked Salvatore if he heard Kupruck say that FBI agents were always fit, and they had high physical standards. He said that he did not hear that comment. I asked him if he heard Kupruck say, "That all ended when they hired broads"? Salvatore said that the only mention he heard Kupruck make about women in the FBI had to do with the physical fitness program, the loss of their jobs, their reinstatement through the courts, and the end of the physical fitness program in the FBI. He said he did not hear any reference to women being broads, and opined that if that were said, Kupruck may have been talking to Robert Johnson, and Salvatore did not hear it"

An interesting twist here. Translation: 'Kupruck didn't say it. Salvatore didn't hear him say it. But, if he said it, Robert might have heard. I'm not saying he didn't say it.' Bull shit. Come on guys! Make it easy on yourself and just tell the truth. It's a hell of a lot easier and makes a lot more sense. I thought they were beginning to sound like a bunch of second graders caught playing hooky, instead of grown adults who had simply stuck their foot in their collective mouth. All they had to do was say, 'Yes. I had a lapse of judgment and said that stupid thing. I'm sorry and I further guarantee it will have no impact on anyone's career.' That's all I wanted. But they kept going. The tale got bigger.

"Salvatore added, 'there was a woman present and I try to watch my mouth. And for the record, I hired women, including blacks, for the auxiliary program before they were on the regular department.' He said he didn't hear Kupruck make any insensitive remarks about women.

Salvatore said he has never seen any problems regarding the treatment of women on the Portsmouth Police Department. He believes that the women are afforded an equal opportunity. Salvatore has never seen an inappropriate behavior by male officers toward female officers. He said that if anything, 'they are overprotective of them. Any decent male would do these things.'"

"My son had contact with a female FBI agent," Salvatore continued, "who wanted to interview him regarding a case she was working on. My son wouldn't speak with her [the apple doesn't fall too far from the tree] and called me for advice. I called Kupruck who spoke very highly of her, and he didn't make any derogatory remarks about her, either. Besides, I don't know how this complaint has gotten to this point. It was just four guys, or two guys, standing around having a conversation."

What Salvatore has left out of his analogy is that they weren't in his barber shop batting the breeze, they were in a police station; the very location that housed the subject of their inappropriate conversation.

Next in the batter's box was Robert Johnson, an old-time dispatcher who'd he been around a long time. This wasn't an important job to Robert; he was already receiving a retirement pension from some branch of the service, and his wife owned a successful clothing shop in town, so, although he knew the game, he never took it very seriously. This whole investigation would have been titillating and humorous to Robert if he hadn't been directly involved. He was a bit nipped that he had to be interviewed, so tried to separate himself from the allegations as best he could.

"I wasn't directly involved in the conversation, you know," he said.

"But you were in the room when it happened," Middleton said. "Just a few feet away, if that."

"I remember saying hi to Kupruck when he walked in. I had met him about a week before when he stopped in. I was impressed because he seemed interested in us."

"Kupruck was with Salvatore, the head of the part-time division," Johnson said. "Then Cooper came in the room. But, you know, I only picked up bits and pieces of the conversation. I remember that they were talking about the FBI academy, and some old war stories."

"Where was the other dispatcher?" Middleton asked.

"She was in the room too. She was on the police side, just a few feet away from me. I got busy, though. I'm responsible for answering all incoming telephone calls, in addition to dispatching fire and rescue units. I think a hot call even came in while they were in there."

"But you heard them talking about a physical fitness program, didn't you?"

"I heard parts of it. I remember Kupruck asking why there wasn't a physical fitness program in place. Then my attention was diverted to the phones. I had to turn away from them to do my job. I didn't hear anything else they said."

"Nothing?"

"Nope."

"Did you hear anyone make any mention of women working in the FBI?"

"No."

"Did you see Captain Cooper talking with Dispatcher Channels?"

"I saw him walk over to her, but I don't know what they talked about."

And so the interview went. Robert was there, but he was no fly on the wall, or better stated, wasn't telling.

Channels was next. She had her own way of distancing herself from the situation.

"Yeah," she told Middleton, "I remember a night in mid-November when Kupruck came into the dispatch room. I'd never met him before and I shook hands with him."

"Were you included in the conversation going on at the time?"

"Yes and no. I was there. At one point I asked Kupruck if he had any questions about the dispatch function. I was working the police side that night, and wanted to be able to explain anything he didn't understand. Then they started talking about the building, itself. You know, construction and stuff. I turned my back to them and continued working on a crossword puzzle I had brought in. Just as I did that, we got a hot call of a possible burglary in progress, so I had to dispatch some back-up to the officers already at the scene."

"But Cooper says he asked you what you thought of Kupruck's reference to broads, and you said, 'God, for once I kept my mouth shut'?"

"Yeah, I heard the word 'broad' used by Kupruck, but I don't know the way he meant it. It could have been used in the phrase 'broad horizon', I don't know. I remember bits and pieces of a story Kupruck was telling about his years in the FBI, but nothing specific."

"But what about Cooper's version of speaking with you about it?"

"Yeah. Cooper asked me if I heard what Kupruck said and I told him 'no'. But I did say, 'God, for once I kept my mouth shut.' But, I can't remember why. Besides. I don't know why Nancy is pushing this investigation since she wasn't there and doesn't know what was said."

That's how my old friend Linda ended her interview. An intelligent woman who very naturally used her knowledge of the English language as an alibi-aid; she used to kick my ass at Boggle. Frustrated the hell out of me. She'd just kicked my ass again and threw in an extra whammy by attempting to discredit me to Middleton. I guess, 'that's what friends are for.'

Daniel Foley was interviewed on December 8. Daniel, a Sergeant at the time, and Vice President of the supervisors union, is most noted for his ability to openly express his feelings. He is very emotional, but honest.

"I had attended a Detective staff meeting, before the general staff meeting."

"Is this usual?" Middleton asked.

"Yes. We meet once a month, at least, and it just so happened that both meetings were on the same day. Commander Brasso told the detectives that Chief Bird was going to give a lecture on sexual harassment at the staff officers meeting. I asked Brasso, why. Brasso told me that the lecture was really for the benefit of police commissioner-elect Ted Kupruck, since he was gong to be in attendance."

"Did you ask why this was going to happen?" Middleton asked.

"Yes. I was told that Kupruck made some terrible statements in the dispatch area relating to women. Craig told me everything. But, what's interesting is that, at the time, Craig told us that Linda Channel had filed a formal complaint, now I hear that Nancy has filed the complaint. It seems like they wanted someone to pin the complaint to as soon as they heard about it. They picked Linda first, because she was in the room; but then Nancy jumped forward. Probably just what they wanted."

"Do you know why they decided to mask this issue in a group setting, rather than speaking with Kupruck directly?"

"No. I asked the same question. I was told that the Chief will be talking about it in the staff meeting while Kupruck was present, in order to deliver the message that this type of behavior won't be tolerated. It didn't make much sense to me, but I'm not the big boss. I think Kupruck should have been pulled aside and spoken with directly."

"You feel strongly about this?"

"I sure do. I happen to know about other inappropriate statements he's made to other women inside the police building."

"Would you tell me about those?"

"I'm dating a reporter named Summer Moon. We've been dating for a while now and about a week or ten days before the election, Summer called me very upset. She said that she had been to a Police Commission meeting at the pd, which she does every month. While taking the stairwell to the second floor, Commissioner Kupruck walked behind her. As she ascended the stairs, Kupruck told her she had shapely or curvy legs. He also told her that her skirt was short.
She didn't respond because she was shocked and uncomfortable. Then, later, Kupruck made another comment to a gentleman sitting beside him, about the shape of her legs, loud enough for her to hear."

"What was the comment?"

"Something like, "don't you think that's a great skirt, and aren't those shapely legs?"

"But it wasn't said to her?"

"No. Kupruck said it to a guy named Riley, sitting next to him, and behind Summer. He did say it loud enough for her to hear though."

"Did she file a complaint?"

"She talked it over with her bosses at the paper and she decided against it. When I got home that night she was very passionate about the whole thing and I could see that she'd been emotionally assaulted by Kupruck. Summer was irritated that she had worked so hard to be viewed as a professional, and in one second, it had all been taken away from her."

"Summer was too frightened to make a complaint. She told me that she was afraid of not being believed, and that, in the end,

Kupruck would continue to be supported as police commissioner for Portsmouth. She saw it as a career ending situation if it were to become public."

"So, what happened after you told everyone in the meeting about Summer's experience?"

"Well," Daniel said, "everyone pretty much agreed that the incident could be contained within the department. We felt containment would be better than a newspaper article that could have a deterious effect on the police department as a whole. The officers were concerned about Summer and what had happened to her. I believe there should be one standard that applies to everyone, including Commissioners and Ranking officers."

"So, did Kupruck hear the lecture at the meeting?"

"No. He left right before the talk on sexual harassment. The chief gave the talk anyway, but the one person who needed to hear it had left."

"How did Truax hear about this?"

"I told her. On the same day of the staff meeting I had given her a ride to the station, and I let her know. She's the President of our union, and I'm the Vice President. I thought she should know."

Captain Cooper was reluctantly interviewed on December 12. Having the rank of Captain, and having been an integral part of the political system for a number of years, John, too, knew the game. He didn't want to spill the beans because he felt it would hurt his career (which later proved true), but didn't want to lie about it either. Whether he told the truth because he had already let the cat out of the bag (he had spoken openly about this with 8 people at this point), or because he felt an obligation to truth, itself, doesn't really matter. He did the right thing, yet the most difficult thing. He told Middleton that he remembered that the incident happened on November 16 when he was working an evening shift.

"I had seen Salvatore and Kupruck enter the dispatch area, so I finished what I was doing and stepped in with them. They were talking when I walked in the room."

"Tell me everyone who was in the room."

"Well, there were two dispatchers. Robert Johnson, on the fire side. Linda Channels, on the police side. Then there was me, Salvatore, and Kupruck. I think that was it."

"Were you all in there at the same time?"

"Kind-of. There were times we were all in there together. I think at one point Channels had walked out for a brief time. Mostly, we were all there."

"Okay. What happened next?"

"Well. As soon as I got in the room, Kupruck asked me if we had a mandatory physical fitness policy. I was feeling a bit guilty because I'm overweight I thought he might have been asking for my benefit."

"What did you tell him?"

"I told him that we didn't have a policy, and to get one implemented would be very difficult because of the union. Then someone else jumped in and told Kupruck that he would be surprised at the things that had to be negotiated through the union. Then Kupruck said, 'I think some people would be surprised, but not me'".

"What did he mean by this?"

"That's when he started his story about women in the FBI. He said the FBI agents were always physically fit and they had high physical standard. Kupruck went on to say, 'that all ended when they hired broads.'"

"He said that? You're sure?"

"Positive. Then he went on to bolster his statement by telling a story about the first two women to go through the FBI Academy. According to Kupruck, they were unable to meet the minimum standards involving push-ups and pull-ups. Kupruck said the person in charge of the FBI physical fitness program was a retired, 30 year Marine-type individual. When the women failed to meet the minimum standards, the man in charge of the physical fitness unit wanted to approach the women in a tactful manner and try to work something out. He was overridden by the commanding officer of the academy who was, as Kupruck described, "an old J. Edgar Hoover guy." His attitude was that if the women could not meet the standards, they would be washed out. That wasn't the case, and the women remained. I think they had to sue or something."

"And?"

"And the point of this story was obviously that because of the women, standards for being an agent had relaxed."

"Did anyone else hear what was said?"

"Everyone should have heard the conversation, including Linda Channels and Robert Johnson."

"Did you talk with Linda at this point?"

"Yes. After Salvatore and Kupruck left the room. I asked her what she thought of Kupruck's comment, and she said, 'God. For once I kept my mouth shut.'"

"Was it your impression that she knew what comment you referred to?"

"Yup. I saw her expression as Kupruck was talking. She rolled her eye balls, like a kid. That's why I asked her what she thought about it."

"What did you do next?"

"I walked across the hall and told Sergeant Lanko. I was upset that a Police Commissioner would say such a thing about

women and police work inside a police station. I
was also afraid that he might have been indirectly letting me know
that I needed to lose some weight."

"What did Lanko say?"

"He just kind of laughed about it. I don't think he thought it
was any big deal, except that he's overweight too. He might have
said something about being worried about that."

"Did you tell anyone else?"

"Sure, the next day I told Commander Beaumont, my boss.
Then later he had the Chief ask me about it."

"What was their attitude?"

"Concern. But they really didn't know what to do about it.
It's like they didn't want to be involved, but knew they had to be."

Right at the beginning of Kupruck's interview, Middleton
asked him if he spoke with anyone about this investigation. Kupruck
responded in the negative, but was later caught in this lie.

"What was the nature of your conversation in the dispatch
area?" Middleton asked Kupruck.

"We discussed a whole number of subjects."

"Such as?"

"I asked Robert about the system that was in place."

"What system is that?"

"The communication system that was in place, and he said
that Sergeant Ellis pretty much designed it and got it up and running.
I don't remember at this point, but we were talking along these lines,
and I was surprised to learn that no one else had been cross trained
on the system other than Sergeant Ellis."

"What else did you talk about?"

"I don't know. We talked about Ron Brigham's retirement
party. I asked who Brigham's replacement was gonna be and we
talked about that for a while. There were probably other things we
were talking about at the time, but essentially we got onto the subject
of retirements."

"Okay."

"Yeah, that's when I asked the rhetorical question about the
retirement age. I think Salvatore and Cooper told me that it was 70.
I was surprised with this, so I asked them,
'You mean as long as they pass the physical'. When they told me no,
I was astounded. I still have trouble believing it. I just can't conceive
of someone coming on the department at age 25, working until 70
without being required to pass a physical, at least periodically. To
me, that's poor management."

"Okay."

"I think it was at this point that Cooper told me that if
someone was out sick with a serious illness, they have to have a

doctor's permit to come back. Then they told me that if someone had a problem with alcohol or chemical abuse, it would be known in the department and it would be handled."

"This really bothered me so I asked if there was any tracking system for physical fitness or physical qualifications. When they told me no, I started talking about the failure
of management in this regard and how it impacts everyone. I couldn't believe there was no incentive whatsoever to track or keep the officers physically fit."

Kupruck rambled on, "I don't know what they said about it, but I was talking about the total failure of management years ago when they insisted on keeping rigid and unrelated physical fitness programs in place. I gave them the example of when the FBI first hired two women who had to go to court in order to keep their jobs. It took them a number of years to win the case. So, as a result, management didn't know what to do, and physical fitness programs came and went. There was no direction, and it took years to bring it back to some sort of order. As a result, the weight program went out the window. Without some sort of physical fitness program, the health of the personnel was put in jeopardy. I was giving them an example of the history of what has happened with physical fitness in law enforcement. I wasn't talking about, I wasn't denigrating women in law enforcement. I was talking about the failure of management." On and on Kupruck went.

"I'm interested in one particular statement that is attributed to you and that's exactly, or words to the effect, that the FBI always had high standards and the agents were physically fit," Middleton said.

"Yeah, that was years ago."

"And this is either a direct quote, or paraphrase, 'That all ended when they hired broads.'?

"That's...I don't...I said broads?"

"I don't know. I'm just telling you the words that are attributed to you.

"I don't remember how I characterized the women. I was talking about management and what management failed to do. Management was not reasonable in what they
wanted to have done. I don't remember using the word 'broads'. But I wasn't denigrating women. If they understood it that way, that was not the import of what I was trying..."

"Is it your sense that the FBI has, as far as the quality of the agency or the quality of the physical fitness program, diminished since women were hired?"

"It's not...no. That doesn't follow. You're talking about physical fitness?"

"Just trying to get to the comment here. I don't know. I

wasn't there. I'm only relying on what others have said, 'That all ended when they hired broads.'"

"What ended?"

"The physical fitness thing."

"No, it didn't end. It was thrown into a state of confusion because the people that are running the bureau were just dense."

"In what regard?"

"They wanted to hold onto an unrealistic, you can't make...(stuttering now), it took the courts to prove to them that you can't make a direct correlation between physical fitness and investigation. But when they tried to do it after they hired women, they finally learned that they couldn't do it. That was because the women had the courage to take it to court. The bureau was in transition in those days because Mr. Hoover had just died. There was a lot of confusion."

"This," Middleton began, "clearly begs the question, as to whether you believe that there is a place for women in police work."

At this point Kupruck and Middleton go off tape. Although we may never know what was discussed while the tape was off, Kupruck's change in attitude clues us in that he may have been told that it was I who filed a complaint against him. This frustrated him because he knew I wasn't present the comment in question was made and, further, we didn't even know one another. It must have seemed like an arrow flew at him from an unexpected direction.

"If someone is trying to take the conversation I had about physical fitness and construe that to mean I don't think women should be in law enforcement, I just don't see how that follows. That's not what I was talking about. I was talking about management. I wasn't talking about women. You're asking me whether women should be in law enforcement? I spent 30 years working with women. I had them working with me undercover. I put my life in their hands. It's ridiculous to say that women shouldn't be in law enforcement, and whoever said that I think they shouldn't be in law enforcement.... Who made this complaint? Truax?"

"I'll give the Police Commission a chance to respond to that. I don't think it would be appropriate for me to identify the statements of any other persons."

"Then they'll have to give me a copy of the entire report."

"There's another incident I want to ask you about. It actually pre-dates this particular complaint. You were a candidate, of three, I guess, for the Police Commission."

"Is this a separate complaint now?" Kupruck getting hotter.

"Yeah. You know Summer Moon?"

"She's with Fosters. A reporter."

"There was a particular evening..."

"I've had many conversations with her. I don't know which one you're talking about. Is she a complainant in this thing?"

"Yes."

"On this particular occasion there was an event, a meeting held on the second floor of the police station. You came into the waiting room, the lounge area, and then she was standing across the room and held the door."

"Oh, yeah, yeah. Okay. I know what you're talking about. Yeah, we had to go upstairs to the meeting."

"Do you remember a conversation with her?"

"It was about 7:30 in the morning. Yeah. Early in the morning. Sure. I made casual conversation with her."

"About what?"

"I told her she looked good and nice. She was well dressed and I might have said something about the meeting, I don't know what we talked about. We were going up the stairs together."

"So you were going up the stairs together?"

"Yeah, and it was very cold out and I told her something like she was gonna have to put a coat on because it's getting cold. She laughed and said something like, 'oh no, not yet. I've got a few more days.' It was very casual and quick. Just a minute or two."

"Which of you went into the meeting first?"

"I don't know. I was talking to one of the commissioners. In fact, I told him he looked pretty good too. He was all dressed up. I think I used the word 'spiffy'.

Kupruck went on to explain that when the meeting began he sat to the back of the room and did happen to notice Moon sitting in front of him.

"Do you remember making any comment to Riley regarding Summer Moon when you sat down?"

"No. She was sitting up front someplace."

"Do you recall saying as you ascended the stairs with Summer, "boy, that's a pretty short skirt you're wearing. Isn't it kind of cold?'

"I may have said that. I don't think so. When I was talking, I said something about it was cold out and I said she wouldn't be able to wear the dress. Something like that. It was just a comment."

"Okay. When you sat down upstairs, do you recall making a statement, 'don't you like the shape of those legs? Not many people look good in a skirt like that.'"

"To who? I don't remember that statement at all. She's a very pretty girl and she was well dressed. If I said anything, I don't remember saying anything about it now. I didn't say anything at all. Are we going to go back to my child hood here?"

"No."

"If this was so offensive to her, why did she wait so long to come forward. What bandwagon is she jumping on?"

"The more important question is, is it true?" Middleton countered.

"I don't know."

"Would you consider that if those words had been said, they would have been derogatory?"

"No, I don't think that's derogatory. It was cold. It was a cold morning. That's a fact."

Not much more was gleaned from Kupruck's interview. Middleton compiled his interviews, and presented his package to the commission in a reasonable amount of time.

By this time, the public had gotten hold of the fact that the investigation was being done, and most were outraged that tax dollars were being used for such a trivial matter. Kupruck stoked the fire with a lengthy, four page, resignation letter which was printed in the Portsmouth Herald (but never given to any city official). "Police Commissioner-Elect Ted Kupruck said yesterday he would not take the post, moments after being censured for remarks in which he...referred to women as 'broads' and commented on a female reporter's short skirt and legs.

Mahoney said further, "to be accused of such conduct by individuals seeking to curry favor with the police administration, and for purposes of self promotion is an insult." Kupruck denied making derogatory remarks and questioned the motives of those who brought the allegations.

Linda Panori, City councilor came out and publicly blasted the commission for using tax dollars on such a bogus claim.

City Councilors, City Attorneys, friends of the barbershop group, members of the FBI, the Portsmouth Police Patrolman's Union, the Ranking Officer's Union, the Auxiliary Unit, and the Taxpayers Association, all felt a need to be publicly involved and come to Kupruck's aid. Most of these people testified to Kupruck's virtue and lack of discriminatory character. Politicians publicly held his hand stating they have never known him to be a bigot and concluded that Sergeant Truax must have an ulterior motive for making her complaint. Perhaps, it was said, she wants to be a Captain and feels this is the only way she can get there.

On January 4th, the day after Mahoney's public resignation, he waffled, and recanted his resignation stating he'd received volumes of support over the last 24 hours, and his phones hadn't stopped ringing. His supporters convinced him to fight the good fight.

I was being attacked from all sides. Home wasn't much different. Vince callously told me that I should have kept my mouth shut. Then in the next breath he would apologize and tell me that if I really felt this strongly, I had done the right thing. But, by opening his mouth, the damage was already done. I didn't believe that he really supported me. I believed that he wished I hadn't upset his world by stirring mine up. This was when my battle with depression became most apparent, and is when I first acknowledged that I was depressed. It had been following me since my hire with the Police Department, but I was keeping tabs on it and trying not to let it overtake me. This is the point at which I collapsed beneath it's power.

I cried continuously for days. Slept my days away for months. Went to work cuz I had to, but hated every moment of it. I didn't want to die, but I didn't want to live this life either. I felt I had been battling a cause all my life and had finally lost. I wanted to give up because I realized that no one else could see things as I saw them. I was weird, and didn't fit with the conventions of the police world.

It took me a while to read all of Middleton's report. I was afraid of what I would find, and didn't feel emotionally strong enough to handle it right away. After reading it for the first time, I felt a mix of emotions. Mostly I was pleased that Cooper had substantiated my claim, and had been brave enough to step forward.

Kupruck repeatedly taunted Cooper after the investigation by turning his back to him, and refusing to speak with him, in any setting, public or private. The boys-club certainly does engender a great deal of juvenile behavior. No doubt, Kupruck believed that Cooper should have been "one of the guys" and lied about what he heard; Cooper should have protected Kupruck. The sad fact was, even if John wanted to lie, he couldn't. He'd already told too many people about it.

That December, I was voted out of my Presidential seat in the supervisor's union because my peers felt I had thoughtlessly over-stepped my bounds when I complained about Mahoney's comment. They were incensed that I had stirred the pot. By sticking up for myself, I had risked the security of other members of our group. Shame on me.

A couple months later, I sent a letter to the Commission and the Chief requesting an apology from Kupruck, based on the facts gathered in Middleton's report. One month later I received a letter from the Commission advising me that no apology would be forthcoming. It read like this,

"Dear Sergeant Truax, The Board of Police Commissioners initiated an investigation into your complaint about the statements of Police Commissioner-Elect, Mr. Theodore D. Kupruck. *(No shit!)* The police Commission received a completed investigation and

acted upon it in a public session. The completed
investigation is in our files, and a copy of this
investigation was made public as well as forwarded to
Portsmouth City Councilors. The Police Commissioners
believe disposition of this matter is conclusive *(but you
never told me what you concluded)* and has received and
filed all related reports."

It was by far, the most preposterous letter I had ever
received; it said absolutely nothing; but I didn't have to read between
the lines to understand that I'd never hear Kupruck say 'I'm sorry'.

Kupruck stepped down from the Commission at the end of
his term three years later. His professional achievements during his
years with us were good; but he did it with such heavy airs of
resentment, that it mildewed and stained those same
accomplishments.

Life's lessons can be tragic comedy sometimes. I'd always
known that values are not absolute; different people have different
value systems rooted (most often) in upbringing, education, and
culture. But I didn't realize that those same values would be so
quickly tossed aside because there was something bigger and better to
gain by doing so. The Ranking Officer's Union, the Patrolman's
Union, and the Dispatcher's Union all believed that Mahoney would
be a "union man" and endorse whatever contract they sought.
Money. So, rather than defend a healthy societal value (fair
treatment of all people), they rallied to Mahoney's side. The local
media was bursting with accolades for Mr. Mahoney and contained
quotes from a number of personalities claiming Sergeant Truax had
undisclosed motives for her allegations against him. I was mud
beneath his feet.

Mahoney soon fell far short of all the unions' expectations
and before long the unions were in constant battle with him over a
variety of contractual and work related issues. I, by then, had lost all
interest in departmental politics and just sat back and watched the
wheels turn round.

Chapter 13

Shot Gun

'Portsmouth Herald (NH) Wed., March 2, 1983'
"RAPE REPORT" Police had few details to release about a reported rape this morning at an undisclosed motel. A 43 year-old woman reported she was assaulted in a motel room shortly after 4 a.m., today. Police responded to the call, and brought the woman to Portsmouth Hospital for tests. Deputy William Hanes, chief of the local detectives, would not release the name of the motel or any other details."

The love-making, sex rather, the night before had been good, but same old, same old. She didn't do it for him anymore, she only did it for herself. She used to believe that if she could be passionate enough, sexy enough, rock his world in the bedroom, she might be able to change his disposition toward her a little bit. Make him be nicer to her. What Nancy didn't understand was that Vince only did it for *him*self, to meet *his* needs. He never said, "come here darling", "you're beautiful honey", "I can't get enough of you". He didn't even say, "you feel good to me." He would say, "let's fuck", or "how about a quickie?". It was like he wanted to know if he still had what it took to excite her. He liked knowing that he was responsible for that pleasurable burst she emitted when she climaxed. It was a power trip for him, and it was only after she came on him, all over him, that he too would allow himself to release. He always waited; but he was waiting for himself.

Always before he came he would fuck her hard. His favorite position was to sit on the edge of the bed, feet on the floor, while she sat facing him. He would grab her tightly at the hips, hard enough to cause finger bruises, and rock her hard, back and forth. As if he couldn't get deep enough inside her. As if he must do this, or be forever damned. When he finally came, Nancy aching from the thrust of him, he grunted loudly, in relief. His body covered itself with goose bumps. Lovely, silly, goosebumps. The universal sign of pleasure, happiness, and satisfaction. The only sign Nancy ever had that he enjoyed her company, even if only for that split second.

What Vince didn't know was that he was not responsible for her excitement during these times. Nancy had learned how to travel to her own world, her own fantasy place that no one knew of, because the thought of being with him was repulsive, even hideous. She pretended that he was someone else, a friend, a stranger, a celebrity, it didn't matter as long as he wasn't in the room while they had sex.

If there were times when she hated herself, it was when she was unable to travel to her special places. It saddened her to remember that it used to be enough to just see him, feel him, touch him, look at him. But she also knew that she wasn't responsible for this outcome. She also hoped that one day she would have feelings for him again. Hope again. But hope is what made her good at pretending; at going places that didn't exist.

So, sex the night before had been the same as always, and served to extend their blindness to what they had become. In so doing, it provided an eerie sense of comfort and stability.

They slept well that night, but not in each others arms. They hadn't done that in a long time. They slept, each sprawled into their own favorite position, each reaching one hand to the middle of the bed as if it, that one spot, were the only neutral territory that provided safety from harm. Neither side could initiate attack unless the neutral territory was a void. It was too often empty.

The alarm went off at 5 AM; much too early for the average person, and she does consider herself average. Day shift. She lay in bed fighting the desire to finish her interrupted dreams. She knew in her head that if she could just throw the soft, warm, covers off her body and force her feet to the floor, she would wake up sometime between her morning shower and the drive into work and be glad she was awake. Just right then, it was awful hard.

As soon as she started puttering around the house, the kids got up too. Of course they maneuvered themselves onto the family room couch and she was jealous as they lounged drowsily with one pillow each, and a thin blanket to prevent a morning chill. Cartoons provided them with some early morning entertainment; she thought this must be some sort of historical ritual for all American children.

What were they doing on the couch? What were they waiting for? The same thing they, and all children of working parents wait for every morning of their young lives. They were waiting for their parents to step into the living room and ask: "Did you take your shower yet? Did you wash your hair when you took a shower? What are you wearing to school today? No, that shirt's not good enough. Find one that's clean. Did you brush your teeth yet? What about breakfast? Who fed the dog? In a child's beautiful world, none of these tasks can be started or completed until the question is asked, even though they know it has to be done. And so on, and hustle and bustle to get everyone out the door to their appropriate bus stops, baby-sitters, and places of employment. The morning is a race to beat the clock, to get to work, so the race can begin all over again.

Her mornings are the same as any other working parent with children. Unless, of course, she's on evening or midnight shift whereupon her evenings are mornings and mornings are night. That's another juggling act to tell you about later .

A woman by the name of Charlene M. kept Nancy busy that morning and most of the day.

"Nancy," Sgt. Smith said, "we've got a rape at the Port Motor Inn. Can you handle that with Joe?"

"Sure," she said. "Anything special?"

"Another tough one. No signs of force. Maybe a date rape. The victim's in the hospital being examined and we hope to get a rape kit done. You'll need to interview her."

"What about the scene?"

"We've got some coppers standing by till you can get over there and do your thing."

"Suspect?"

"Yeah. Guy by the name of David Smith."

"Phony name?"

"Sounds like it."

"Joe here yet?"

"Yup. He's already been briefed. I think you'll find him at his cubicle getting ready."

Joe had always been okay to work with until that sergeant's promotion. After that, things between them deteriorated as neither trusted the other. Nancy, however, had *always* felt suspicious of Joe's motives - even before the sergeant's promotion. It was that seemingly insignificant, incident wherein he told her he was waiting to take her seniority from her when she had her next child. This incident refused to remand itself to her deep subconscious.

She knew that Joe must have his own feelings About *her*, and tried to understand that, and his resentment of her. She tip-toed around him, refusing him tangible ammunition for the feud simmering between them.

"Joe, you ready?" she asked.

"Let's go," he said.

"Will you do the interview with me at the hospital?"

"Yeah, but then we're going to have to process the scene."

"Yup. Have you called Sexual Assault Support Services yet?"

"Yeah. They're on their way to the hospital now. We should hurry up. I don't want them shutting her down or making her so upset that she won't talk. You know what I mean?"

"Sure," she lied. SASS was a civilian, non profit, agency put in place to help rape victims. As long as the victims were getting help, who cared if they shut down for a while? It seemed like a natural reaction to Nancy. Maybe even a process one had to go through before reaching recovery.

Charlene lay fully clothed on the sterile hospital bed, glancing furtively from the SASS worker, to detectives, to the doctor, and then the nurse. The small room was full, and in some ways it felt like over-kill, but everyone had a job to do. The nurse helped the doctor who examined the patient. Part of the doctor's examination would include the Johnson Rap Kit; this kit required the collection of very specific evidence, such as, pubic clippings, pubic combings, vaginal swabs, and so on. Once this evidence was collected by the doctor, it would be secured in the box, and turned over to police for laboratory examination and DNA testing.

The detectives, in addition to conducting interviews, would also gather the victim's clothing as evidence. This was done by having her stand atop a large, white sheet of paper and carefully remove her clothing. The purpose of the white sheet of paper was to assure the collection of all particles that fell from the victim's body or clothing. Each article of clothing was placed in a separate, sterile bag, labeled as evidence, and, later, signed into a secure area at the police station. Finally, the white sheet of paper was slowly and neatly folded, and placed in a brown paper bag also.

Charlene appeared frightfully pale to Nancy, and very alone in a room full of people. Nancy could see it in her eyes; they were vacant, lost, gone. Nancy guessed that Charlene was in her mid forties or so. Her face was very wrinkled, as though some bad habits had aged her prematurely, and she was short, a bit chunky, with long blonde hair.

"All I wanted to do was kill myself," Charlene said, not to anyone inparticular. It seemed to explain why we were all there. Concise.

"I know," the SASS worker said, "we're glad that didn't happen, and we wish we didn't have to be here at all." Nice, but rote.

"Charlene," I said, "would it be okay if Detective Ellis and I asked you a few questions now? It shouldn't take too long. Are you feeling up to it?"

She nodded her head, and shrugged her shoulders to imply it didn't really matter either way. Her uncombed, greasy hair fell forward, into her face, as she made an effort to look at me.

"I'm going to have to ask everyone else to leave, Charlene. Will that be okay? They can come back in when we're done."

"Okay," she said.

"If you need anything, Charlene, I'll be waiting for you in the hallway." the SASS worker explained. Then she looked at me and said, "You know where to find me if you need some help."

"Sure," I said. What she meant was that if Charlene needed some emotional support, she'd be willing to come in and comfort her until she calmed down. I couldn't question Charlene in front of the SASS worker because the worker would then become a witness to the interview, but I could ask her to remain available in case the flood gates burst open. One of the reasons these volunteers are so wonderful for police investigations is because they allow the police to stay focused on the facts and details of the case while the volunteer helps maintain the emotional balance the victim needs.

Joe stood in a corner of the room that Charlene couldn't see. Sometimes a victim felt more comfortable talking with just one person, so even though Joe was in the room to lend me some assistance, the idea was to allow Charlene to forget he was there. Over the years, I had discovered that the best way to get a concise and complete statement of the events, was to first allow the victim to tell her whole story from beginning to end, with little or no interruptions. When she has finished, I would back track and fill in the blanks by asking questions. I wouldn't turn the tape recorder on till the sequence of events was clear in my own mind. Once the tape begins, it's my job to keep the victim on track, with no digressions. Or, minimal digressions. This takes a lot of time; anywhere from several hours, to several days, depending on the complexity of the case, the incident, the victim, the evidence, or the suspect.

"What did you mean when you said you wanted to die?" Nancy asked.

"I was just trying to kill myself, and this happened."

"How?"

"I stole some of my mothers pills, percosette I think."

"Why, Charlene? What was going on that made you want to kill yourself?"

"You name it," she said. "I've been depressed lately, and I've been seeing a doctor, Doctor McGlaughlin. Nothing seems to help."

"Okay," I said allowing the air to be quiet for a moment.

"Then my daughter called me; yesterday she called me. She told me that she was going to kill herself, and I just couldn't take it. I figured that if she didn't want to live, neither did I."

"Your daughter?"

"Yeah. She's twenty, and she's also seeing a doctor for depression. She sees Dr. McGlaughlin too."

"Why did she want to kill herself?"

"Her boyfriend broke up with her and I guess it pushed her over the edge. I've been admitted to the State Hospital before because I was upset about a guy. It happens. Anyway, I went out last night to get drunk, get a motel room, and then take my mother's pills. I didn't want to wake up this morning."

"Where'd you go to get drunk?"

"First, at about 5:30, 5:45, I went to this place called Wally's Cafe; I think it used to be called Ricco's. I'd never been in there before cuz I figured it was a real dive, but I didn't care about too much last night."

"5:30?" she asked, not because she hadn't heard her, but to let Charlene know that she was listening.

"About that. It was a dump. The tile floor was all grimy, and the bar looked like it had never been cleaned!! The people inside looked as though they'd been there since the place opened. The place smelled like booze too; which I suppose is natural, but isn't something I enjoy. Maybe I went in that place in order to remind myself why I wanted to die."

"So," she continued, "as I was sitting at a table waiting to get a drink, this guy came and sat down next to me. I had never met him before, but he asked me if I wanted a beer. I asked him where the waitress was, and he told me that I had to go to the bar and get it myself. But, he said, he'd get it for me if I wanted. I told him okay, and he brought me a light beer."

"Did this guy have a name?" I asked.

"Sure, if you believe it's the right name. He told me his name was David Smith, but I think he was lying. I must have scared him, because within the first couple minutes of talking to him, I told him I wanted to kill myself."

"What did the guy look like?"

"Well, he was about 6 feet tall, dark, curly hair, and he was wearing jeans, and a blue telephone company jacket."

"Okay. Do you think you could tell me what you guys talked about?"

"Sure. I told him that I wanted to kill myself. I had showed him the pills, and told him that I was going to get a motel room and do it there. You know, take the pills and kill myself."

"How many drinks did you have with him?" Nancy asked.

"We had 3 or 4 drinks at Wallys. From there he asked me to walk down town with him to the State Street Saloon. So, that's where we went next. I guess David is kinda young because he got carded by the waitress at the State St. I guess if you want to know his real name, maybe the waitress would remember his name."

"Okay, that's helpful. How long did you stay at State Street?"

"Probably, just for one beer. It was getting close to last call, and we wanted to hit the Hammer before they closed."

"Okay...."

"So, that's what we did."

"Were you still talking about wanting to kill yourself?"

"Yes I was. At one point David told me that he was real sad too because he had just buried his fifteen month old daughter. I told him I could understand, and asked him if he would come to the hotel room with me and hold me while I die."

"You asked him to do that?"

"Yup. But, he told me he couldn't do that or that he wouldn't do that. When we were at the Rusty Hammer I asked him where a close hotel was. He gave me the name of one, I don't remember which he said, then I remembered that I had stayed at the Port Motor Inn before, so I asked him to tell me where it was. So, after the drink at the Hammer, I told him I was leaving to get a room at the Port. He asked if he could share the cab with me because he didn't live too far from where I was going. I told him he could."

"Do you know where he lives?"

"No. I asked him earlier, when we were in the State St., but he told me I didn't need to know."

"Why did he say that?"

"Like I told you, even though we were having a good time together, I think he was trying to remain anonymous in case I did show up dead in my hotel room."

"Okay."

"Then, we got in the taxi, and I told the driver to take me to the Port Motor Inn. David and I were both in the back seat of the taxi, but David had gotten in after me. When we got to the Port, I gave the driver a fifty dollar bill, which she couldn't change. I had to go inside the hotel office in order to get change. After I paid the taxi, I went back into the hotel office to register for a room."

"Where was David when you did this?" Nancy asked.

"Last I knew, he was in the taxi, and he was leaving."

"What next?"

"I registered for my room in the office, and I walked to my room. As I was putting the room key into the knob, I noticed David standing by the Pepsi machine, drinking a Pepsi. I tried to ignore him and just go into my room, but he came running toward me and asked if he could talk to me."

"Did he ask to come in?"

"Yes. I know I should have told him no, but we had been talking most of the night and I had already told him some deep secrets, so, I said yes, but told him, 'no sex'. He said okay. It seemed like he understood. He also said something about talking me out of killing myself."

"Can you give me a better description of what he looked like? We've got the clothing, but what about shoes?"

"I think he was wearing a pair of construction boots. Like,

with rubber soles on the bottom."

"Any distinguishing characteristics? You know, something about him that might make him stand out a little more; something unusual?"

"I think so. I noticed that he had three teeth missing. Left upper jaw. A scar above his left eye, and a tattoo on his right shoulder with the letters "RB"."

"Once inside the room, can you tell me, step by step, what happened?"

"First, he sat on the bed, and I sat on the chair, and we turned on the t.v. We watched that for a while. He asked me if I wanted to talk about why I wanted to die. I told him 'no'. I figured I'd already talked enough about that, and was even tired of hearing myself talk about it. Then he turned on some stupid game on the tube, and I didn't want to listen to it, so I got up and went to the bathroom. When I was sitting on the toilet, he opened the bathroom door, and stood there watching me. I was shocked as shit to see that he had nothing on from the waist down. He had a shirt on, but he had taken his jeans, underwear, and boots, off."

"Did he say anything to you?"

"Yes! He said, 'Look how big I am! Look how big I am!' I told him to leave because I wanted my privacy. He just kept saying to me, 'but look how big I am'. He wouldn't leave, so finally I stood up, pulled my pants up, and walked toward the door to leave the hotel room."

"Okay."

"From there, he attacked me from behind, took my jeans and underwear off, unhooked my bra, but left it on, and pushed me down on the bed."

"How?"

"He took his hands and shoved me down with his hands on my shoulders. When he did that, he fell down with me, on top of me, and pinned me down. then he reached over and grabbed one of my wrists, as he straddled me at the waist. I kicked and I yelled that I wanted him to get off me; but he stayed. Then he put his penis on and around my mouth. He kept telling me to eat him and suck him."

"Did he force it into your mouth?"

"No, because I was yelling, I told him that I was gonna tell on him. He said that was okay cuz he was gonna kill me when he was done. Then I started to get really scared and that's when I asked him if he was the one who killed the girls from the Beauty School."

"Did he reply to that question?"

"No. He just kept looking at me. By this point he was trying to put his prick inside me. My legs were flailing, and I kept telling him to get up, but he wouldn't. Then his dick was inside me, and he just kept saying, 'isn't this wonderful? isn't this wonderful?' He made me sick."

At this point, Charlene began crying some very quiet tears. They trailed down the side of her face, leaving the slightest stream. I looked up and saw Joe behind Charlene, giving me the old 'time-out' signal. He was telling me to give it a break, and let her finish crying. I gave him a silent nod. I sat in front of Charlene, knowing that any words of compassion from me, wouldn't be heard.

After just a few minutes, she was ready to begin again.

"Anyway," Charlene said, "it wasn't wonderful, and I was scared. When he was done, he came inside me. After that, he laid on top of me for several minutes. I was scared to say anything, so I just let him stay. Then he rolled off me and said, 'well, I suppose you want me to go now, in the rain?' I didn't say anything. He got dressed and left; but, before he walked out the door he looked at me and said he was sorry."

"Is that when you called the police?"

"Yes. No. I didn't call right away. I didn't know what to do, so I called my daughter first. She told me to call the police."

Joe, seeing that the interview was just about over, slid out the door as Charlene and Nancy were having their last words. Nancy explained to Charlene how the investigation would continue from this point forward, as Joe walked in with a SASS worker.

Perfect timing, Nancy thought. The interview had taken up a good part of their day, and she knew they still had a scene to process, and was anxious to get started.

The SASS worker expertly positioned herself to take over where Nancy had left off.
This happened just as Nancy was saying her goodbys to Charlene and letting her know she'd be in touch.

Without even grabbing lunch, Nancy and Joe went directly to the Port Motor Inn. Having gathered their statement from Charlene, they were curious as to what they would find at the hotel, and whether or not there would be any corroborating evidence. As of yet, they still didn't know the true identity of Mr. David Smith, but they felt as though there were enough clues to lead them in the right direction.

When they arrived at the Port, they were immediately recognized by the coppers holding the scene, so there was no need to badge themselves in. The Port Inn is a dumpy little place, with no frills. One of those tiny row motels, with about ten rooms attached to each other in a long, thin line. Each room would have the basics, but that was it. She was willing to bet that some of the televisions didn't work. As Nancy looked around room number 2, a distinct feeling of empty, loneliness came over her. It was obvious that a great deal of activity had taken place in the room, but between people void of any deep understanding as to what they had engaged in. The blankets were skewed from the bed, and left on top was the stained, and disheveled remnants of the rape. Without a magnifying glass, Nancy could see body hairs on the bed, seminal stains, and a few small drops of blood. She made a note to ask where the blood had come from, as Charlene hadn't talked about it in the interview. Neither had Nancy noticed any injuries on Charlene that could have caused blood and further wondered if this could have been the result of her menstryl cycle. Or, whether David had been so aggressive during the sexual assault, that he caused her to bleed.

Retrieving several sanitary paper bags, Truax and Ellis neatly and carefully folded all the bed clothing, and placed each item into a separate paper bag. These would later be brought to the lab to be tested for DNA, hairs, blood-type, etc. As they were packaging the sheets, Nancy noticed a straight-edged razor blade sitting atop the lamp table nearest the bed. As she looked closely, she notice that it had dried blood on both sides and some white powder dried onto the blood. This too, was gathered. In all, Nancy and Joe spent another 2-3 hours processing the room. When they left, they carried with them all the evidence they had gathered and packaged; this included the bed clothing, a 12 oz can of Pepsi which David Smith had been drinking from, razor blade, and a copy of the room voucher. The voucher showed that Charlene paid a grand total of $26.70 for one room, for one night, at the Port Motor Inn. She paid with cash.

As was mandatory, they brought the evidence directly to the PPD evidence room, in order to maintain proper chain of custody. Before they could leave for the day, they had to brief Commander Smith as to what they had learned. Jerry listened intently, but seemed most interested in the true identity of David Smith. He pushed for as much information as they had on Smith and promised to take it home and come up with the name of this guy. He appeared to have the name of an individual on the tip of his tongue, but couldn't seem to push the name from the recesses of his brain, to his tongue.

We all parted company for the night, each feeling a sense of accomplishment. At what , I don't know. Possibly it was just that feeling you get after completing a full day of work, and knowing that what you've done will result in something positive.

As Nancy arrived home, she was glad to see that the house was empty. That would give her just a few minutes to rest, and clear her mind. Sometimes, after a day like this, all she wanted to do was to crawl into bed and sleep until the next day. Knowing she couldn't do that (homework assignments to help with, dinner, and lunches for the following day), she laid on top of the bed spread, trying not to wrinkle her work clothes, but allowed her eyelids to slip downward, for a rest. She had a sweet, peaceful, hazy, dreamlike, sleep that allowed her to travel limitlessly through time and space. She traveled through the bright, cloudy, sky until she tired of that and wished for the ocean. In the ocean, she could swim and breathe beneath the water, while exploring the beauties of the marine world. Sometimes, before she went to sleep, she tried to program her mind to go to specific places. On this day, however, she just floated softly and easily from one beautiful world to another and simply enjoyed each existence for what it was.

Nancy awakened to the slamming of her bedroom door, and the growling of Vince's anxious voice.

"Wake up, Nancy," he said.

He wasn't really talking, but he wasn't really yelling either. It was an order more than a request. It was a demand, more than an order. It was a hateful demand, more than it was a demand. Nancy's mind struggled to reconnect, and as usual, did so slowly. Her eyes slipped open, just as slowly as they had closed. Her vision needed to adjust to this new galaxy.

She opened her eyes, and looked with curiosity as her husband stood beside her, a baseball bat in his hand. That's funny, she thought to herself. 'It's not softball season, he's not wearing his ball uniform.....

The bedroom door opened suddenly because Mike had just entered to do some after school visiting with his parents. But, as soon as his head popped in the door, Vince hollered for him to get out of the room, go to his own, and do his homework. We're talking and don't want to be bothered.

Nancy remained still as she scurried in her mind to connect with whatever fragments of logic that would explain her current situation. What had gone wrong now?, she wondered. Why was the baseball bat swinging in his right wrist, like the pendulum of a kookoo clock. Motionless, but her eyes wide open now, she faced Vince, and asked him as sleepily, and nonthreateningly as possible, "What's the matter?"

"What's the matter!!" he yelled, "what do you mean, what's the matter? Didn't you see it?"

"See what," she asked.

""The car," he yelled, "somebody keyed the car again."

"No, I didn't see it. Where?"

"Driver's side door. Looks like they took off about 7 layers of paint. Somebody did a real good job."

"Vince, the only place I went with that car today is to work."

"Where did you park it?", he asked.

"In the police parking lot."

"Well, goddammit.   This is gonna cost another couple thousand dollars to fix. I'm sick and tired of those assholes you work with damaging my stuff."

"It's my stuff, too," she said.

"Yup. And speaking of which, why don't you just tell me what it is you're up to over there, that these people keep doing this stuff to you."

"Are you blaming me, now?"

"Yes. I want to know what it is you're doing to them to make them do this to you."

At this, she became enraged, but knew the conditions were unsafe for any kind of release.

"Vince, I'm just doing my job over there," she said. "Nothing more, or less than what anybody else would do. Whether you understand it or not, there are still a few people over there who have a hard time accepting me."

"They owe you protection," he yelled. "They owe you at least that much. Besides, that's nonsense. You must be screwing somebody over for them to be treating my property like this."

"I'll report it to the station tomorrow, when I go in."

"Yeah, and what good will that do? Those people over there are useless." He brought the bat over his head, brought it down onto the bed, and as it bounced up, he screamed, "Just useless."

Now Nancy was screaming. Although he hadn't threatened it, she was afraid that she would be the next target for the bat. She sat up, screamed, told him to stop. He put the bat down and suddenly flipped the mattress over, with her on it. She landed on the floor first, then the mattress was on top of her. Vince's logic was beyond her. What had she done to deserve that anger. As that thought was rushing through her head, she felt a sudden pounce on her back, as Vince jumped from the box spring, onto the mattress. He gave a loud grunt as though he was satisfied that he may have done some injury. She squirmed beneath the mattress, in a vain attempt to get out from under it. She screamed, telling Vince to get off. He ignored her by pouncing up and down, squishing her further. He was going for a ride, she thought, and he was taking Nancy with him, a ride to hell and back. Will these days never end? Will he ever stop, will he ever learn? Will he ever lay down his sword of anger, and pick up the cup of love. Right now, it didn't seem as though this was an eventuality.

"You son-of-a-bitch," he yelled, as he got off the mattress. Everything of mine is destroyed because of you. The red jeep is totally scratched, now the new Saab. Is there anything else of mine you want to bring to that place you call work so they can destroy it?"

When she felt him leave the back of the mattress, she pushed with her hands and knees in an effort to stand. The mattress popped up, and over, Angry, but not humiliated, she looked at him square in the eyes, and said, "Vincent Truax, you knew who I was and what I was when you married me. You were so anxious to keep me, you insisted on eloping, right away. I did that for you. But now I'm gonna do something else for you.."

As she said these last words, she saw a ball of white spittle flying in her direction, toward her face. She allowed it to land on her left cheek. She left it hanging, dangling, for him to see, so he would know what he had done.

"As I said," she continued, spittle now beginning to hang, "now I'm going to do something for you. I'm leaving." She stepped toward the bedroom door to make her exit.

Vince rushed in front of her, slammed the bedroom door and hollered that she wasn't going anywhere.

"You just spit in my face, and I'm not going anywhere? You throw me on the ground with a mattress on top of me, you jump on top of me, and I'm not going anywhere?"

"You're not going fucking anywhere." He opened the bedroom door, slammed it behind him, as he yelled, "You're not leaving this fucking room!"

To cry or not to cry. Crying really is a waste of time. It keeps you from planning a way out. It keeps you tied down to your own sorrows, rather than planning a future without them.
Exhausted, she sat on what was left of the box spring. She thought about calling the police. The phone, after all, was just within reach. But, foolishly, situations like these always embarrassed the
living hell out of her. She ignored the phone, and instead went to the bedroom door, where she started down the stairs. When Vince heard her, he screamed in his rage, "You're not going anywhere!! I'm getting the shotgun, NOW!"

The shotgun, Nancy thought. He's never gotten the shotgun before. It's funny how stable thoughts can run through your head at a time like this. Then it was, 'he can't be getting the shot gun. Well, yes. He's pulled a gun on me twice, threatened to shoot me twice before, but never a shotgun. She heard some doors slamming, and the next thing she knew, she heard footsteps, and the ever distinguishable clanking sound of a shot gun loading one round into the chamber. Calm, yet petrified, as Nancy crossed the upstairs hallway into the kids bedroom she saw Vince turning the corner to go up the stairs with the gun. In all her life she'd never imagined this; this of all things. How could one man be so insanely evil? He really was coming up the stairs with the shot gun, and Nancy had enough experience to know that he had at least one round ready to go. She wondered if the safety was on or off. As he rounded the corner to come up the stairs, Nancy saw that he was holding the gun toward the ceiling, but figured as soon as he got to the top, he'd have it as his shoulder.

Mike and Matty, fully aware of the argument, looked immediately up at her as she entered their bedroom. Their eyes were big with fear, and she suddenly felt more shame than she could have imagined. This is what she had led her children into, this is what she had allowed them to survive. What kind of a mother was she to give birth to them in this environment, and then keep them in it; it was one thing if Nancy made the choice to stay, but she shouldn't have allowed her children to live and breathe this life.

With the strength that adrenaline graciously gives, Nancy gathered her children in her arms and hauled them down the back stairway, and into the garage. They were crying hard, but she couldn't pay attention to that right now. Right now, they needed to be safe. She threw them into the car, started the engine, and ripped out of the driveway.

Nancy knew Vince pretty well and knew that he would be too lazy to get in his car and follow her. About a mile down the road, she pulled over to the side, and safely secured the kids.

"Where are we going?" they asked.

"We're going to visit Nonny," she said, "Nonny hasn't seen us in a long time, and I bet she'll be real happy to see us." Nancy smiled big at them, like the time when she got to take her T-shirt off, hoping they would smile big, back. They didn't. Unlike Nancy, at that age. They had been caught in a trap of sorts. Rather than a trap of convention, this was a cycle, a whirlpool that refused to release its victims until they were pulled beneath the cold water, and into it's depths. Those who entered the whirlpool rarely escaped. The longer one remained in the whirlpool, the greater the fatigue as the victim tried over and over again to escape. The greater the fatigue, the greater the chances of being pulled under, of succumbing, of dying.

Safe at Nonny's, the kids tucked in bed, Nancy blurted the whole story to her mother, and felt again, empty and lonely as she watched her mother's expression of disbelief. It's not that her mother didn't believe her, it's that her mother found it difficult to believe that another human being would behave this way, or that Nancy would put up with it. For the first time ever, Nancy shared the history of her marriage to Vince with her mom. It was something she never wanted to do, but the time had come.

She told her about the untold holidays she'd spent alone because of Vince's hatred of them. Every holiday, Vince would suddenly, without reason, become angry and volatile. This is why, she told Nonny, that on so many Holiday occasions, she had to cancel the family visit to her house. She told her about the time when she was pregnant, that Vince had become so angry with her that he

had thrown her to the ground, kicked her in the stomach, and left, swearing he'd never come back. About the time when he
punched her in the eye and she lied and told her parents that she'd walked into a doorjamb. And about the time he punched her in the nose and made it bleed. About all the times he told her he didn't want her, didn't love her, didn't want to spend time with her (so go out and find your own friends). She talked, cried and sobbed, until she passed out in her mother's bed. Nancy's last thoughts were about how she wanted to smile BIG, because she could take her shirt off. She wanted to smile BIG, and know that life was the way it should be. She wondered where every thing, of her, had gone, and whether she would get it all back again.

Sure, she would. Sure.

The next day she worked long, tedious, hours, sinking her soul into the search for "David Smith". She found him, arrested him, and returned home.

Chapter 14

DCIT

Between mid and late 1996 the Portsmouth Police Department learned they would be the recipient of grant monies from the Federal Government totaling almost $100,000. The purpose of this grant was to establish an elite unit within the department that would concentrate specifically on domestic violence cases. At the time the grant money was received, I was still serving as a patrol sergeant working rotating shifts, and, coincidentally, it was just after my awakening experience with Commissioner Kupruck.

Once the money was received, the department had to choose someone to head-up the new division. Hopefully, this person would be capable of doing the research necessary to determine which new programs should be put in place, and decide what changes were needed within the department, in terms of how we were handling domestic violence cases. There were only two people interested in doing the job: Sergeant Lanko and myself. Sergeant Lanko, to his credit, was responsible for actually writing the grant, along with officer Jen Sives. As you may recall from earlier chapters, it was widely known and accepted that Lanko was not one of the most sympathetic persons when it came to women's issues. As a matter of fact, he was known to be downright chauvinistic, and not afraid to let anyone know that men are the center of the universe; it's very reason for sustaining synchronisity. Women, he thought, should not employ themselves outside the home as doing so took jobs away from healthy men who were more qualified.

This quality put the fear of God into the Administration with regard to having him as the forerunner for this division. As a result, various members of the upper administration, including Craig Brasso, set about gently dissuading him from taking the job, while I stepped forward declaring my interest. I think that the department wished there had been another, third person option for the position considering, though I tried to keep it hidden, it was generally known that I had experienced some domestic problems at home. I believe many members of the department thought I would be overly aggressive in my pursuit of these cases. I understood this concern and, once I received the job, made every attempt to be fair, yet aggressive identifying every case, and bringing it to a fair resolution. As a safety measure, it was agreed that all my cases would be thoroughly reviewed, and all arrests authorized by both Commander Beaumont, and Attorney Bob Simmons (the Department's prosecuting attorney).

The conditions of the grant were multi-faceted. One of the first components mandated department wide training on the issues of domestic violence. At the time this money was received, though there had been new and aggressive laws pertaining to domestic violence, our Agency still handled them in a very casual manner. Officers were reluctant to identify domestic abuse, except in the most extreme cases, as anything other than a "family problem". As a result, most times the arguing couple was simply separated for the evening in hopes that they could come together the next day and resolve their own problems.

This resulted in officers responding over and over again to the same homes, so they could easily name the "regulars" involved in most of our domestic disputes and enumerate specifically what their problems were, i.e., crack, cocaine, heroine uppers, downers, alcohol, or simply temper or anger problems.

By educating the officers on the advantages of a more aggressive approach, we were hoping to diminish the incidence of domestic violence response by police. The training was set up and held in September of 1996, and was comprised of three parts.

During the first portion of the lecture I laid out Departmental history of response to domestic violence cases by showing that in 1995 the Department responded to 421 domestic violence calls but only made 23 arrests. Only 5% of the domestic violence dispatches resulted in arrests. When this small percentage of arrests was more closely analyzed I learned that only four of those persons were charged criminally; the others were brought in for protective custody drunkenness). This means that in all of 1995, less than 1% of all domestic violence dispatches were charged criminally.

Thus far, in 1996 we responded to 311 domestic dispute calls for service. This resulted in 49 incident reports (15%), and 28 arrest reports (9%). When reviewed more closely, only 16 of the 28 arrests were charged criminally (5%).

These statistics were appalling considering domestic violence calls encompassed approximately 20% of our overall police responses. When I outlined the facts, the officers in the room became defensive because they thought I was pointing the finger of blame and further implying they were not doing their job. I explained that that was not what the statistics were meant to do; simply, they were meant to point out one area of much needed change within the agency, and promote discussion on how to achieve this.

At the second part of the training, I had Barbara Dennett and Dr. Greg Schwartz speak on the social and psychological ramifications of domestic violence, which led into a conversation on why it is so important to concentrate on these issues. Dennett taught us about the "cycle of violence" saying that violence within the family continues generation after generation if we do not make an attempt to stop it. She also explained why it is so difficult for a person caught in this cycle to permanently leave the situation, and therefore why an officer responds to one home time after time after time. She explained further that perhaps if we understood why it is so difficult for the victim of abuse to leave, perhaps we could be a bit more compassionate, rather than frustrated, when again we are called to the same home we had been to the night before, or even the hour before.

Dr. Greg Schwartz told about a new program he was using that focused on the perpetrator's anger. This is a 26-week course which helps abusers learn how to better manage their anger. By making arrests on these domestic violence cases we would then be able to have a Judge mandate attendance at the "Anger Management" course, which might further assist in reducing the incidence of domestic violence.

For the third and final portion of the training I invited the County Attorney, Bill Champagne, to talk about the new laws that had been set into place focusing on domestic violence and stalking, and explain how the officers could easily utilize them when they responded to a call.

I believe the officers left the training having gained some information, but still individually doubtful as to whether or not the program would work. There were many officers who privately approached me expressing worry about this new and "fanatical" approach to domestic violence. To them, it seemed too rigid leaving little room for situational discretion at the scene.

They were concerned about their own home lives too. One officer asked: "You mean to tell me that if I have an argument with my wife, and she blocks the door to prevent me from leaving, I can't push her aside to walk out because I've committed a crime? I could be arrested?" Lots of questions like this were asked, as though they were demanding to know the possibility of their arrest; as though they needed to know how far was too far. I explained to each that all he had to do was use his common sense. If he needed to leave the home in order to prevent further argument or violence, brushing by his spouse, or squeezing through, or a gentle push to the side, was not going to result in any kind of arrest for assault. I have to say, though, that for the number of concerned officers that came to me with these questions, I had to wonder if it was actually *just* a shove or push they were anxious about.

From that day forward some officers, in abject protest to the new policy, simply refused to make any arrest on domestic violence cases unless it was absolutely necessary. Others begged out of doing their job by, rather than taking immediate action when they responded to the scene, referring the call to me to handle the next day, or whenever I could get to it. Others, mostly younger and more eager officers, latched onto this new philosophy and honestly helped to make the program work.

By the end of 1996, domestic violence statistics were rising rapidly. November through December of 1996 logged 225 domestic calls for service, 76 police reports, and 33 arrest reports. Additionally, many cases were being referred directly to Dr. Greg Schwartz, and other social service agencies; another plus for the program. The project was beginning to work, so I pushed forward with great enthusiasm in spite of a silent resistive undercurrent.

Around the 20th of January 1997, I stepped into my small, 4' by 7' office located directly between the station officer's desk and the Captain's office, eager to begin my daily routine. I mention the location of my office because it was situated in a place where foot traffic from police personnel, arrestees, local dignitaries, and any citizen, in addition to phones ringing from the dispatch center, the station officer's desk, and the Captain's office made it extremely difficult to concentrate, get work done, and conduct interviews. As with many jobs in police work, I had to be very good at doing ten things at once, but at the same time strictly focus on the task at hand.

This job was no different. I turned on the newly purchased, government funded, computer to check my CAD entries. CAD is an anachronism for Computer Aided Dispatch. This means that I was checking the dispatch log for the last several days to see what had happened over the last forty-eight hours. What kind of police calls had the officers responded to, and how did those calls impact my division? There were several reasons to do this; one was to be sure that all domestic violence cases were labeled appropriately in the computer so that when I did the administrative task of tallying domestic calls as compared to arrests and referrals, I could make any necessary corrections, which would better enable me to gather *accurate* statistics at the end of the month. Additionally, I reviewed each and every domestic violence call to be sure that appropriate action was taken by the responding officer. If this was not done, I would seize that case and do any necessary follow-up. There were times when I would take the call information and hand it back to the responding officer and have him re-investigate. This was one of the worst parts of my job. Each time I had to kick a case back to a police officer they resented being told that they didn't do their job right, and they had to redo it. It was around this time that I was beginning to be viewed by my peers as a staunch femme-nazi who wanted to arrest all men, even if they hadn't committed a crime.[1]

As I was spinning through the dispatches I happened to notice that on January 18, 1997 at 1:20 AM, Officer Mark Houston had been sent to a local club called 'Spin' for what appeared to be a domestic dispute; but the notations on the call were vague, so I couldn't be sure. The original CAD report is labeled number 970180012 and reads, "female has been assaulted by male." Then all it says is: "#303[2] advised spoke with husband and wife. Was verbal argument. Will be all set".

The hairs on the back of my neck began to prickle because I had learned by this time that, often, when the dispatcher receives the initial information, as noted in the first line of the CAD call: "female has been assaulted by male", that is the more accurate piece of information because it is called in by a third party with no outside interest as to how the case should be handled, *and* received by an impartial dispatcher. The second line in the CAD call, being information given by the officer who responded to the scene, has more of a bias attached to it in that the officers may have any number of reasons for not wishing to pursue the case further. I will admit that often their reasons are noble and just; but, due to our 'zero tolerance' policy, I had an obligation at this juncture to ascertain whether a woman had or had not been assaulted. The key words that jumped out at me on this particular CAD call were the words "husband and wife". These words led me to understand that the call *was* domestic related, and therefore fell into my jurisdiction.   Further,   the words "verbal argument" smacked me in the nose. Often times, even when an officer had solid evidence that a domestic fight was physical, the officer would sometimes articulate *differently* to dispatch as he[3] cleared the scene, alleviating any necessity for follow-up or in depth investigation. Simply put, laziness was the dominant factor for many decisions made by responding officers; a cultural habit that I, and

---

[1] It is here that I wish to note that I do not believe that only men are abusers, or that only women are victims.

[2] That would represent the police unit number.

[3] Gender non specific.

other supervisors, were desperately trying to stop by the diligent policing of the officer's actions.

Another, glaring aspect of this police call was the absence of a police report number. There was no report to retrieve in order to read the details of the incident. This, in and of itself, went against policy as, whenever officers responded to a domestic disputes, they were supposed to take an incident number and generate a report about the incident. Even if no arrest was made, they were supposed to generate a report. The fact that no number was issued led me to believe that the officer had either been lazy, or there was something to hide. This prompted further concern, and added to the urgency of looking into the event. It should be noted, that at this point in time, I had no idea who the arguing couple had been, or the seriousness of the case. I decided to do my own footwork to get the answer to these, and many other questions.

If, in fact, this domestic dispute turned out to be a physical argument rather than a verbal argument as the officer specifically had the dispatcher notate in the CAD call, I was dealing with an officer of poor credibility. Without credibility, an officer becomes ineffectual. Sometimes arrests, and whole cases are built on an officer's word, which is his promise that everything he says is true. Judges and Juries depend on this. If an officer is shown to be a liar of any degree, his testimony can no longer be taken seriously.

There are many aspects to an investigation of this type, and one of the steps I always take is to obtain a copy of the emergency (voice) call to the police station. Listening to the call itself will often give greater insight into the exact nature of the call and perhaps the height of, or lack of hysteria at the scene.

As I sat numbly absorbed in completing the request form for for the 911 call, my office door opened allowing a noisy stream of daily-police-activity to filter in, bringing with it Detective Sives.

"Have a seat," I said without looking up. I knew it was Jen because she carries with her a mellow, sweet, musky scent that billows about her as an invisible cloud. Its such a pleasant smell that I've often contemplated asking her about it, but only when I had a chance to be still and review certain moments of my day. I, obviously, never had those times during working hours. Now was no different.

"I'll be back in a sec," I said as I quickly twirled my seat toward the door; my intention was to turn the form in immediately, to get that tape as quickly as possible; but I stopped short when I saw the look on Jen's face. At 5'7", carrying a proud and sturdy build, she stood in front of me openly allowing her chin to tremble. As her apparent grief registered, she continued to let go by sinking into the vacant interview seat, and letting her silent tears flow. She was neither embarrassed or ashamed.

My first reaction was to pass her the same box of Kleenex I had passed to so many victims of domestic violence as they told me their sad stories in this dank, puny office. But this was so different. This woman was different. Police officers, especially police women, don't cry. Can't cry. Tears are a funny thing to police officers. Tears are a symbol of weakness rather than strength, and if caught crying, it could be the end of all respect by our peers. Right or wrong, history dictated that, during work hours, we armored ourselves with uncaring callousness to protect us from hurting when a child was killed in a horrible traffic accident, or when a woman cried for help because she found her husband had hung himself from a rafter in their newly built garage. The same twisted logic applied to the inner politics of the department. No matter how badly a knife was twisted into one's back, tears at work were a 'no-no'.

"Jen! What's wrong?" I asked simultaneously returning to my chair.

She took a moment to slightly compose herself and, while blowing her nose liberally, and clearing her throat as needed, began talking.

"Nancy, I don't know what to do. Ever since I got the promotion into Youth Services, I feel like I'm starting all over again, like I have to break through that invisible barrier again and I don't know if I can do it. No one in the office is talking to me, or when they do, it's empty prattle, or rude jokes, or cutting down women, me especially. The Sergeant gives me assignments, but with no direction or no support. They know I've got no training for this stuff. I feel like Sergeant Lanko is purposefully setting me up to fail."

"They haven't sent you to training yet? You've been there two months already. What assignments are they giving you?"

"I'm supposed to be teaching for the Dare Program as soon as Detective Smith gets his promotion, so Lanko's asked me to develop some new lessons for all the students in grades five through eight. That's no problem, but every time I ask him what the classes should focus on, he says we'll have to meet with the teachers and ask them. I've told him over and over again that I want to go introduce myself to the teachers at the middles school, and find out from them what they want."

"That sounds reasonable. What's the problem?"

"He says he doesn't want me to go over there on my own, till he's ready to come with me, so that *he* can make the introductions. He also said he was afraid that if I went by myself they'd have some misconception about the new "bitch" coming into the schools to work with the kids."

"What?" I said. "The new 'bitch'? What's that supposed to

mean?"

"He said that there's always been a man there before; you know, they loved Kevin, so he thought it would be too forward and pushy for me to go force myself on them. That's how he sees it."

I knew Lanko was an asshole, but I didn't know he was so daft as to openly display his chauvinism to a well-liked, successful, female employee. That part astonished me the most. Now *I* was taking deep breaths and inwardly trying to reassure myself that neither I nor the whole world was insane. 'It's only a few', I chanted inwardly.

"The problem is," she continued", he never has the time. He refuses to make the time. He comes to work late every day, drives fifteen miles home for a two hour lunch every day, and leaves the office at three in the afternoon, *every* day. Now, here we are, two weeks before I take the program over, and I have nothing to teach my kids."

"Jen, you've got to get your ass over there whether he wants you to go or not. Don't let him set you up like this. I shouldn't say that. I don't think he realizes the impact his schedule is having on you, so you've got to just cover your own butt. You can explain later why you disobeyed an order. You can't allow yourself to lose face in front of the teachers or the kids. It wouldn't look good for the department, and I'm sure the Chief would be pissed."

"It's too late," she said as, again, her cupped hands received more sobs and tears.

"What do you mean, 'it's too late'?" I asked impatiently. She was never going to win this battle if she didn't take things into her own hands.

"That's what I'm talking about," she said. "Lanko received a scathing letter from Captain Wilson demanding to know where the outlines for the lesson plans were, the ones I was supposed to do, and Lanko blamed the whole thing on me. He told Wilson that he had given me the assignment two months ago, that he had continuously reminded me to get them done, but I had failed to do it. They want to suspend me for a week for disobeying an order."

"You've got to be kidding me!" I said. "Did you tell Caption Wilson what happened?"

"No, Lanko won't allow me to speak with him. He told me I had to use the chain of command. He doesn't want me to rat him out."

I knew Lanko well; I knew his tendency to use coworkers to get what he wanted, as a shield for protection, or as a stepping stone for advancement, regardless of who he hurt.

"But a suspension of any length is wrong, Jen. You have to speak out."

"Yeah, right. Speak out. Talk to *him*? Are you crazy? How do I speak with a guy who tells me that his dream job was to be a gynecologist, but his fingers are too big?"

"He said that to you?"

"Yeah. That and other stuff. You know. I should wear shorter skirts, lose weight, bake muffins at home and bring them in for the office. Stuff like that. Last week he told me I shouldn't try out for the SWAT team because I'm a woman."

"He said that?"

"Yeah. He had a long conversation with me about that one. Lots of guys in the office are on the team. They must have heard I was planning to try out, so I'm guessing they complained to him, and he took it as his duty to prevent me from joining. Anyway, he told me that there are no women on the team, like I didn't already know that, and if I should be lucky enough to get on, my presence would so destroy the moral of the other members that they would all quit, and I would be the only member. Basically, the eradication of a good team would be my fault. Can you believe that?"

I was stunned. "How long did this ridiculous conversation last?"

"About half an hour."

"He spent a half hour talking to you about the SWAT team? Was anyone else there? No. Wait a minute. When did he spew this psycho babble at you? How long ago?"

"About three weeks ago."

"So it was *before* he and Wilson came up with this idea about suspending you? As far as you know, I mean?"

"Yeah. I just found out about the suspension today."

"Okay, Jen," I said as I grabbed her by the shoulders and looked her in the eye, "stay in here as long as you need, but do yourself a favor and don't make it too long. You don't want anyone else to know you've been knocked for a loop over this. I'm going to go take care of a few things."

"Where are you going? What are you doing?"

"Never mind. Concentrate on pulling yourself together and getting back to work. It's still early enough. As soon as your face is clear, and your nose stops running, get your ass over to the middle school and introduce yourself as the new Dare Officer in the most cheerful and professional way you can muster. If they ask you about the lesson plans, tell them you're working on them based on the specific DARE guidelines, but ask for input. Got it?"

"Got it," she said.

And I was off.

"Commander Brasso," I said after knocking on his door, "have you got a minute?"

"That's about all I've got. I'm late for a meeting with Captain Wilson and Sergeant Lanko."

"Perfect," I said. "I've got the other side of the story for you before you attend that meeting."

He gave me a puzzled look and said, "I'm glad you know what the meeting is about, because I've got no idea."

"Well, let me tell you," I began; and I told him what I knew. When I was finished, I said, "You've got to put a stop to this suspension. It's absolutely unjust; and, along with the other things that have been going on in that office, Jen's got the ability to put this whole Agency in a negative spotlight with a great big law-suit, and I don't think you want that."

"No I don't," he said. "I'll take care of it."

"The sexual harassment too?" I asked.

"I'll take care of it," he said.

And I left it at that.

As I expected, the emergency call to dispatch did give a bit more insight into what was happening, however, it should be noted that since the call was made from a public, pay phone, inside the bar, a mere foot from the actual incident, it was short and to-the-point. The following is a transcript, in total, of the emergency call to the police department. Imagine as you read the words, behind the caller there are people partying, drinking, a band is playing, and some sort of fight is happening less than a foot from where he is standing. All those sounds can be heard in the background of the tape.

Dispatcher: "Portsmouth emergency."

Caller: "Yeah, we got, ah, a assault going on down here. This guy's beatin up his wife down here at Spin, and, ah, come down here right away please."

Dispatcher: "Okay"
Caller: "Whassat?"
End of call.

There was definitely an urgency in the caller's voice created in part by the incident itself, and furthered by his frustration in attempting to relay a compelling message in the worst of circumstances. Now it was clear to me that I was dealing with a physical dispute, as opposed to a "verbal argument" only. Receiving this piece of information, I obtained a control number that would generate a police report, in order to get the facts down on paper, and later make a clearer determination as to how to resolve the case.

After receiving the 911 tape, information traveled quickly

through the police department that I was investigating the call. I couldn't understand the frenzy that arose, until seven days later, on January 27th. In the course of my investigation I called a witness, Joe Moore, whose name I got from a third party who heard he might have been there, and might have seen something. Contacting him was a long-shot in terms of gleaning any valuable information, but, why not? A few minutes of my time couldn't hurt.

With this ten minute conversation I unearthed the reason for the angry, backward, scurry of police foot steps from both me and the case; I learned why no police report had been done, and I sadly discovered why the officers wrongly insisted that this was nothing more than a verbal argument, and logically no arrest or follow-up was made.

Bingo!! Joe told me that he was the 911 caller. Oddly enough, when I first received Joe's name, I didn't realize the impact his information was going to have on this case, so my first interview with him happened via telephone. A day or two later we had an in-person interview which I taped.

Joe arrived at Club Spin at about midnight on the 18th of January 1997 with his friend, Jeff Whitman. At about 1 AM, and two beers later, he and Jeff happened to notice a man, later determined to be Matthew Patterson, leaving Spin. In order to exit the Club you have to pass through an inner membership door, which leads to a flight of 20 steps, which takes you to another, outer door. Bouncers were placed at both sets of doors, as well as throughout the club.

In any case, Joe and Jeff were exiting the club directly behind Patterson. Joe saw Patterson forcefully pushing a woman up the stairs in front of him. This woman was later identified as Theresea Patterson, Matthew Patterson's wife. Joe saw Matthew grab his wife's beautiful, long hair from behind, trail it over her head as he continued to step in front of her, then proceeded to *pull* her up the stairs, using her hair like a dog leash. Matthew was also purposely and aggressively bumping shoulders in a side-to-side motion with other club patrons as he walked by them with his wife in tow. Joe told me that he was a bit curious about this, but wasn't sure if the man was just joking around because Theresea seemed to be walking up the stairs willingly, and she wasn't crying out.

When Joe got to the outer door at the top of the stairs, he stepped to his right to speak with one of the bouncers for a moment. After about five minutes, his friend Jeff turned to him and frantically said, "Hey, Joe, are you gonna do something? You gotta stop this guy."

Joe turned to the direction that Jeff indicated and saw that

Matthew Patterson was holding onto his wife by the back of her neck and forcefully bending her upper body over a cold metal rail that guarded the sidewalk entrance. Patterson was telling his wife:

"It's none of your business about the woman in the club. I can do what I want. It doesn't matter if I had my arm around her. Fuck you!!" Patterson wasn't yelling, but talking with a madness in his voice that eerily shattered any previous thoughts of playful harmony between the couple.

"Hey buddy," Joe said. "Let go of her."

Matthew lifted his head, refusing to be told what to do; he simply glared icily at Joe Moore. In response, Matthew grabbed Theresea by her left arm and jerked her off the sidewalk to a nearby dumpster situated in a dark corner of the club parking lot. Here, Matthew grabbed onto his wife with both hands and proceeded to shake her violently, her head bobbing forward and back, her hair flouncing this way and that.

Joe bravely stepped into the vicinity of the fight and grabbed Matthew by his right shoulder and shoved him around, turning him 180 degrees, placing Patterson's back to his wife.

Jeff stood by and watched as the scenario continued. Jeff later told me that he is not at all violent, and doesn't like people who are. He felt that Joe was more capable of handling himself physically than he was. "At least," he said, "I stayed nearby so that I could help if I had to. This Patterson guy made me real nervous. A psycho, you know?"

As Matthew spun around, he simultaneously reached toward his rear pant pocket. Joe was suddenly afraid that Matt could be grabbing for a weapon, so he stepped back and to the side as quickly as he could.

Matt thrust a rectangular, leather wallet toward Joe and snapped it open with a flick of his wrist, and pressed it in Joe's face. "Mind your own fuckin' business. I'm a cop and this is my wife." Patterson demanded.

Joe was shocked to see that Patterson had pulled out a police badge. So shocked that he wasn't at all sure what he should do. Baffled. Mortified. He pontificated that perhaps, if this person had not been a police officer he would have taken more aggressive action to prevent the following course of events; but he felt intimidated and threatened, and also feared some sort of retaliation by the police officer. After processing these thoughts he dared to step forward and ask Patterson to get a closer look at the badge number. Seeing that the badge was real, Joe and Jeff stepped to the side, but remained close enough to watch what was happening and be sure that Theresea didn't get hurt.

From behind the dumpster, Theresea walked away from

Matt.   Matt followed her and shoved her against a car. Bouncing off the fiberglass, she walked away, yanked her wedding ring from her finger, and threw it into the blackness of the parking lot yelling, "Keep it!"

"Go pick it up, Jeff," Joe ordered. "She might want it later."

Joe watched as Jeff picked up the ring, and Theresea ran toward a lawyer's office at the other end of the parking lot and ducked behind some evergreen bushes that blanketed the face of the brick building. "I've never seen anything like it," Joe confided. "She was scared of her own husband. And her husband hated her. I mean, at least at that moment, he *hated* her. How can people live like that? It was a question that didn't need a response, least of all by me.

"Anyway," Joe continued, "she must have thought Matt split because she came out from behind the bushes. Then he pounced out of nowhere, like a "Tigger", but a mean one, chasing her again. When he caught up to her he slammed her against another car in the middle of the parking lot. Just like that! Pow! This time she crumpled to the ground and Matt stood over her just laughing and yelling at the same time. Jeff and I knew something bad was gonna happen if we didn't get there quick, so we ran to her. I grabbed onto that asshole, Matt, just as he was pulling back to give her a heavy kick in the ribs and I yanked him onto the ground and we began scuffling. I didn't really hurt him; I didn't want to hurt him, just distract him from his wife. He was pissed off, man, but only toward her. He seemed totally focused on her."

"During our little fight, Theresea was able to get herself off the ground and run for help. She ran toward the club, but as soon as Matt realized that his wife had gone, he ripped away from my clutch and ran after her. Nuts, I tell you. He didn't give a damn about me or anyone else watching. Just her."

Joe and Jeff followed them and watched as Matt ran down the stairs, back into the club. He grabbed onto Theresea by the collar and, again, slammed her against the wall, but this time he had the force of a mad sprint propelling him. It was here that Joe picked up the phone and called 911. Even as Joe was speaking with the police, the fight between Matt and Theresea didn't stop.

Mo, a black man that towers a lethal 6'7", with shoulders about four feet wide, was situated at the bottom of the stairs; he was one of the bouncers that night. He interceded by attempting to pry Matt's fingers from Theresea's dainty neck. All the while Mo's deep voice hollered for Patterson to release his grip.

Patterson stupidly retorted, "Hey, that's my wife, and I'm a cop."

Mo countered, "Well, buddy. Those two facts have nothing to do with what's going on here. You're in my club. Let go of her."

"Do you drive in Eliot?" Patterson hissed.

"What are you talking about?" Mo demanded.

"Do you ever go to Eliot? If you do, you better watch out for me," Patterson spit.

By now, Patterson had become so violent that he had drawn the attention of other club members. Patterson had slid his hands onto Theresea's shoulders and made further attempts to slam her against the wall by pulling her toward him and shoving her backward again. Members on the other side of the club door grabbed onto Theresea and pulled her in one direction, while Mo pulled Matt in the other direction. Club members were able to pull Theresea into the club, closing the entry door. This left the loving couple physically separated by a closed door.

"But, wait a minute," I said, "When the police came, did you give them all this information? You know, at the scene?"

"No. By the time they came, we were gone. Are you kidding me? I didn't want anything to do with this mess."

"So, the police didn't get any of this information?"

"Sure they did," Joe said. "I told Mo everything; on top of which there were at least four or five witnesses, workers at the club, who saw Patterson grab onto his wife and slam her against the wall when I was calling the police. I know the police got that piece of information."

"You know," Joe continued, "I was talking with people from the club just a few days after this happened, and they said they told the cops everything. Even the stuff that happened outside in the parking lot. There were other witnesses, friends of mine, who told the cops about that."

"Do you know which cop they spoke with?" I asked.

"Naw. I just know that Kilty said he was pissed that no one was arrested. He told me that if he'd ever done anything like that, he would have been arrested in a heartbeat. He was also mad because the Portsmouth Police Department had, at one time, arrested *his* brother for domestic violence. It was obvious to Kilty, and lots of others, that the reason Patterson wasn't arrested is because he's a cop."

"Who else told you this?" I asked.

"Yeah, every one who saw it happen. Patterson told just about everyone that he was a cop. When all the witnesses saw the cops clear the scene without an arrest, they were disgusted. Word travels like wild fire when something like this happens in a small town. You guys otta be a little more discreet with who you protect."

My thoughts were screaming "cover-up" when I placed the receiver in it's cradle. The nerves at the tips of my fingers were pulsating with the rhythm of my heart. This was my body telling me that I needed to pay attention to what I had just been told. No. Not just pay attention; pay it tribute. Take action.

Who else knew that Patterson was a police officer? Did my co-workers really fail to arrest a man who had just beaten his wife to a pulp in front of no less than a hundred people? How could they have been so dumb? The least they could have done was to make it *look* like they arrested him so the witnesses wouldn't be so outraged, and therefore so willing to talk. I learned from my conversation with Joe that the witnesses *were* talking. They were telling anyone who would listen that the Portsmouth Police Department had, on that night, failed to arrest another police officer for something any one of them would have been arrested for on-the-spot. Now I, the overly-aggressive-man-hating-femme-nazi was in a position to correct the wrong. Great. Just what I needed. Would I do it? Yes. Was it going to be as fun as a pony ride at the fair? Nope. It wasn't. And I knew it. But, wrong is wrong; and, a wrong looks even worse when it's covered up by a bunch of key-stone cops trying to help their buddy. The Blue Brotherhood is nothing more than a bunch of shitty propaganda used to validate cover-ups such as this. I also knew that I would be expected to "leave it alone" once I learned the whole truth. But that wasn't going to happen.

Don't get me wrong. Having heard the bitter truth, part of me wanted to leave it alone. I wanted to drown the information in a tub filled with cement and launch it from a cannon into the deepest, darkest, most deserted sea. I momentarily coddled these selfish desires rooted in self preservation as I imagined the natural outcome should I fail to ignore the facts. I just didn't need the hassle this would cause.

"Don't forget," I reminded myself, "you can squash the information *you* received, but all those people who are witnesses will *never* forget what they saw, nor will they stop talking about it until it's made right again. I had to continue with the investigation and report my findings to Beaumont and Simmons so we could make a joint decision. It was my only option, but not my only wish.

Another week passed before I saw Jen again as I learned that, in lieu of the suspension, she had been given 48 hours to develop a years worth of DARE-lesson-outlines for four grades. Knowing her, she was back on her feet again showing "them" she was no softy, and couldn't be beaten down. I knew she would survive; but I also recognized that she had no concept of the high toll she'd have to pay the Lord of Humanity when she ended her journey.

"Jen, how's it going?" I asked.

"Oh my God! You're not gonna believe this, but Lanko is up to his old tricks again. I don't think anyone's talked to him about his behavior, and the other day he made some comment about going to 'watch the sweaty high school girls finish their gym class, and run to their lockers'. He's sick. Can you imagine what those kid's parents would think if they knew a Youth Services Sergeant was talking about their daughters that way?"

I just shook my head and walked away, directly to Commander Brasso's office. I asked him if he spoke with Lanko about the sexual harassment and he explained that he hadn't had time yet.

"You better make time," I said, "because it hasn't ended and people are talking. Apparently he's been making open comments about watching sweaty high school girls. Do something about it Craig."

A few days later I learned that an internal investigation had been initiated against Lanko. The same day Jen had told me about his latest comment, she also told Sgt. Daniel Foley, who immediately put everything in writing, filed a report, and demanded an investigation. Good for him. Now the administration was forced to do something; and, they hate it when that happens.

They did do something. They put Captain Rudolph Shilling, Lanko's long time personal friend and biggest supporter, in charge of the investigation. All I can say to that is, typical.

Continuing with my case, I interviewed over fifty people and spent more than eighty working hours on the investigation. I interviewed everyone from club bouncers, coat-check persons, bartenders, patrons, drunks, drug addicts, police officers, and State troopers, who all corroborated Joe's version of the events (all, that is, except for Matthew and Theresea Patterson). But, by far, the most damaging piece of evidence was the internal police investigation of Matthew Patterson's actions that night completed by the Eliot Police Department.

The following pages are a representation of what the investigation entailed, and what it looked like. Of course, most of the names have been changed.

Page 1:
"Town of Eliot
Police Department
Inter-Departmental Memorandum

Date: January 22, 1997   To: Officer MatthewPatterson   Subject: Suspension from duty.

Effective immediately you are suspended from duty with pay pending further investigation. Signed by: Chief Al Bennington, Eliot Police Department"

Page 2[4]:
"Date: January 21, 1997
Time: 0625 hours
Officer: Matthew J.Patterson

Upon arrival to the Eliot Police Department...I was greeted by Patrolman Matthew J.Patterson.   Patterson was accompanied by his wife Theresea. Matthew stated, "I have to talk to you, I have called Sergeant Russo and he is on the way in also. I will talk to you as soon as he gets here. Upon the arrival of Sergeant Stephen Russo, Theresea Patterson, Patrolman Matthew Patterson, Sergeant Russo, and myself went into his office. I asked, "What is happening?" Patrolman Matthew Patterson stated, "I screwed up. I made the department look like shit."   He explained he was at Spin in Portsmouth, New Hampshire on Friday evening, he was drunk, got into an altercation with his wife ..., he shoved her, a doorman or bartender attempted to stop the altercation, he shoved the black individual.   Portsmouth Police and New Hampshire State Police showed up on the scene. He began arguing and shoving them, he was arrested then unarrested by the officers on the scene. Patrolman Matthew Patterson claimed he was drunk and does not remember everything that happened, however, he did make the Eliot Police Department and himself look like shit.   ...Patterson stated that the reason for this is the pressure and stress from: family problems, Karen Richards incident[5], and doing away with the K-9 program[6].

Prior to leaving, Patterson asked if he could take the next couple of days off as vacation in order to cool down. Vacation granted."

Reading this I wondered if the "vacation" is what the paid suspension mentioned on page one was about. Were they paying him to stay away, without making him use his earned vacation days?

Page 3:   "Sergeant Stephen Russo reported Patrolman Matthew Patterson came to his home on Saturday January 18, 1997

---

[4] The author of this report is not named, but is possibly Chief Al Boston

[5] An internal investigation agains Patterson

[6] Patterson was a K-9 officer

at approximately 1400 hours and told him he was involved in an altercation in Portsmouth, NH with his wife... and he made Eliot Police Department look bad. Sergeant Russo advised Patrolman Patterson to report the incident to Chief. Russo was surprised to learn on Tuesday, January 21, 1997, that Chief Al Bennington was not aware of the incident. Russo reported the following:

1. ..Patterson was at Spin on the evening of 1/17/97, into the morning hours of 1/18/97

2. ..Patterson assaulted Theresea Patterson by pulling her by the hair and throwing her on a dance floor in front of several individuals.

3. ...Patterson made several racial remarks to a male individual.

4. ...Patterson waved his badge around and stated "I am an Eliot Police Officer".

5. ...Patterson shoved a bouncer.

6. ...Patterson shoved a Portsmouth Police Officer.

7. ...Patterson was arrested, then unarrested.

8. ...Patterson got into a fight at home with other officers...Officer LaMont cut his finger on hood ornament of Eliot Police cruiser; the result of a subsequent fight with Patterson. It is believed that the mirror or windshield may have been broken as someone was thrown against the cruiser.

9. Incident continued on and Patterson's mother was called to remove Patterson to Kittery, Maine for the evening (her home).

10. Officer Stilman of Eliot was contacted by Mrs.Patterson to go to assist with calming Patrolman Patterson down.

Page 4 of the internal investigation states: "They (Portsmouth Police Department) gave him (Patterson) a courtesy by sending him home (and not arresting him)."

Page 5 is a report of an interview of Graham Gerry, another officer present during portions of the incident.

"Gerry reported that at 1830 he picked up Robert Baker at his home in Berwick, Maine, and they went to a club called Rusty Hammer in Portsmouth, New Hampshire, where they met Zach Chauncer, Chris LaMont, Matthew Patterson, Ronny King, and David Worthington. We arrived at Rusty Hammer around 1945-2000 hours. Robert Baker, David Worthington and myself sat by themselves while Matt and the others went over to hit on some girls. After a few moments a woman went over to Gerry and asked if he was an Eliot cop, they also asked Baker and Worthington. They decided the situation was getting out of hand, and left. They were irritated that Patterson was bragging about being a cop.

Gerry drove Baker home, but later went back to Bananas to pick up his wife, Emily. When he got to Bananas Theresea came out, and she sent Emily over to see why I was leaving early.

Theresea asked Gerry if Matt was cheating on her. Gerry went home.

The next morning Robert Baker called. He said something happened at Spin. Matthew Patterson was extremely drunk, he had his arm around another girl, Theresea came in and she was not happy, they had an argument. Matt threw Theresea on the floor, and Matt assaulted two other individuals, one of them was Mo the bouncer. Around 1245 the police were called, Portsmouth Police, along with New Hampshire State Police showed up, Matt was arrested. Matt told them he was a cop and they couldn't do that to him. LaMont came out and they turned Matt over to him. LaMont took Matt to Baker's home in Berwick, Maine and Baker let him in. Matt said something to Baker that offended him, and Baker subsequently kicked him out.

Page 5: I[7] had the opportunity to talk to Chris LaMont, a patrolman with South Berwick Police Department. He stated on Friday evening he was with Matthew and Theresea Patterson at Spin.....

First Chris went to a club called Rusty Hammer in Portsmouth...he was with Zach Chauncer, Matthew Patterson, Theresea Patterson, and Ron King. At Rusty Hammer he met Robert Baker, Davidin Worthington, and Graham Gerry, who were sitting at a separate table. "Matt and I ran into some friends who were sitting at a separate table, and we went to sit with them....We went to Spin....and met Theresea on the way to Spin. When I was in the club, Theresea came to me and told me she got into an argument with Matt, and he shoved or pushed her.

The police finally turned Matt over to me. We dropped Theresea off at her home, we went to my apartment in Berwick. Matt was upset and he realized he screwed up.

I did not see any handcuffs used by the police. There were two officers one was a Portsmouth Police Officer, and New Hampshire State Trooper. Theresea got upset because Matt had his arm around the other female. I understand the shoving match or pushing took place in the hallway of Spin."

The rest of the document merely reiterates many of the same. The document doesn't say so, but the Eliot police department did fire Matthew Patterson as a result of these events. They had to because I eventually arrested Patterson and charged him with three counts of domestic violence assault against his wife, and another count of

---

[7] Unknown speaker

assault against the bouncer. He was eventually convicted on a plea-bargain because his wife refused to testify against him and even loudly professed his innocence. In the State of New Hampshire, once a person has been convicted of a domestic assault, they can no longer have or carry a firearm. This is what makes police officers scared to death about domestic squabbles.

Matthew and Theresea Patterson have moved from the area hoping to start a new life together, away from people who know the details of this, and probably many other, domestic incidents.

One day in February, as I was completing some paperwork on the Patterson case, I received a phone call from Captain Shilling.

"Nancy," he said with his harsh New York accent, "we're gonna have to have a talk." He meant interrogate.

"Yeah? What about?" I asked.

"This Lanko thing. Sives is willing to testify that she told you *all* the details of what was going on in her office. She went to you for help with this sexual harassment stuff. As a supervisor, it was your duty to report it to a boss so that we could put a stop to it. It looks like you could be in a bit of a jam."

"Really?" I asked.

"Yeah," he said.

"Wow," I said, "Do you know what my testimony will be?"

"Whhhat?"

"I reported everything to Commander Brasso, in detail, on two occasions, for which I'll gladly retrieve the exact dates and times and notes of my conversations with him. I demanded that he take action immediately before the situation got any worse. He told me, and I quote, 'I'll take care of it.'"

Silence.

"Do you want those dates and times?" I asked.

All I heard was a dial tone. I guess he didn't want them.

I never heard anything from Shilling again on this issue. I guess he didn't really need to talk to me afterall. I have a feeling that Commander Brasso was never confronted about his inaction either, because Lanko was soon exonerated of all sexual harassment allegations based on some bullshit theory
that basically meant they swept it under the rug. The next year, Sergeant Lanko became Lieutenant Lanko, and Commander Brasso became Chief Brasso. All I have to say to that is, Wow!

Chapter 15

The Final Straw

August 11, 1998 was a significant turning point in my personal and professional life. Commander Craig Brasso had been selected to replace Chief William Bird, as the new Chief. His assignment was, however, conditional. He was told to devise a plan that would successfully reorganize the police department with an eye on fiscal responsibility. The situation, however, was oddly designed in that there would be a six month time frame wherein we would have two Chiefs. The public was told that this time period would serve to train Chief Brasso. Insiders know that various political factions were in such a rush to get rid of Bird, they made Brasso the Chief as soon as possible. They hoped to push Bird out early.

The Commission wanted to cut expenses and hopefully lower the budget; they were not open to maintaining the current department structure. Where they came up with this mandate is anybody's guess, since a formal needs-assessment wasn't done. I was further puzzled as to what qualifications the Police Commission had to order such a sudden and seemingly unwarranted restructuring of the department. I guessed that it was most probably rooted in their political desire to discredit Bird.

Brasso's plan was fraught with self indulgence and pay-back for those *he* thought deserved it. He was able to convince the Commission that the department needed to be better unified; divisions needed to stop their senseless competition and in-fighting. His resolution to this was to promote his best friend, Michael Irons, from Commander to Deputy Chief. This way, they formed a stronger team, like Fric and Frac, or Tom and Jerry, or Laurel and Hardy. If they had one more member, they could be Larry, Curly, and Moe.

Brasso explained that the D.C.'s responsibilities would include being Lord and Master of Patrol and Detectives. This way, should the usual controversy between the divisions arise, the D.C. had the power and authority to make a final ruling. The concept is, and was, a good one.

In the past when police divisions argued, the two commanders, one heading each division, would have to battle it out. The usual result was a compromise that seeded childish contempt between a winner and a loser. A winning division and a losing division. The creation of one Deputy Chief, running two divisions, was a focus on diminishing this problem.

One year, when I was a Sergeant in charge of the Court Office, there happened to be a prisoner that was late for Court. He was supposed to be brought from the County Jail to the Court room by 8:30 in the morning. When the prisoner wasn't there by 9:00 am, Judge Taylor became a bit upset, and as a general rule, we try to avoid pissing off the Judge. As the Court Prosecutor, I was responsible for assuring the prisoner was in Court on time. I knew I had filled out the appropriate paperwork and documentation, and was a bit puzzled as the whereabouts of the prisoner. I called the Patrol Division with my inquiry because it's their job to follow through with getting the prisoner to Court, after I submit the paperwork. It was nothing big. I just needed to know where the prisoner was, so that I could tell the Judge.

That phone call prompted an angry shift Captain to come all the way to the Court House in order to have an explosive confrontation with me. Upon entering the Court room, the Captain marched directly toward me; I was standing by the prosecutor's table, directly in front of the Judge. It wasn't until I heard him whisper my name, "hey, Truax," that I turned around and saw that he was red faced and angry. He began speaking at me in a very agitated manner, so I suggested we speak privately in one of the conference rooms. Once inside the room, he physically backed me into a corner and demanded to know what I, a Sergeant from another division, was doing ordering him, a Captain of Patrol, to have prisoners delivered to Court. More accurately, he was questioning my gall in challenging him. He must have forgotten that I was only following procedure. This encounter resulted in a cold war between the administrative division and the patrol division. Truly, this was an unnecessary complexity caused by the pompously, righteous attitude of one division leader versus another.

Chief Brasso also planned to diminish the number of Captains in Patrol by doing away with, what we call, our relief shift. The result of this would be that the promotion coming up on
August 11, 1998 would be the last promotion that allowed a jump from Sergeant to Captain. After that date, we would establish the rank of Lieutenant. This structure would provide three Sergeants, three Lieutenants, and three Captains in Patrol (the old structure consisted of four Captains and four Sergeants)
. The error in the new plan was in it's implication that three ranking officers for each shift would provide additional coverage, and thereby save money. The hope was that all shifts would be filled and overtime budgets, normally required for annual leave, sick and funeral leave, would be diminished. But, the obvious result was that we had less people to cover the shifts, so we spent more money on overtime.

There were five of us competing for the promotion; but, only four were interviewing. One Sergeant, Lanko, decided not to present himself for the interview, but did submit his resume and cover letter for consideration. He did that because of the recent, scandalous, sexual harassment investigation wherein he was eventually cleared. No other agency would have cleared Lanko of the charges against him; no sanctions were issued against him. Within six months of that investigation, he was promoted to Lieutenant.

August 11, 1998 finally came. I was nervous, excited, and anxious for the day to end. For many reasons I was expecting to get this promotion. Of all the Sergeants going in, I was the most senior, though, admittedly, Joe Ellis was not far behind. I wasn't too concerned about this factor as, whenever promotional candidates have been so close in capability and experience, PPD administration had always gone with the most senior candidate. Additionally, at this point in time, the Agency had set in place an affirmative action policy that specifically stated that we would use whatever resources necessary to assure that women and minorities are hired and promoted within the department.

Additionally, by this point in time, I had worked every division within the police department, and was a more well-rounded candidate than the others. Joe Ellis had not worked in Juvenile Division or the Court Office. Neither was he a practiced public speaker, as I was by this time due to a series of lectures I'd been giving around the Country.

Because I was the most senior candidate I was to be the first person interviewed. Once again I found myself waiting in Cindy Place's office. I had personally chosen an outfit that was professional and smashing. I was wearing a pair of wide-legged black pants that cuffed at the ankle, black high-heeled shoes that laced up the front, a white blouse, and a black, plaid, jacket. My hair was long at the time, down to my waist, and I had it tied very neatly in a bun to the back of my head, but not so tight that my facial skin pulled backward. On the floor beside me I had placed five 3'X3' placcards I planned to use during my interview.

"Cindy," I said as I sat in front of her desk, repeatedly snapping my left leg, up and down, up and down, "What should I say to them to help them understand that it's my turn for promotion?" Of course I had already prepared some ideas in advance, but I liked talking with Cindy before going into an interview of this importance. Cindy had the inside track on just about everything going on at the PD, and every now and then she'd squeak out a clue or two.

"Just let them know, from the bottom of your heart, that you want it and you deserve it."

"But, Cindy, I always tell them that. I feel like a broken

record during my opening presentation. Is there anything special, that you can think of, that they're waiting to hear?"

"If there is, I don't know about it."

Just then, Commissioner Hanes walked up the stairs, his 70 year posture looking like that of a 90 year old. He is a tall man, about 6'5", and thin. He wears coke bottle glasses and is bald; well, what hair he does have is so white it's clear. He barely gave me a glance, although I've known him all these 18 years, and he continued walking into the interview room. This lack of acknowledgment conveyed an aura of doom. Directly behind him was Chief Bird. Chief Bird walked by me toward his office and began shuffling some papers as though he were looking for something very important. He lifted his head, looked directly at me, and said, "Nancy, I wish there were a better way to do these things."

In the back of my head, I knew what he was trying to tell me, but didn't want to believe it. Cheerily, I looked up to him and said, "Well, Chief, as they say, this is all we've got right now, so we've got to make do."

Commissioner Kupruck recused himself from this interview but insisted on remaining in the room and acting as a monitor. I told him openly, and on tape, that I didn't wish for him to recuse himself. My intuition told me that between Bird's remark before the interview, and Kupruck's distancing himself during the interview, they'd already decided the next Captain, and it wasn't me. I allowed the intuitive twinge to pass and I forged ahead.

The interview setting was fairly casual, as it was in a room familiar to all of us, because we meet there often for staff meetings. It held three long mahogany tables positioned in the shape of a 'T'. The three police commissioners and two chiefs sat across the top of the 'T'. Each candidate sat at the opposite end, giving the feeling of having to shout down a long, airy, tunnel.

I left the interview feeling great. I had really nailed all the questions, and felt I had presented myself well. My voice was solid, and not shaky. My gestures were firm, but not aggressive. My diction was clear, my words were well chosen and I was comfortably seated in the top slot for the promotion.

When I walked out of the interview room, Joe Ellis was sitting in Cindy Place's office, awaiting his turn. He was wearing a rather nice suit, but looked quite nervous, and he made some vague comment indicating his apprehension. He said something like, 'if they want me, they want me; I guess I'll find out.' I told him very confidently that he would do well.

I walked through the maze of a police building, to get to my office. I sat and waited while again pretending to occupy myself. I checked my phone messages and learned that an old friend of mine,

Attorney Randy Means, had called to see how my interview had gone. Randy is a very busy attorney who lectures and speaks around the Country, but is based in North Carolina. I called Randy back, and spoke with him at length. I told him that I felt very positive about the interview and expected to know within the next hour whether or not I had gotten the promotion.

Shortly thereafter, Jen Sives came into my office and wanted to know how the interview had gone. I told her the same that I had told Randy. She was interested for her own reasons, in that she was coming up for promotion to the rank of Sergeant. My promotion to Captain would surely make an opening for her in the very near future. We sat for a moment, playing out the promotional odds, and trying to pick the most likely scenario. For example, if I were promoted to Captain, that would leave an opening in the Domestic Violence Division, which Detective Sives is more than qualified to be promoted into. On the other hand, if Joe Ellis were promoted to Captain, that would leave a sergeant's opening in general investigations, which we didn't believe would be filled right away because of the current state of the budget.

Before we tired of our titillating conversation, and just before we had the problems of the world fully solved, an announcement was made over the p.a. that all promotional candidates were to report to the upstairs interview room area. Upstairs, there were four of us standing around waiting to be allowed back into the room we had just exited. Inside, the three Commissioners and the two Chiefs were casually discussing our individual futures. We, on the other hand, or the others, I should stay, were discussing sports. Nel Parson talked about his latest golf match with the Chief, while Joe Ellis spoke of his recent experience coaching his son's lacrosse team. 'How typical this is,' I thought to myself, 'that no matter what kind of setting men are in, the issue of sports will come up.' Most of the time I don't mind, and I can be just as capable of joining in, but I found myself thinking, 'what is it about this topic that so conveniently allows it to be brought up in some of the most stressful situations?' It's as though, when the topic of sports arises, the original reason for the gathering completely disappears and is forgotten; as though 'sports' was the reason for the get together. I don't know if I've got the right answer, but I've concluded that sports provides a fantasy life that men have always wanted. It's an outlet for them, an escape, an abandonment from reality, just as any trip to the Caribbean Islands might be for me. When I acknowledge this, I have to giggle to myself because I can't imagine any sport being compared to a magical, tropical island. But, this is part of what life is about...the differences between us make life so colorful.

Chief Bird opened the door and invited us to parade in, single file. As I ducked under the Chief's arm, and into the room, Bird pulled me aside quickly, whispered in my ear, "Nancy, you gave the best interview."

I knew the promotion was mine! When it came time for the Commission to announce the name of the next Captain, I was sure my name would be called. Chief Bird had just told me so.

We stood, like trained dogs, lined neatly in front of the commission, each of us fully involved with our own thoughts. Commissioner Hanes turned on the tape (all interviews and announcements are taped in case of future grievances). As is customary, Hanes began by saying, "I want you to know that all of you standing here, and even Sgt. Tom Lanko, who's not with us today, are excellent candidates. Those of you who interviewed, did an excellent job and, you've made the selection process very difficult."

At this point I was thinking to myself, 'Come on, come on, come on, this is usual and customary. As I stood there listening to the mundane opening, I was stricken by stomach pains so strong I wanted to grab onto myself and yell at Hanes to hurry up. Nerves.

"At this time," Commissioner Hanes said, "I would like to nominate Sergeant Joe Ellis as the next Captain."

In a deep haze, my body conducting itself in a way I had never felt in my life, even during the worst fights with my husband, I heard Commissioner Burke say, "seconded." This all done as Ted Kupruck, my favorite Commissioner, sat in the middle, looking smugly, directly at me. My extremities began to have no feeling. I became dizzy and lightheaded, seeing a few speckles in front of me. The most odd phenomenon, that I have rarely felt since, is that I could feel each and every tooth tingling in very sensual way. I panicked. This had never happened to me before. Aside from the feelings of loss, abandonment, betrayal, I was also feeling frightened that I would faint in front of these people, my judges. This caused more panic, and even more tingling of the teeth. The more my teeth tingled, the better my mouth felt; the better my mouth felt, the more I panicked, and the more my teeth tingled. It was a helpless situation to be in, considering I had previously committed to myself, that if I didn't get the promotion, it would be okay. I would move on with plans to get my Masters Degree in Social Work. No big deal. I felt forsaken by my own body's reaction.

So, afraid, surprised, and confused by my own reaction, I quickly congratulated Capt. Ellis, in the most professional manner I could. I shook hands with the Commissioners and the Chiefs, and worked my way down the stairwell, toward my office. I don't know if I was in shock at that point, but if I wasn't, at the very least, I was dazed. I felt as though I was going to crumble, break apart, fall apart, become a million pieces, cry in front of everybody; I was losing control. I wanted to sink into myself, the floor, anything that would allow me. I wanted to be in hiding so I wouldn't have to walk by the many faces still in the police building, wondering who had received the promotion. I walked down the empty flight of stairs, alone, and keyed myself out of the echoing stairwell, into the main lobby. I then keyed myself into the main doorway that prefaced the hallway leading to my office. I managed to skip by the station officers desk without being noticed. I passed the dispatch center praying no one would stick their head out to try to congratulate me prematurely. Commander Beaumont's office was dark and empty as he had recently retired, and his position had not yet been replaced. Being near his long-time office reminded me that he had let me down also. I found out that Beaumont, who was with me from the beginning as my FTO and friend had failed to recommend me for the promotion to Captain. I knew, without being told, that he had advocated for Joe Ellis to receive the Captaincy over me. That's where I felt the most betrayal; especially when it was confirmed as fact the following day when I spoke with Chief Asshole, I mean Brasso.

What gets me, is that the decisional factor leading to Joe's selection over me, was his technological and electronical expertise. This angered me beyond reason because I had gone to Joe Ellis, and other members of the police department, and offered to learn the dispatch center, and any other duties that Ellis was doing. I was categorically denied the ability to be taught or learn these skills. In order to balance the scales between Joe and I, had to bone up on certain technological skills, on my own time. I began taking a variety of computer courses offered by the city. I took every one that I could, passed them all with flying colors, and learned a great deal. Even though I out-skilled him in other areas, I knew that I had to far surpass him if I were to be promoted before him.

I later learned that what I was dealing with here was a promise. Joe Ellis had been promised that if he developed and managed an upscale dispatch center, he would be rewarded for it. In recollection, I have to say that, at the last promotional interview to Captain, when John Smith received the nod, Joe Ellis was absolutely livid. He didn't show up to work for several days, and when he did show up, he was a bear to be around.

In any case, I meekly continued walking the gauntlet to my office, which seemed to be about a mile away. I was still at the station officer's desk, all these thoughts having run through my head, when I was tapped on the shoulder from behind. I jumped. It was kiss-ass Joe Ellis, long lanky arms and all. The tap on my shoulder took me by surprise as I was deep in thought. I turned around and looked at him, now wondering if I would be able to keep my composure. I said weakly, and disgusted with myself, "Hey Joe, what's up?"

"Oh. Commissioner Kupruck wants to see you back upstairs in the interview room."

'Great.' I thought to myself. 'This is all I need. I can barely keep myself together; my body is doing things to me that I have never known it could do; and, the Commissioner wants to see me. The Commissioner who recused himself from my oral interview, and further made hay-day with the inquiry I filed against him for his overtly discriminatory remark about women. This man wanted to speak with me privately. I took a deep breath and calculated my odds. What would happen if I didn't go upstairs and speak with him, but instead, rushed my office door so that I could collapse and hide? Should I go face my adversary?'

Not wanting to insult a police commissioner, and thereby bring additional animosity on myself, I stoically and quietly followed Captain Joe Ellis, up the dark, dank, stairway to the big-wig gathering. They were clustered in small groups, talking and chatting, as though nothing had just happened. Nel was talking with Chief Bird about their latest golf game, while Chief Brasso was talking with Commissioner Burke about a most recent budget issue. Nobody seemed to even realize that I was present, as requested. I was invisible. The temptation arose to turn around and leave. Just as I was turning to reface my exit, Commissioner Kupruck came from the hallway and stepped in front of me. I couldn't believe I had to face him this closely. I was two inches away from his ruddy, red face and I was forced to look deeply into his eyes, and acknowledge what he had just done to me. I couldn't believe he had the gall to seek me out and speak with me in person, after what he had just done. I felt as though he was, again, making a joke of me.

As I was thinking these thoughts, he stuck out his hand for me to shake. I accepted. He said, "Sergeant Truax, I just want you to know, that your thoughts and beliefs in running this organization, and your ideas about where we should go, are more in tune with mine than any of the other candidates. Please, for the benefit of this organization, continue striving for excellence.
Know that I want to see you in front of me again for the next set of promotional interviews."   Now *I* was being given a promise; they dangled the carrot hoping I'd bite.

I don't know if I was thinking clearly at that point. My feelings were still running amock, and I just wanted to burst out and cry. I'm sure my eyes were brimming with tears and I think Kupruck saw it. I was having a hard time keeping my emotions down. I continued shaking his hand, up and down, up and down, while he said these things. I issued a very meek "thank you" when he was done talking. I turned quickly to my left, and again made the exit to my office, where I knew I could have some privacy.

Did Commissioner Kupruck have any idea how much he had tortured me by bringing me back upstairs and saying those things to me? Did he know that Chief Bird had already told me that I gave the best interview? If I gave the best interview, was philosophically parallel, was the senior candidate, was more than qualified, why did they promote him first? This was beyond my understanding. Even if politics were involved, I couldn't understand how they thought they could get away with this. I slinked as best I could, through the same route I had already traveled, in an attempt to get back to my office.

Just as I was about 20 feet away from my door, Officer Schwartzmiller, who is a big brusque guy, said to me, "So, Truax, who got the promotion?"

Squeaking it out, I said, "Ellis got it." Saying those words had been a task, an effort.

"Oh, what the fuck!" he said, "Fuck 'em, right Truax?"

"Right," I said as I closed my office door. The moment I closed the door, or perhaps the millisecond before the door actually closed, or perhaps even the millisecond after my hand touched the door with the purpose of swinging it closed, I broke down uncontrollably. I cried and sobbed in my own office with the door locked. I was disgusted with myself, as well as angry with the administration. I was ashamed of myself for allowing them to effect me in this way. I had allowed them to touch me deeply. I wasn't in control. I knew full well, that I was as qualified, equally qualified, if not more qualified than Joe Ellis. I was crying so hard, I found it difficult to muffle my heaving sobs of anguish. I tried as best I could, and hoped, no, prayed to God, that good old Jimmy Schwartzmiller wasn't outside the door listening to me.

I knew that Vince was home waiting for my call, to tell him whether or not I'd gotten the promotion. He too, believed that this would be my day. I hated to call him with this kind of news, as I knew he would be upset, and there was always the possibility that he wouldn't respond in a supportive way.

I knew as soon as Vince answered the phone, that I wasn't going to be able to talk. I was crying so hard, all he could hear on his end were my painful sobs. They weren't even sobs; they were more like muffled puffs of agony signifying betrayal and mistrust.

He knew I was wounded. He must have understood my pain. For once in his life, before I was even able to spit out the words, 'Joe got it', I heard him say, "Nancy, what can I do for you?"

This was the first time in our marriage that Vince had uttered those words, 'what can I do for you?' My feeling of betrayal compounded at that moment. We had been married so many years;

why did it take him till now, this, to finally say the words that I had ached for, for so long? With this thought in my head, I cried even more. Of course he didn't know that at this moment, he too, was part of my agony. He didn't realize that what he had just done, aside from give to me without asking for anything in return, was to let me know that he always had it in him. That, in my mind will always be the first time, and so far the only time, Vince ever gave. Just gave.

"Do you want me to come and get you?" he asked.

Barely able to speak, and through my tears, I said, "Yes."

"When do you want me to get you?" he asked.

"I don't know. I have to stay behind this door for a while. I'm a mess. My eyes are swollen and red, and I don't want anyone to see me like this. "

"Okay."

I sat on my end of the phone line and cried, while he listened. After a moment or two passed, I told Vince, "You know what? I don't want you to come and get me. I know I'm still crying pretty hard, but I don't want them to see you coming to get me. I don't want them to know that I wasn't strong enough to take this. I'll be home. I just need some time to calm down and clean up. As soon as I've done that, I'll come home." I hung up the line and continued to sob. It seems as though the more I tried to remain calm, the harder I cried. It was as though my body was telling me, 'you deserve this. You need to do this. Go ahead.' And so, I gave into it even more and allowed my body to shake with the pain of 17 years of harassment, discrimination, torture, pain, agony, humiliation, gossip, lies, and betrayal. Betrayal of an entire administration that I had worked so hard for; betrayal of a man with whom I'd had an affair, and maintained loyalty to all these years. Betrayal of my coworkers, peers, and subordinates, who seemed to see no injustice in my failure to be promoted; and even said so openly. Officer Les Hill told many officers that the reason I didn't get this promotion is because 'men don't want to take orders from a woman'. It seemed that nobody saw things the way that I did, and per usual, I was alone, on my own little island, after having been lulled into the belief that men and women are equal.

So, this is where I found myself on August 11, 1998, at about five o'clock at night. In my office at work, with the door closed, and locked, sobbing uncontrollably, in a fit of j'en se qua. I went into the ladies room which is just across the hall, and tried to quell the swelling in my eyes by placing pockets of cold water on them. At the same time I tried to stifle any tears that continued to emerge. It was at this point that I realized my physical and emotional reaction to this was out of my control; no matter how hard I tried to get-hold of myself, I just could not do it. I knew I had to leave the building soon, before it got worse. I quickly scurried from the bathroom, to my office, locked the door, and exited the rear door of the police station, feeling ashamed of my display of emotion, and again, praying to God that no one would see me. I walked through the back parking lot, cut through a woodsy pathway to the front lot, jumped into my car, and quickly drove home.

Once out of the lot, I again felt free to let go, and, even as I was driving, cried to my hearts content. All I could think about was getting home, getting behind the doors of my own house, closing them, locking them, and never coming out again. My concern about home was that I didn't want my kids to see me in this state. Then I realized, well, hell, if I can't show my kids who their mother is, and what she is about, then who can I tell? Knowing I would explain myself to the entire family, I allowed myself the freedom within my own home to let those feelings flow.

Sure enough, when I got home, they were all waiting for me. I told them all about it between hiccupping sobs. I tried to explain to the kids that there are disappointments in life, and that is okay. I told them I was feeling very strongly disappointed, and was still unable to control my tears, but they needed to understand that they shouldn't be afraid. I also told them that I was trying to stop, but was feeling so intense about the whole situation, I found it difficult. With this explanation, they openly accepted me and my reaction, and tried to cheer me up in many ways. They eventually gave up, but walked away knowing that I loved them and this was not their fault.

I told Vince that I expected the police station to call the house in order to make excuses, or justifications for doing what they did. It was usual and customary practice by administration to (attempt to) quell the gurgling volcano of the rightful 'winner'. Politics at it's best. I told him that under no circumstances would I accept any phone calls from the police department. I was fully intending, however, to be at work the following morning to face the music.

Sure enough the phone began ringing off the hook. We tried to ignore it, but it became incessant, and even though I was drinking a bottle of wine (and I do mean, the whole bottle), my feelings had not dulled enough to allow me to speak rationally with anyone I worked with. Finally, feeling surrounded by the enemy, I asked one of the kids to pick up the phone.

"Mom," Mike said, "it was work."

"Did they leave a name?" I asked.

"No. They just said to let you know that work had called."

"What did you tell them?"

"I told them you weren't here, and you wouldn't be available for the rest of the night."

"Perfect," I said, drinking my wine. It seemed as though there was nothing I could do to prevent my body from doing it's own thing. I hope to God I never have to go through that again. This wasn't the same as a child throwing a tantrum and becoming angry because they didn't get their way, or a teenager pouting in their room because they couldn't hang out with their friends, or being an adult who lost a lover. All that I can tell you today is that it was the deepest sense of betrayal I have ever had, including the betrayal of my very own husband. On that day, at that moment, when Joe Ellis's name was called, something inside of me withered up and died and I was mourning it's loss. It was the inside of me that believed vehimately that hard work produces great things. The credo of the Protestant work ethic. The credo of equality, credo of hope, belief in your fellow humans, trust, the belief that work and ethics outweigh sexuality, politics, racism. Some day I will have the right words to explain this time in my life. My feelings, emotions, desires, hopes, and fears. That may not come until I'm 90. So, now, I am only doing the best that I can to explain something I don't come close to understanding, and maybe never will. Having said that, I know that life is mystical, magical, and mysterious, and that some day I must let this all go. I only hope that the writing of these feelings and events are a helpful part of that process.

My deepest wish, however, is that no human being in this entire universe of ours, should ever have to face this type of political, racist, sexist, ambiguity. It is a most tortuous experience. The good thing is, that I am only one person; imagine the Jews during the Holocaust. I cannot fathom the emotions, sorrow, contempt of an entire nationality that was overridden with an even deeper hatred and a blatant attempt to exterminate them like roaches. At least, in my case, they just failed to promote.

In any case, that night I drank the entire bottle of wine. Vince found himself attempting, as best he could, to soothe me, but we both knew he couldn't.

So, August 12th turned out to be a cool rainy day, which I thought appropriate, as it matched the way I felt inside. I knew as I sat in my office that I must surely look like hell and, smell like wine. I'm sure that my presentation to the office that day was that of a tired, disheveled, wino. But I didn't care. My objective for the day was to show up. Period. I wanted to avoid being labeled by administration as a 'cry baby'.

Sure enough, right around 8 am, Big Chief #2, Brasso, walked into the back door of the police station, located not too far from my office. As soon as he saw my door open, he stepped into the archway, wearing a long, wet, trench coat. I was thinking to myself how adequately his outfit demonstrated his true character; a drip. He looked at me and smiled. He said, "we'll have to talk today, Nancy."

"Well, come on in, Craig. We might as well get this over with now."

His hands in his coat pockets, he shook the tails of his coat to cast off the remnants of rain, gingerly removed it and hung it on the back of my door.

"Well, Craig," I said, "nothing surprises me anymore."

Again he smiled.

"Go ahead," I said, "tell me."

"Well," he said, "the commission wanted Joe, so they took Joe."

I said, "That's bullshit, Craig. That commission takes recommendations from you and the other commanders. Would you mind explaining what their reasoning was for picking Joe?"

"Well. That's the funny thing. There really is no reason."

This statement, coming from the Chief of Police, knowing that he had promoted someone below me, to a rank higher than me, 'for no reason'. How could this be? He's admitting to me that there was no reason.

"What do you mean, 'no reason'?"

"Well, you know. Joe's got skills in different areas than you've got skills, and we just weren't really sure which we should go with."

"Craig! I am senior to Joe, I have been since I got here, I am as talented as he, if not more. Why are you castigating me?"

"I'm not, Nancy. There will be other opportunities in the future. We're going to be having some Lieutenant promotions,"

I cut him off again. "Lieutenant!? You're gonna give me Lieutenant? Gee, thanks Craig. You want to give me dog food when I deserve steak. What the hell is wrong with you? Didn't you give us a lecture, very recently, about doing the right thing? That was supposed to be your theme for your reign as Emperor, I mean, Chief?"

"Yes."

"It doesn't seem to me as though you've done the right thing here, at all! How did the commission come to finally say Joe's name?"

Even more incredulously, he said to me, "Well, Nancy. I won't deny my responsibility in recommending Joe instead of you."

"Okay, but there's no reason?"

"Well, he's handled the dispatch center,"

"I'll tell you what the reason is, Craig. You promised him this promotion over two years ago. You promised him, and then John Smith was promoted instead of Joe. A fluke, yes. I remember when Smith got the promotion, and Ellis didn't; he pouted and banged around this place for months afterward, he was so angry. This tells me you had promised it to him then, and by some quirk of the commission, he didn't get it. So, what you've done is promote a crybaby. Because you promised it to him two years ago, even though I'm the better candidate, and I'm more senior, you're gonna give it to him. After all, boys clubs must keep their promises, mustn't they. I just have one more question, Craig. Where's the sign outside the club-house door that says, 'no girls allowed'?"

"Nancy, don't say that. That's not what this is about."

"Oh really, then let me ask you a different question. If rather than being myself, and going into that interview dressed as I was, a small, 5'2", 120 pound person, with long blonde hair, and a bun in the back of my head, bringing with me a high pitched female voice, I came in a 6'2" body, power suit, shoes, deep voice, but having all the skills I have now, can you tell me you wouldn't have given me the promotion then?"

Craig thought a moment, and said, "Well, I guess I can't really say that I wouldn't have given it to you."

I was astonished he made this admission to me. I looked at him, my mouth half opened like a guppy, and said, "my point, exactly, Craig. Aside from which, do you know how much of a fool you made of me during that interview process?"

"What do you mean?"

"Well, Chief #2, three of you on that board, three of you, winked at me, as if to say, 'atta girl!! Good job. Good answer. Were any of the male candidates winked at when they gave their responses, Chief?"

"Who winked at you?"

"You, Chief Bird, and Ted Kupruck."

"I winked? I don't think I winked. I don't even know how to wink. I'm not good at winking at all." He demonstrated his lack of talent in this arena.

"You winked at me, Craig. Specifically, after a response to one of your questions, you winked at me."

"Nancy, it's just that Joe had some technical computer skills that you didn't have," he said in an attempt to change the subject.

"And, yes, I have some skills that he doesn't have. I'm more well-rounded than he, I've worked in more divisions, handled more cases and made more arrests. I'm also much better with personnel issues. Every time he works in patrol, he winds up getting an Unfair Labor Practice filed against him by the union. You can't tell me that's not a waste of the City's money, time and man-power. Why do you want someone working for you that cannot appropriately relate with people? Aside from which, I have offered two or three times to assist Joe Ellis in order to learn some of those skills. Each time I've offered, he has flat-out refused, saying we need to limit the number of people that have access to this equipment. How can you fail to promote me for something over which I have no control? What control I did have I used to attend computer classes offered by the City."

"I know that Nancy. It's not that you are less qualified than Joe. You're not less qualified. You do an excellent job. You work very hard."

At this point, I snapped, and I said, "I know I work very hard and you don't have to tell me that I work hard. Don't patronize me. I work harder than you, for Christ sake! But apparently, that's not something this organization values."

"But, Nancy, you need to remember that the other Commanders, Beaumont, and Irons, also advocated for Joe"

"I'm well aware of that. It doesn't take a rocket scientist to figure that out. But, what were their reasons for promoting Joe over me?"

"Well, same as mine."

"And yours was...let me remember...'no reason'?"

"Yes," he said and shook his head up and down.

This conversation was getting more and more ridiculous. The more we talked, the less I could believe what I was hearing from this man.

"Craig," I said, "this is what I think . Although our affair ended many, many years ago, and it didn't last but three months, you are feeling guilty about it, and you don't want anyone in the world to know. Taking into consideration that I know for a fact that Commissioner Hanes has asked you if you had sex with me, my guess is that you will do anything to prevent him from knowing that you had an affair with me. As a result, you cannot openly advocate for me, so you advocated for Joe. And, thereby, we have your infamous, "no reason". The "no reason" is that you fucked me many years ago, quite literally. Now, you're fucking me again. This makes no sense. If I had been considered a legitimate and true candidate, that fact never should have come into play, Craig. Should not have entered your thought process. That affair isn't something I wanted. You pushed it on me. And now because I gave you what you wanted, you find yourself in a position where you cannot give me what I deserve. This is just making less and less sense as we talk, Craig."

At this point, Officer Tibbetts stuck his head in the doorway and told me that my appointment, Mrs. Taylor, was in the lobby waiting to see me. I looked at Tibbettes, the chief, and back at Tibbetts, and said, "Tell her to have a seat and wait. I've got to strap on my penis before I can talk with her; because, I guess that's what I've been forgetting all this time." Lloyd kinda grinned, but knew there was something deeper to my comment than just a simple loss of tact.

I returned my gaze to Craig. Not a friendly one, by the way. "Well, Chief. Before I go to my interview, I'm gonna put you on notice, here and now, that I'll probably file a grievance."

"Okay," he said, "I understand. You gotta do what you gotta do."

"Yup."

"Just remember you only have five working days."

"I know the rules. I used to be president of the union, remember? Until I was voted out for complaining against Kupruck. It all comes full circle eventually, doesn't it Craig?"

It was here we had reached a point where I had nothing left to say to him, and he had no convincing words to allay my anger. Craig slowly stood from his chair, reached for his coat, and gently pulled it off the door, all the while looking at me as if there was something else he needed to say, but couldn't. I watched as he turned his back to me, a long thin spineless back. As he walked out of my office, he must have known that a storm was brewing, and was headed in his direction. That could have been the night. The night he went home and told his wife about the affair he'd had with me, just before he married her. If I were him, that's what I would have done.

During my 'post-failure-to-be-promoted' conversations with Chief Brasso, I had been assured many times that the next promotion would be mine.

Over the course of the next few days I sought advice from many people as to how I should handle the situation. I talked with my husband, my Mom and Dad, friends, lawyers and colleagues. It was apparent to everyone that I was emotionally rocked by the administrations failure to promote me. Every time I talked about it I started to cry. I wanted, though, to be absolutely sure that if I did file a grievance, I was doing the right thing (not out of anger), and that I would have the strength to follow through....all the way to the end. I took the full five days to make my decision.

At three p.m. on August 18, 1998 I filed the grievance with Chief Bird. As I walked back to my office I bumped into Brasso.

"Can I talk to you for a minute, Nance?" he asked.

"Sure," I said, a bit nervous because I hadn't told him my decision about the grievance. He gently pulled me by the arm into his office, as if we were old friends.

"I was upstairs ten minutes ago and happened to notice you hadn't filed a grievance about the promotion," his voice sounded relieved and ecstatic.

"I want you to know," he continued, "that if you don't get the next promotion, I don't want to hear you tell anyone that I promised it to you."

My heart rose to my throat, and like a swirling dervish, did a kamikaze dive to my toes, skillfully passing that butterfly pit in my stomach. He hadn't even planned on feeding me that carrot he so skillfully dangled. He'd been taunting me; again.

"I guess you checked too early, then," I snapped. "I just delivered it to Chief Bird. Thanks for the warning, though. I appreciate your thoughtfulness." I turned around and walked out.

That slimy, spineless, back stabbing, carrot dangling, political, sexist, mother fucker, I thought. When I filed the grievance I wasn't angry; I was standing on principle and justice. Now, now, I was angry. I knew it would pass, but as I reveled in its hot and steamy residue, I came to the solid conclusion that I had made the right decision. If I wasn't sure when I filed it, I was sure now. His comment had boosted me to a higher level of clarity. This too, is the moment when I realized that Craig Brasso was the furthest thing from an ally; he wasn't to be trusted.

Once a grievance is filed, the aggrieved party has the right to meet with the Chief of Police in order to prevent a drawn-out battle. In most cases, the meeting is a waste of time, and this one proved to be no different than the others.

Ten days after this meeting Chief Bird approached me, smiling but plainly nervous, with a rather puffy envelope.

"Nancy, I believe you've been looking for this," he said.

"What is it?"

"It's our final response to your grievance. You may want to be alone when you read it."

"I think I'll save it for when I get home so I can relax with a glass of wine while I'm reading it."

He chuckled and appreciated my ability to make the situation light; but, as he scampered away, I tore the envelope open, fully expecting the negative response it held. The letter was several pages long, and noted that a primary reason for Joe's promotion was his technical, computer skills. Further, the Chief and Commission denied my grievance and suggested I "take it to the next level." It seemed like a challenge.

Twenty minutes later I was standing at my mailbox as Bird walked by.

"Hi, Nancy," he said as cheerily as always.

"Hi, Chief," I said pleasantly.

He straightened his back in a slightly surprised motion, and said, "Oh, you're talking to me. You must not have read the letter yet." I guess he thought I would be livid, but I wasn't.

"I read the letter," I said as we walked the hallway together.

"Oh...good then. Business is business, right Nancy?"

"Right, Chief," I said as I patted that spot between his shoulder blades, "business is business. Just remember that when the lawsuit comes down," and I chuckled.

He chuckled too, but his face turned bright red. He was a tomato. We parted ways, each knowing that enemy lines had been drawn; but, I wasn't about to let him, or anyone in the administration upset me anymore than was necessary. That, I could do without.

From this point forward, I set my sights on correcting an injustice. I filed a lawsuit against the City of Portsmouth that threw the sleepy community into a tail-spin.

SEX, LIES, DIRTY BOOKS

By **Susan Maddocks,** Portsmouth Herald Staff Writer

PORTSMOUTH - The Portsmouth Police Department is a place where officers have sex while on duty, drink alcohol, and brag about extramarital affairs, two police officers have charged in a civil action filed against the city of Portsmouth, Police Chief *Craig Brasso* and other current and former civic officials.

City Attorney Robert Sullivan yesterday strongly denied the allegations and today added they have to be proven in court.

Capt. Nancy Truax and former Officer Karen Johnson[8], in a complaint filed in United States District Court, allege it is a department where lewd magazines are circulated throughout offices and restrooms, where discriminatory jokes are made about blacks, where junior female officers are targeted by senior male officers for sex and where an officer can take his penis out and wave it at a public official and later get promoted.

If the aftermath of the allegations requires the Attorney General's Office step in, it will, said Senior Assistant Attorney General Mark Zuckerman.

In the meantime, Sullivan said an internal inquiry will be conducted.

"I think that the actual litigation process over each of those claims is going to require a significant amount of inquiry be conducted," Sullivan said. He added, "At this point, those are allegations. All of which remain to be proven. All of that stuff is going to be addressed

---

[8] Officer Johnson later joined me in the lawsuit; we filed together.

during the litigation process. It can't be addressed (now)."

Police Chief *Craig Brasso* said he was "troubled and disturbed" by the allegations made in the lengthy complaint filed this week at the United States District Court of New Hampshire, against the City of Portsmouth, Police Chief *Craig Brasso*, Police Commissioners *Hanes* and *Burke* and former Commissioner Ted *Kupruck*.

The charges are untrue, *Brasso* said.

"We believe the allegations are without merit, and that we will be vindicated in court," *Brasso* said. "I am not going to litigate this in the media."

A meeting to acknowledge the complaints was held at the department Tuesday after Russ learned of the civil discrimination suit against him and the department. He has asked officers to continue doing the "excellent job they do" and to try to leave their troubles out of the office.

David Slawsky, a Concord attorney who represents both women, said the city needs to take a good look at the goings on inside the department.

"A big part of the case is to convince the city to take this seriously," Slawsky said. He said the case is so important that he hopes it will receive a trial date quickly. "We will be meeting in the next few weeks to schedule a trial date," he added.

Among other things, the lawsuit, filed by Slawsky on Feb. 8, alleges Truax was removed from a departmental post after rebuffing sexual advances allegedly made by *Brasso*.

"As a direct and proximate result of Ms. Truax's refusal to agree to maintain an affair with Chief *Craig Brasso* while both were away from Portsmouth participating in the federal Office of Juvenile Justice and Delinquency Prevention (OJJDP) program," the court document stated. "Ms. Truax was removed by Chief *Brasso* (who was then Captain who had appointed her to that position) from the OJJDP program."

The court document continued, "Despite her communication to Chief *Brasso* that his romantic advances were unwelcome, Chief *Brasso* continued to make such advances."

In the suit, the female officers also allege the following:

- A notebook known as "The Book of Gross Reports" with lewd comics, "Playboy" photographs and similar papers was circulated among the male members of the department.

- X-rated photographs from "Playboy," "Hustler," and similar magazines were placed into the police log book.

- Phony affidavits containing sexually explicit and degrading descriptions were circulated within the department.

- Officers made crude, demeaning comments about the supposed inability of women to serve as police officers.

- Junior women officers were targeted by senior male officers and supervisors of the department to obtain or attempt to obtain sexual favors.

- Officers used crude language and lewd jokes on a regular basis by male officers about women.

- Male officers refused to work with female officers.

- Male officers referred to females as "f...ing c..ts."

- Female officers who take maternity leave were discriminated against.

- A former police officer who was at a firearms qualifications event saw a former police commissioner; he pulled his penis out of his pants, waved it in public and shouted to get (the commissioner's) attention. The officer was later promoted to captain.

- Female officers were routinely directed into positions involving children and schools.

- A former Commissioner Ted *Kupruck* commented that the FBI had high standards when he worked there but, "That all ended when they hired broads."

- A sergeant once asked a female officer under his supervision, "Why don't you wear your skirts a little shorter?" The officer reportedly told a female officer he had always wanted to be a gynecologist. "Don't you think I'd make a good gynecologist? What's the matter, do you think my hands are too big?" The same officer was also quoted as saying, "Let's go out and watch the sweaty high school girls play soccer." When these comments came to the attention of upper-level management, the department conducted an investigation and determined that there was insufficient evidence to establish that the officer had violated the department's sexual harassment test. The officer was later promoted.

- In 1998, Truax was passed over for a promotion. Three members of the interview panel winked at Truax during the course of the promotional interview. Afterwards, then-Chief Bird pulled Truax aside and congratulated her, telling her she had given the best interview of the candidates. A few minutes later, the three candidates were advised that Sgt. *Joe Ellis*, one of the less senior male candidates, got the promotion. Only after Truax filed a grievance challenging that decision did she receive the promotion to captain.

- (*Brasso*) recommended that Karen Johnson's position with the department be terminated ... because of a dispute Johnson had with a male officer under circumstances substantially similar incidents involving two male officers that have resulted in much lesser discipline, or no discipline at all.

"As a direct and proximate result of the above-described continuing discrimination, plaintiff Nancy Truax suffered a tangible job detriment when the Police Commission refused to promote her on Aug. 11, 1998, despite the fact that she was qualified and the most senior candidate for the position," the court document stated.

The court document continued: "As a direct and proximate result of the above-described continuing discrimination, plaintiff Karen Johnson suffered a tangible job detriment when Chief *Brasso* ordered her to be suspended without pay following an argument with another officer, and when the Police Commission adopted the chief's recommendation to terminate her position with the city ... in September, 1999."

At this point, the allegations are to be dealt with in civil court. However, the state Attorney General's Office could become involved with the running of the Police Department if the repercussions are severe, according to senior assistant Attorney General Mark Zuckerman of the Public Integrity Crime Unit of the office. As of this point, his office is unaware of the allegations, he said.

"The Attorney General's Office is the chief law-enforcement office of the state," Zuckerman said. "When we have good reason to believe there has been a systematic breakdown in a police department, we wouldn't just sit back and wait; we'd find some way to get involved."

Mayor Evelyn Sirrell last night refused to comment. She said city officials have been asked to keep quiet about the matter. She did venture to say that she has known Truax for several years, that the two women once served on the police auxiliary unit.

Truax has said she will not comment about the case. She continues to serve on the Police Department, but is off for the next two days. Johnson did not return a phone call.

Chapter 15

High-Speed Chase

Foster's Online, **Police at odds over Seacoast Chase, Kittery, Maine (AP)** - A police chase that began in Maine and spilled into New Hampshire has led to recriminations between police officials in the two states.

Portsmouth, NH - Police Capt. Nancy Truax said Kittery police refused to call off their pursuit of a speeding teen-ager who led them on the perilous chase Friday night into the city's busy downtown section. Kittery Police Chief *Dick Young* defended his department's action, saying the continued pursuit was meant to stop the driver before he killed someone. Truax had called Kittery cruisers off and sought to de-escalate the danger.

"It was a packed downtown. There was no reason to endanger anyone," Truax said. "There were several reasons why I called it off," she said. "I followed our protocol. That's all I can say." *Young* bristled at the notion that his cruisers were 'called off', and said he wished Portsmouth Police were more cooperative in putting up spike mats at the Memorial Bridge to stop the suspect. "Portsmouth doesn't call my cruisers off," said *Young*.

The chase began when a 16-year-old driver failed to stop for police while heading up the I-95 on ramp in Kittery. The driver and his 14-year-old passenger sped north to York, exited onto U.S. 1 and sped South to New Hampshire. The chase ended when the vehicle crashed in Dover, NH, causing minor injuries to the two teenagers. Because of possible injuries and fatalities, police pursuits have stirred controversy in recent years. A National Highway Traffic Safety Administration report found that five people in New Hampshire and six in Maine were killed from 1994 to 1996 as a result of police pursuits.

About a year had passed since my eventual promotion to Captain. They promoted me on October 29, 1998, two months after Joe's promotion,

two months after I'd filed the grievance, two months
after the final straw, two months too late. I'd gone
through another oral interview in front of the
Commission (Kupruck didn't recuse himself this time,
and no one winked at me) and two chiefs, which
lasted about a half hour. This time around, the
number of competitors increased because my peers
theorized that if the Commission passed me over
once, they just might do it again, and this increased
their odds of being selected. It was survival of the
fittest.

I didn't put as much effort into preparing this time, and I
found the interview itself very boring. I was so tired of hearing
myself talk, trying to convince five conservative men that I was the
woman for the job, that I yawned repeatedly during the oral.

We, as usual, survived the ritual of standing in front of the
Commission as they made their announcement.

"I hope nobody brought their gun in with them,"
Commissioner Burke said. Everyone politely chuckled.

"Some of you aren't going to like this," he said, "but, I'd like
to make a motion to promote Sergeant Truax to Captain."

I began to blush with embarrassment.

"Seconded," said Kupruck.

"All in favor?" asked Burke.

Hanes raised his hand in agreement also.

I'd never before heard a promotional announcement quite
like the one I received. What was that? 'Hope no one brought their
guns? Some aren't going to like this?' What kind of support was
this? More of the same mentality whose not-so-subliminal message
told me I was still in a time-warp. With this insight, even with the
promotion, I was beginning to want out.   I'd had enough
humiliation. I know that if I'd been an unproductive employee, or
even marginal, I wouldn't have cared, and none of this would have
mattered; but that wasn't the case.

Well, even though the promotion was anticlimactic, publicity
on the promotion was plentiful and positive. I was toted as the first
female to achieve the rank of Captain in the entire State of New
Hampshire. The Portsmouth Herald said, "At five feet, two inches in
height, Nancy
Truax lives tall. She plays basketball with a competitiveness learned
from being raised with brothers and most recently conquered one of
the last truly male bastions: she became the first female police captain
in the state." A sad fact indeed, considering it was 1998. Chief
Brasso, who was fully aware of my pending lawsuit against him, and
was busy trying to keep it quiet, was quoted as saying 'Capt. Truax

could be the next Chief of Police in the City of Portsmouth'. That's funny. Then why didn't he promote me to Captain when he should have? Why did he force my hand? Why did he make me back him into a corner? I never wanted to do that. I am upset with him for making me take such harsh measures, to make a point that shouldn't have had to be made.

The City used my promotion as a tool to proudly announce, "We promote women." Since I'd been with the p.d., I'd allowed them to use me in this fashion. I never minded; I was happy to do it, if it meant that other's could benefit from this role model. I had believed the City was serious about the accolades they were throwing at me. It wasn't until the fated August 11, 1998, that I began to see that it was just political fodder to them, and their opinion of me was far different from what it appeared to be on the surface. So, by the time they gave me the bars, and while the Community lauded Brasso as an advocate for women, with me as his example, I was growing more resentful toward the administration's shameless political maneuvers.

Further, because I filed the suit against them, it was made clear to me, in a variety of ways, that if they could hang me out to dry, they would. In the past, when I had angered members of the patrolman's union, I'd had my locker broken into, all four tires flattened, a windshield cracked, a new car keyed three times, and most recently, someone jumped onto the trunk of my car and scratched a shoe print into the paint. All acts of criminal mischief were done during highly stressful eras of my career; during times when I felt compelled to speak-out against someone or something. But this was different. I had openly challenged the Administration, and they weren't about to let me get off that easily.

They were looking for something on me; I knew it, so I was constantly on the alert. Always aware of 'cya', 'cover your ass'.

"Cap. We gotta high speed chase coming into town from Kittery. We've been listening to the chase on the Kittery channel for about ten minutes now. You better come listen.

Sounds like it's getting pretty hairy. The cop handling the chase is yelling and screaming. He sounds more out of control than the bad guy," said Sara Falls, one of our better dispatchers.

"Who's the officer? Do you know?" I asked.

"No. You'd better come listen."

The dispatch center is directly across the hall from the patrol captain's office. It was built to be the envy of all New England, and I think it had succeeded in that arena. Agencies from all over the coast came on tours of the facility in hopes of convincing their towns to invest in our type of equipment. One of the many advantages to our center was the quality with which it was soundproofed. Each time I walked into the room I was amazed at the noise level inside. Loud sirens wailed through the radio waves. I stood at the console and listened carefully as the Kittery officer blared wildly over the air.

"Coming down Route One by Mrs. and Me," he screamed. It was Howe. Quitter. Shit. Nothing good would come of this. Although Howe is a man with a unique personality, he is forever the center of adversity at his job in Kittery. One day he shot and killed a family dog claiming that he had been in fear of his life. A huge controversy and investigation resulted; Howe was cleared. Imagine that.

One day Chief Young, the Kittery Chief, called my house looking for Vince, and I happened to answer the phone. The Chief had always been friendly with me (until this particular police chase). Anyway, before I put Vince on the phone, Young says, "Hey Nance. I got my face slapped by my wife after that wedding we went to the other day. Yeah, Yeah," he chuckled, "she noticed that I kept looking at your ass, and she didn't like it too much. You got a nice butt." I gave the phone to Vince.

I consider Howe to be less than cautious in his policing style, and didn't want this high speed chase anywhere near our town. I had a lot to be concerned about because Mrs. and Me is a straight shot from Kittery, right into Portsmouth.

"Oh my God!" Howe screamed. "He almost hit another car. I think he tried to ram it. Get me some units with stop sticks." A 'stop stick' is a device with spikes in it, that can be placed on the roadway, in front of a car being chased, and it will deflate it's tires. It's not dangerous for the suspect because the tires flatten very slowly, to avoid throwing the car into an uncontrollable spin.

"You will not use that cruiser as a battering ram," his Sergeant yelled. "Acknowledge receipt Kittery 12."

"Got it." Howe said.

"Sara," I said, "what's the cause of this chase?"

"Don't know yet. We've tried to find out over the teletype, but Kittery won't answer. They must be too busy".

"Well, find out. Call them over the phone if you have to. I want to know the reason behind this chase before we get involved."

She shook her head up and down in acknowledgment, and was already dialing the phone.

"Kittery, unit 10," the Kittery Sergeant spoke calmly, "position yourself at the traffic circle in case he goes in that direction."

"Sara, you also need to find out if Kittery knows who's driving the suspect car, and how many people are in it. I don't want anyone getting hurt." Again she acknowledged by shaking her head at me, but, continuing with her exceptional radio and phone skills.

If we knew who was in the car, we could call the chase off when it got to Portsmouth, and fill out paperwork for an arrest on the driver, later.   This would reduce risk and injury for everyone involved, and, at the same time, guarantee capture of the bad guy.

I knew Howe well, and figured this whole mess was the result of a minor infraction. If that was the case, I planned on calling it off as soon as it hit the border. This was a Friday night, at 8 PM, and downtown Portsmouth was buzzing with tourists, pedestrians, and regulars, out for a fun night. But I needed to know fast, because I imagined that most, if not all, the Portsmouth cruisers were getting closer to town, trying to get themselves set up to be involved in the chase. Most cops love high speed chases so much that they'll even leave the donut shop to be part of the 'fun'.

"All Portsmouth Units," I called over the air, "do not become involved in this chase until I give the order. I'm trying to retrieve some necessary information now. Stand back, and stand by for further orders."

I could almost hear their collective grunts of displeasure at the order, but I smiled knowing they would comply. In the mean time, our dispatcher was desperately trying to reach the Kittery dispatch center, but kept getting put on hold because they were busy with the chase. If it weren't so dangerous I would have considered the radio chatter comical. It reminded me of an old cowboy scene.

"Kittery 12," Jimmy Howe again, "still on 1A, approaching Haley Road. NO, NO," frantic now, "he's taking a left onto Haley." As Jimmy talked, the sound of his wailing siren nearly muffled his words.

"Anything yet?" I asked Sara. She shook her head, frustrated too.

"At least they've taken the other road. They've gone further into Kittery. Maybe they won't come this way."

"Hopefully. But keep trying."

"I've got stop sticks and can set up on this side of the bridge," said officer McDonald.

"Negative," I said. "Stand back. The chase has taken an opposite turn."

"State Police says it's a speed violation. That's all they've got." Sara said.

"NH State, or Maine State?" I asked.

"NH State," she replied.

"Is Maine State involved?" I asked.

"Don't know. No one's saying much."

Then, "Kittery 12, Kittery 12. He's taking another turn and we're headed for the traffic circle by Dairy Queen." His tires screeched as he made the announcement.

Shit. My stomach dropped. If they continued south from the circle, they'd be in Portsmouth in minutes. They were headed right through the center of town, right toward all those people. I had already been advised that the streets were packed with tourists and pedestrians and I knew Howe's style. He'd come ramming through town without a care in the world for the people walking the downtown area. Someone could get very badly hurt. I just knew someone would be, and I didn't want any part of it. Nor did I want the City of Portsmouth to have anything to do with it. This had the stench of a lawsuit all over it.

Sara had just told me that the driver of the car was *believed* to be a kid by the last name of Dubois, and he had one of his friends in the car with him. Dubois was a local trouble maker who Howe knew, and was determined to catch.

My interpretation of these facts was that Howe knew who was in the car, no major infraction had occurred, but there were two spunky juveniles in a car being chased by an irresponsible policeman, who was also driving at speeds in excess of 90 miles per hour. I became immediately frustrated with Howe, and the Kittery style of policing. Mad at them for playing with innocent lives, and putting the City of Portsmouth in a position of having to bail them out.

I so much wanted to take a completely hands-off approach, but couldn't take that extreme yet. I was still waiting for confirmation from either Kittery or Maine State Police as to why Howe was chasing the car. Nothing. The chase was coming our way quickly. I had to think fast. Not panicking, I realized that I had to trust Kittery's judgment, until I heard differently. It was always possible that they knew something I didn't. Why they weren't communicating it to us was another matter.

"All units, be advised that the chase is headed our way, over the Memorial Bridge, straight through the middle of town. I anticipate they'll be here within the next minute." I expected no response as I continued, "Only two Portsmouth cruisers will assist Kittery." I knew that at least 6 cruisers had already strategically placed themselves in hopes of being chosen. Knowing this, I quickly assigned two officers, McDonald and Page. I had to specifically order that no other officers become involved, using harsh words to assure myself that none of them would allow temptation to sway an otherwise logical order. I knew that if I didn't specifically order them to stay away, they might try to run parallel with the chase, in hopes of finding themselves in such a wonderfully, strategic position that their services couldn't be denied. This would only cause more danger. Anyway, I told them, NO OTHER UNITS, per policy.

By the time Howe busted into town, there were three cruisers already involved in the chase, from his side of the bridge. Two

Kittery units, and one Maine State Police unit. The Memorial Bridge is narrow and short, and the travel portion is made of metal grating that creates a lot of noise when the car tires drive over it. You can't pedal a bicycle over it because the tires get caught in the grate holes. When you walk on it you can see through the road into the water below. The river's current is very fast and you can get dizzy or disoriented if you stare at the water for too long. The water beneath the bridge carries the third fastest currents in the world, and not too many people have survived a fall into the Piscataqua. I've seen huge moose get carried away in its current as they desperately yet futilely attempted to scrape their way onto shore.

"McDonald," I ordered, "position yourself on Daniel, just past the bridge. Put out the stop sticks. Page, position yourself at the intersection of Daniel and Penhallow, and be ready to follow. When the chase gets into town, I want you to take the lead, just behind the suspect. You or McDonald. Page, if you take the lead, McDonald will follow directly behind you and transmit updates on the conditions and speed."

"10-5," they said.

Just then, "Kittery 12, just passing Warrens Lobster, headed to Portsmouth. Did you advise Portsmouth yet?"

We heard the Kittery dispatcher telling Jimmy that we were already aware and were willing to help.

"Ask her the details of the chase, maybe she'll respond now." I told Sara.

"Portsmouth, home base, to Kittery home base."

"Go ahead Portsmouth."

"Inquiring as to the purpose of the chase. Original infraction?"

"Stand by."

Then Jimmy, "Where are the Portsmouth units. Coming through town now. Where are they?"

Shit, McDonald said as he picked up the radio. "No stop stick in my car, repeat, no stop stick."

It was too late. Kittery units were visible and audible to McDonald; they were in Portsmouth and there was no time to wonder where the stop sticks might be. McDonald jumped in his cruiser as he heard the familiar sound of sirens, joined by tires going too fast, rackety rack, over the bridge. "I'll take the lead," McDonald told Page over the air.

Vroom, sirens, tires hitting the sidewalk curb. McDonald pulled his cruiser into the chase and attempted to maneuver himself to the lead chase position. He got on the radio and told Howe to pull over and allow him to take control. Howe refused by instructing McDonald to take a position that would block the suspect's access to the highway. McDonald pulled into the oncoming lane and again ordered Howe to move over and allow him to take charge. Howe veered his cruiser to the left, and tried to run McDonald off the road. Whether Howe wasn't aware of proper procedure or just didn't care, is of little significance compared to officer Howe's obsession with catching the car. He was willing to ram another cruiser off the road in order to become a hero.

"Pull over," McDonald ordered.

"Cap," said Sara, "Kittery finally advising that the driver of that car is wanted for speed."

"Speed?" I asked.

"Yup. That's it."

"All units. Break away from the chase. Do not continue." I said.

The chase continued down Market St. Extension.

"Do you want Kittery to continue?" Sara asked.

"No," I said. " I want them to stop immediately."

"Do you want me to tell them?"

"No, I'll take care of it." to Sara, but then over the air, "Portsmouth 14 to Kittery Dispatch, discontinue the chase in our town. Repeat. Discontinue the chase."

No response. The chase hummed on.

"Did I push the right button, Sara?" I asked.

"The one on the left, then key the Kittery channel. Right here," she said and pointed to the appropriate ICON.

"Kittery, did you copy? Break off the chase in our town. NOW," I ordered.

"Yeah, yeah, yeah. Don't worry about it." This was Howe, and as he keyed the mike, I could hear his siren continuing to wail. He wasn't stopping.

"14 to McDonald. Give me the location of the chase and rate of speed."

"Market St. Extention, just beyond K-Mart, we're going about 85 mph. But, I'm breaking off now."

"10-5. Kittery is chasing them for speed. Speed only. Pull out."

"Kittery 12, I'm reaching the Newington Line. Still involved in the chase. There's a Portsmouth cruiser right behind me," said Howe.

"That is not a Portsmouth unit," McDonald squawked. "14, no Portsmouth units still involved in the chase."

"10-5. Captain Truax to Kittery Officer Howe," I said on his channel, "if that car turns around, you will not chase it in our town."

Silence. Disrespect.

"Acknowledge receipt, Kittery 12."

"Don't worry about it, don't worry about it," he said over the air. That bastard, I thought. This is my town right now (being the highest ranking officer on duty), it's my job to worry about it, especially when I've got some hotshot playing cowboy on my streets. I didn't reply, but crossed my fingers that he would not bring this mess back into our town.

We continued to monitor the chase and I wasn't surprised to hear Kittery 12 announce that the suspect car had crashed, and rolled over on its side, at the Dover toll. The accident was bad. Two kids were locked in the car and the jaws of life had to be used to get them out.

"202. Would you like me to slide into Dover to see if they need any help?"

"Negative. All units stay away from that scene. They have plenty of help." I said this because, again, I wanted to distance us as far as possible from this accident, which was sure to become a law suit. I didn't want there to be any appearance of wrongful Portsmouth involvement.

The phones started ringing off the hook before the chase even ended. The media had their scanners on and wanted to know the scoop.

"Nancy, I could have sworn I heard you order them to stop the chase. Did you?" one reporter asked.

This is where I faltered. I know, now, that the correct response should have been that the chase originated in Kittery, and the media should get their information directly from them, not us. this is policy. But, I wanted so badly to have nothing to do with the ramifications of this reckless chase, that I told them that I had called the chase off. When they asked why, I told them, 'to protect the citizens of Portsmouth from being hurt'. This statement was enough to fuel the press.

They came out with headlines like, "Police discuss high speed chase", "2 Hospitalized in chase", "Portsmouth Police say Kittery took the car chase too far", and so on.

Just as I was getting ready to handle my umteenth reporter, Sara burst into my office.

"Cap, I've got a woman on the phone who says her car was stolen. It's the same car involved in the chase. She walked out to get in her car, and it wasn't there."

"Has it been reported stolen yet? Is it in NCIC[9]?" I asked.

---

[9] National Crime Information Center

"No. She just discovered it."

"Is she credible? Maybe she let the kids take it, heard about the accident, and is trying to cover her butt."

"I have no idea," she said.

"Send a cruiser to take the information. Make sure the officer knows the circumstances. It might make a difference as to how he approaches the interview."

"Got it," she said.

As it turned out, the complainant was telling the truth. This becomes of interest later on as members of the Kittery Police Department made public claims that they'd been chasing the car *because* it was stolen, as if they knew this at the beginning, and throughout the chase.

Chief Young became so angry that I had violated the "police code" by speaking the truth to outsiders (that Kittery had been reckless in their actions and had caused needless danger to numerous people) , that he filed a formal complaint against me which he hand delivered to Chief Brasso in one of their 'pow-wow', meetings. The complaint named me, specifically, as having made *false statements* to the press, by telling them that I had called the chase off, when in fact I hadn't. The following is a copy of a letter written by Chief Young to Chief Brasso:

"Now that I have turned over to you, all the information that I have pertaining to this incident, I am requesting that your department conduct an internal investigation of the events that transpired the evening of April 9, 1999. Upon review of this information (police reports and audio recordings of the chase), it is clear to me that the statements released to the news media, apparently by a member of your department (Captain Truax), immediately following this incident were contrary to my findings. The various articles mention that we were ordered to terminate this pursuit and failed to comply.

The result of having had this type of publicity has created a firestorm for my department and me. I have come under fire from the town manager, the town council and citizens from both Kittery and Portsmouth for failing to comply with requests from your department to terminate the pursuit on that evening. My council has ordered me to appear before them with an explanation of why my

officer and supervisor disregarded your
department's orders. ...you also indicated to me
that either in your reports or from information that
was given to you that you were of the impression
that we had prior knowledge of the identity of the
individual driving the vehicle that night. This
information was false. At no time during the
pursuit were we able to identify or even get a good
look at the driver. The information that was
published in the Foster's Newspaper was
erroneous information. I told the Foster's that
once the individual got stopped and was in our
custody, he related to all officers that the reason he
did not stop was that he did not want to get
arrested and return to the Youth Center. ...we did
get a commitment from the State of Maine
ordering him to be held at the Youth Center. All
of this transpired after we were able to ID the
individual once the pursuit was over. I would
appreciate it if you would inform me of the results
of your internal investigation as soon as possible so
that this matter can be closed."

We had indeed told Chief Young that we believed Officer
Howe knew the identity of the driver because Howe made the
statement on the police radio that he thought he could tell who the
driver was 'because of the way his ears were sticking out."

This complaint was candy in Chief Brasso' hands because it
gave him an excuse to make my life a little more difficult, harass me,
maybe even push me out. You see, he felt that I needed to be
penalized for filing the law suit, and this was a perfect tool. He knew,
however, that it would look bad, under the circumstances, if he had
the City conduct an investigation into my actions, so it was somehow
decided that investigators from the NH State Police would handle it,
and report to the Chief.

Portsmouth Herald: An independent investigator has been
brought in to clear up an interstate turf war over who had the final
say - Kittery or Portsmouth police - on a high speed chase through the
city.

New Hampshire State Police Lt. John Stevens (who
mysteriously retired in the midst of the investigation) will settle a
matter between the two departments stemming from a high speed
chase through downtown. Kittery police were chasing a young
automobile-robbery suspect when they all crossed into Portsmouth.

Portsmouth Police Capt. Nancy Truax tried a number of times to call
off the chase; she said the downtown was too crowded, the chase too
dangerous. Kittery police continued, finally catching the teen when
his car flipped in Dover.

After several meetings about the chase, Kittery Police Chief
Richard Young and Portsmouth Police Chief *Craig Brasso* agreed an
independent investigation should be done."

As I've already said, the reference in this news article to the
fact that Kittery was chasing a robbery-car theft suspect is a blatant
untruth, which Kittery used to their political advantage. Kittery,
Officer Howe, had no idea that the car had been stolen until *after* it
crashed at the Dover tolls. While the chase was going on, all Howe
knew was that he was chasing a speeding car that contained a
juvenile he believed to be Dubois. That's it. He had no additional
information to lead him to believe a felony had been committed, or
that Dubois intended to harm anyone if allowed to escape and
therefore the chase was unwarranted.

To complicate matters even more, my husband worked for
the Kittery Police Department, and I had great concern as to how he
would handle this recent development. As we all know by now,
anything was possible. I was worried that he would feel squeezed
between the opinions of his fellow officers in Kittery, and his
obligatory loyalty to me. I had no idea whether he would agree with
my point of view, or side with his Kittery cohorts. This would
determine his demeanor; but nothing would stop him from wishing I
had just kept my mouth shut....that much I knew.

I was feeling torn over the damaged relationships that would
follow this new political skirmish. There was no doubt I would no
longer be considered a friend or colleague of Chief Young's.

This bothered me, not for myself (at least he wouldn't be
looking at my ass anymore), but because I didn't want to be
responsible for creating a negative work environment for my
husband. I knew too, that this incident would be a major strain in
the professional, working, relationship between Kittery and
Portsmouth. Being border towns, even though we are in different
States, we need good communication and I knew a controversial
public argument would hinder that.

I predicted in-fighting within our own agency over whether
the chase should have been called off or not; and, the same at the
Kittery Police Department. As it turned out, there was more fighting
within Kittery than Portsmouth. Vince would often return home
frustrated, because the "guys" would daily hide the local newspaper
from him, and would stop discussions when he walked in the room.
It was during these times he knew they were arguing the merits of his
wife's (not Captain Truax's) actions. Whatever he overheard, he

reported to me. I was appreciative of that because it gave me a three hundred and sixty degree picture of the political maneuverings of the upper echelon of both agencies. It certainly led me to understand that I would need an attorney for this "impartial" investigation; especially since I had learned from an anonymous source that James Devon, the NHSP lead investigator, was an old high school buddy of Craig Brasso. So much for impartiality. Government agencies must have a different definition of 'impartial' than Webster. And so it goes, in Politics.

Although torn over the controversy, I was also upset that Kittery dug it's heels in, and refused to admit any wrong doing. They squewed the story to fit their purposes, and denied that they should have done anything differently. Even though I believe that I had conducted myself appropriately throughout the chase, retrospect gives a clearer picture, and I would definitely say that I could have handled certain things better (such as comments I made to the press, although true). Not once during this six month process did Kittery make any such statement. In their mind, I, or my big mouth (if it could be a separate part of me over which I have no control) was the sole reason for any problems they were currently having.

Additionally, although I held the rank of Captain, and was supposed to be considered part of our agency's upper management, I was treated like an inept clod, with no status, throughout the investigation. What we had was one Chief, Young, scrambling to save his ass from being fired; and, another Chief, Brasso, embarrassed that someone from his department had insulted another Chief by speaking out to the press. The two Chiefs stuck together, and left me to battle the piranhas.

This is how it happened.

Everyone involved in the chase was interviewed separately by New Hampshire State Police. I was the last to be interviewed. Does that tell you anything? Any good cop will tell you that the *suspect* in a case is interviewed last; that way the investigator has all the information he/she needs, from all available sources, to 'go after' the targeted person if it's deemed necessary. I was the last, so I was the suspect. They were going after me. They knew it; I knew it; and they knew that I knew.

As I walked down the familiar hallway that houses the station officer's desk, the communications center, and the Deputy Chief's office, I was accompanied by my attorney, Jim Loring, and my union representative. Jim is an average sized guy, with stark black hair that curls nicely when it's long. Since I've known him he's always worn a heavy, dark mustache that magnifies his dark features. He's always been a startlingly handsome guy in my eyes; but it's only enhanced by his intelligence. He has a rare intelligence that I've only ever found in one other person, my husband. Jim and I have had many talks over the years about the seductiveness of intelligence.

We walked by Deputy Irons's office, where he was standing behind his desk, preparing to leave for the interview. He saw me, saw Loring, and gave us a look that told me he wasn't expecting me to bring an attorney. We just smiled as if it were par for the course, and continued down the hallway.

The interview was held in the detective's lunch room; apparently the Chief's conference room was booked. This room had a table large enough to hold all the parties involved in the interview; but also held the odor of expired food, with several crumbs on the table to add to the atmosphere. I positioned myself at the end of the table with Loring to my right, and my union rep to his right. All three of us were squeezed at the end.

If you can believe it, three representatives from State Police were present to handle my interview (what a laugh); one was the Lieutenant that they talked about in the paper, another was Brasso's' good buddy, Devon, and a third whose name I don't recall. Deputy Irons was in the room, too. To add further to my humiliation, Mildred Peas, the Chief's secretary was also present, handling the recording device. I felt surrounded by the enemy, but was determined to hold-up, and give them the simple truth. That couldn't be too tough, right?

"....name is detective James Devon, NH State Police."

I shook my head up and down, looking directly into his eyes to let him know I wasn't bothered by what was going on.

"I've been assigned to investigate this case, and so far have interviewed everyone that I believe was somehow involved. It's been a long process, but we hope to end it today."

All eyes were focused on him. As an investigator, I knew that an opening statement can be crucial to an investigation, especially when interviewing the 'bad guy'. You don't want to say anything that's going to turn the suspect off, or let him know that you have feelings one way or another about his involvement in the case. 'Hey, man. You're just there to gather the information and do your job. No big deal. No hard feelings. Let's just get to the truth.'

"....can I call you Nancy, or would you like me to call you Captain?" he asked.

This threw me off a bit. He had been nicey, nicey, and now he wanted the privilege of calling me by my first name, even though he had no rank, and he was charged with tripping with my career. What a ballsy question, I thought.

"Since this is a formal proceeding, you can refer to me as Captain, detective." I said. Now I was getting nervous, but I wouldn't let him see. I recognized a ploy when I heard one, and this was definitely a ploy. He wanted to be my friend, and then screw me over. Fuck him, I thought. He was actually using criminal interview tactics on me; and, I had no doubt that Brasso had ordered him to do so. There was Irons, Brasso' best friend and new DC, sitting directly across from me, smirking. What a web I was caught in!! A web spawned by Brasso, Young, Irons, and Howe. A web I was going to have to fight hard to get out of. Or, perhaps the best tactic would be to lay low until the spider thought he had the advantage, and then suddenly spring loose.

Devon gave me a stern look, demonstrating his reluctance to refer to me by my appropriate title. I returned his gaze with an empty, blank stare.

"Fine, Captain then," he said. "I've got to read you your administrative rights."

I nodded my head in acknowledgment. When a police officer belongs to a union, the administration is required to give notice of his or her rights. It's just like Miranda in the sense that, if the administration fails to explain these rights to the officer, it will become more difficult to take any kind of disciplinary action against the officer. By reading me my rights, they were reserving the right to discipline me for any action they considered inappropriate. It is here that I would like to point out that no one else involved in this incident had their administrative rights read to them. No one in Kittery or Portsmouth.

Devon read directly from a document, and when he was done, said, "Do you understand your rights?"

"Yes, I understand," I said.

"Sign here, indicating you understand," he said.

"No," I said.

"Are you refusing to sign?" he asked.

"Yes. I'm refusing to sign."

"Okay, I'll just indicate that on the signature line," he said.

I said nothing. I watched him as he wrote the word "REFUSED" in bold letters across the straight, black, line, as though I had committed a horrible sin by denying them my signature.

"You're aware of the high speed chase we're taking about?"

"Yes."

"Tell us your version of what happened," he ordered.

As I started telling my side of the story, I was sure to look my foe directly in the eyes. I wanted him to know that I had nothing to hide. I could tell by the way he was listening that he was waiting for me to falter; when I faltered he would pounce hard, knock me down, and go in for the kill. All eyes were on he and I, as though we were playing out some inevitable drama, the outcome of which would effect everyone's fate.

It didn't take long for Devon's temper to come out, as he was frustrated with my attitude, and my answers; but, I wasn't sure whether this was a role he was playing, or whether he was serious. After brief consideration I decided that this didn't really matter. What did matter was that I understood that his flare-up was designed to unseat me, make me nervous, make me afraid of him. Kind of like the emotional abuse I had been experiencing at home and work. Little did he realize that I was far more skilled at this game than he was, or ever could be; I had been living on the emotional edge for eighteen years now and had learned well how to protect myself, and how to attack, leaving my victim wondering what had just happened. It wasn't a game I liked to play, but if I had to, I could and I would.

"Isn't it true, that once you realized it was officer Howe that initiated the chase, you made a judgment that you weren't going to allow Portsmouth to get involved?" he asked.

"No." I said.

"Isn't it true that you don't like officer Howe?"

"It's not a matter of like or dislike," I said, "it's a matter of professionalism and whether or not someone is doing their job correctly."

"Didn't you decide from the get-go that, because Howe was the initiating officer, you wouldn't allow Portsmouth to assist with the chase?" he demanded.

"No. That's not true at all. I was attempting to fairly evaluate all the circumstances. It was a hot night, downtown was busy, and the car chase was way out of hand. Howe was ramming parked cars and nearly had two head-on collisions with cars driving in the opposite direction. He tried to ram one of our cruisers, for heaven's sake!"

"It was a felony chase," he said.

"How is that?" I asked.

"The car was stolen."

"The fact of the matter is, that no one, not even Howe, not even his Sergeant that night, knew the car was stolen until quite some time AFTER the car rolled over. All he had was a speed violation. When the chase came into Portsmouth, a good twenty minutes after the chase started, all Howe had was a speed violation. In my judgment, that is not a good enough reason to endanger so many lives."

"In your judgment?" he asked, as though I had no right making such a decision.

"Yes. In my judgment. It was my shift, and it was my call."

"Did you order Kittery to stop the chase, once it got into Portsmouth?"

"Eventually I did. Yes. But, not at first. When they first got into Portsmouth I hadn't yet learned the reason for the chase, so I decided to support their decision until I could find out what they were chasing this kid for."

There was no response, or even any indication that I had been heard by any of the men in the room, so I continued, "Our pursuit policy has some very specific guidelines. I was trying to follow policy, but found it very difficult considering Kittery has a completely different pursuit philosophy. It seems like our policy is geared toward safety, while Kittery's, if they even have one, is focused on catching the bad guy at any cost."

"What makes you think you had the authority to call Kittery off the chase?" he asked with a disbelieving tone.

"Almost all the facts in this situation gave me that authority," I replied.

"Which fact exactly?" he snipped.

"I was the patrol Captain that night. I was the highest ranking police official on duty. Safety for the citizens of Portsmouth was My responsibility during those hours. Kittery, a town in another State altogether, had no jurisdiction or authority in our town. It was their obligation to honor Our policy."

"At what point did you order Howe to stop the chase?" quicker now, the questions came.

"Right after I ordered our units to pull out of the chase."

"Where were they when you gave the order? Where was the chase?" quicker now.

"Market Street Extention."

"Where on the Extention?"

"From radio transmissions with McDonald, I would guess that it was somewhere near the Market Basket."

"Did you give the order?"

"Yes."

"Really?"

"Yes," I said, wondering why he had asked.

"You're sure," he persisted.

"Yes. I'm sure." Now, I was puzzled.

He glared at me. This was a glare that told me he thought he had me. He thought he had pinned me to the wall, caught me in a lie. But, what was the lie?

"We've listened to all the radio transcripts, and can't find that transmission anywhere. Now, let me ask you again, did you actually give the order for Kittery to stop the chase, like you told the newspapers?"

"Yes!" I said, adamant. "I gave the order."

"I don't think you did. Did anyone else hear this phantom order? It's not on the transcripts."

"Then the transcripts are wrong."

"I'm going to ask you again," he steamed, "did you give the order for Kittery Police to stop the chase?"

BONK!! It was suddenly clear to me. My realization came so quickly that I didn't feel it's conception and birth; my body responded with a delicate buzzing in my head, as though a gentle vibrator were tickling my brain. It gave me a 'silly' feeling, along with the terrifying realization that they had altered the tapes. The piranhas were set up to eat me. I was fish bait.

No matter how upset I was, I had to play it smart. I had to play it their way. If I'd learned one thing in all the years I'd been there, I knew that when you're under the gun, when you're in the hot seat, you can never let 'em know you're nervous. Never. Also, a good tactic is to play naive. Don't let 'em know you've caught on to their game. Play dumb.

He persisted. "You told the papers that you gave the order, yet, we couldn't find it. Did you give that order?"

Now they'd given me their game plan. A police officer can be easily fired if caught lying on any issue. This is because credibility is such an integrated part of a cop's career that honesty is a must. Once there's been a breech in that ethic, it can't be repaired. Assured honesty is needed for testimony in the court room, the swearing of search warrants, arrest warrants and complaints.

I flashed back to 1990 when Officer Karen Johnson had released information to a local newspaper that she was experiencing discrimination at the PPD. Director Hanes was bullshit with the accusation because by making the problem public, Karen had finally put the administration in a position of having to investigate the problem. She'd put them on the dime. At that point in my career, I was so occupied with the success ladder that I wasn't seeing, or admitting to, the problems Karen spoke of. They asked me to assist with the investigation. In a briefing, prior to the onset of the investigation, we were told that if we could prove that Karen had lied about any of the allegations that had been printed in the paper, she would be fired. The subliminal message was that we were to look for a lie, so that she could be terminated. They were doing the same with me. They failed with Karen; they would fail with me.

I slowly laid my hands on my lap and tried to give the impression of calm. I looked directly at my lawyer so that he would know I'd caught on, and he looked back, letting me know he was onto the scheme also. My union rep shook his head from side to side as if he were ashamed to be in the same room with these people. He probably was.

"I don't know what I can tell you to help you understand that I gave that order. I was standing at the dispatch console. When I realized I would need to call the chase off, I turned to dispatcher Falls and asked, 'which button do I press?' Have you been in our dispatch center?" I asked.

"No."

"Our dispatchers use a computer that's much different than the ones we, as police officers, use. They use a mouse with three different controls, and the computer screen has a number of frequencies to choose from. I had to ask Sara which button to push, and which frequency to click on, to be sure I was doing it right, you know, to be sure I was transmitting over Kittery's frequency."

"Right. So you can't be sure you transmitted the message, can you?" he demanded.

Speechless and appalled, I glared at my accuser. I decided I had nothing left to say on this issue. I had answered his question several times, and I wasn't going to repeat myself any more.
We'd been in the interview room for two and a half hours, and I was tired, and mentally exhausted.

"Have you interviewed Sara Falls yet? She would have heard me give the order."

"No. You're the last."

"Don't you think it would be a good idea?" I asked. "If you're really looking for the truth, she might help." I was starting to get sarcastic now. "I thought you had interviewed everyone. That's what you said."

Loring slammed his hands on the table and stood up saying, "Well, I'm addicted to cigarettes, and I need a smoke. What do you say we take a break. It's getting a little hot in here." His usual jovial self, trying to make light of a tense situation. I glared at the interviewer. I wanted to tell him to fuck off, but I couldn't, not now anyway. Maybe later. Maybe when I retire.

Loring and I met outside the building. Loring expressed his concerns and sudden realization that the administration was gunning for me, and reminded me to remain calm and answer the questions as best I could. Loring's only allowed function at this administrative interview was to take notes in case I needed him for another proceeding later on. He wasn't allowed to interrupt the process. The administration had the right to ask me any question they wanted, and I had to answer.

The remainder of the interview lasted another hour and a half, and it went much the same way as the first half. Devon grilled me, while I tried to keep calm. When it was over, I felt like I'd been publicly striped, raped, tied to a horse and dragged along a lengthy dirt road. It would take me a long time to bounce back from this betrayal; but I figured it would be okay in the end, because Sara would verify my actions. I was hoping that her testimony would be proof that, not only did I give the order, but the tapes had been tampered with.   I was partly right.   Sara testified that she heard me give the order, and that she heard the order being transmitted over the air.   But, in order for all the guys in positions of power to 'save face' on this issue, Chief Brasso issued a press release which prompted local newspapers to print the following article:

"**Kittery's high-speed police pursuit through Portsmouth was never asked to be called off**".   Kittery police officers involved in a high-speed chase through downtown Portsmouth never received any request to terminate their pursuit, an independent investigation by the New Hampshire State Police determined.   State Police Sgt. James Devon, who conducted the investigation, told Portsmouth police Chief Craig Brasso and Kittery police Chief Richard Young that while the ranking officer on duty in Portsmouth thought the request to terminate the pursuit had been broadcast to the Kittery Police Department, it was determined the broadcast never occurred.   Brasso chalked the miscommunication up to a technical problem.   He said the Kittery and Portsmouth police officers were using different radio frequencies.   The Portsmouth Police Department issued a statement in which it publicly apologized to the "men and women of the Kittery Police Department for comments made to the media that were unfairly critical or inaccurately represented the facts in this incident."

   By telling the media the truth about the incident, I had broken a long-held ethic of law enforcement, that is formally documented, even today, as a valued, even mandated, principle.   By documented, I mean that it is actually written down, and placed in the Portsmouth Police Rules and Regulations Manual; and I quote, "Whatever I see or hear of a confidential nature or that is confided to me... will be kept ever secret..."

Chapter 16

The Lawsuit

Portsmouth's callous treatment of me before, during, and after the high speed chase made me realize that my continued employment with the Organization could only be fraught with unending turmoil and controversy. By the end of the investigation I was being avoided by most members of the agency, even if only for fear of "guilt by association". When someone in our agency is permanently, politically shunned, it's like being thrown into a leper camp. No one wants to be around you for fear they may be seen as having empathy for you, and therefore be labeled as a sympathizer, which in turn would be career suicide for them.

The Administration, of which I was now a part, was excluding me from meetings that I would normally attend. I would often walk by the D.C.'s office and see a group of supervisors inside conducting a meeting; when I would later ask what it was about, I learned that it was a meeting I should have attended as I was on the committee.

On another occasion I was handed a written order from Chief Brasso advising that I could no longer have conversation with a Sergeant Thibideau about personnel matters. This was the result of a private conversation I had with Thibideau as to why he had been involved in usurping my position as Leader of the Fire Arms Team. It was a lengthy conversation, but not angry or heated. Thibideau told me that he was not responsible for taking the position away from me, but knew of other members of the team who did not want to be guided by a woman...any woman.

In any case, I guess he didn't like being confronted by me, so he reported the conversation to Chief Brasso, who took it upon himself to write the order. Basically, Brasso was telling me I couldn't talk to Thibideau anymore. I was ordered to bring any personnel issues to D.C. Irons, and he would handle them for me. What a relief! (Definate sarcasm here).

Subsequently, in February of 2000, I complained to D.C. Irons about the state of the men's locker room (as Captain, one of our duties is to police the building to be sure everything is in place, nothing has been stolen or damaged, and there are no illegal persons inside the building). My reasons for being there were quite legitimate, and before I entered their sanctuary I made sure no one was in there.

You can imagine my shock when I faced a series of walls and

lockers plastered with pornographic pictures of nude women, with hand crafted drawings and writing added for humor. Even the walls were written on. Sayings such as: "lick me baby", "you're better than an ice cream cone", and other unmentionables were penned onto the walls and lockers. One officer had "Stud Boy" posted on his locker; another coupled pictures of his new baby with the latest hustler pin-up, while another included a pornographic cartoon of a dog having sex with a woman.

My reasons for complaining were pretty simple. This was not a sports team locker room. This was supposed to be a professional setting, and I didn't appreciate knowing that the officers I managed were being allowed to devalue women. It bothered me immensely to know that the entire Administrative Division (those with rank of Sergeant and above, including the Chief of Police) had lockers there too, and used them every day. It seemed to me that the City of Portsmouth still didn't get it.

After putting Irons on notice that I was dissatisfied with the nasty pictures and rude writings, he issued an edict that (because of the mess Captain Truax found down there) the entire locker room would have to be cleaned, strict rules would be set in place, and sanctions issued if officers did not comply. The officers were blatantly pissed that I had invaded their territory; a place they considered an inner sanctum, private, holy, and untouchable by any female. Irons fueled their anger by implying that, 'hey, if it weren't for Nancy, we wouldn't have to do this.' Good thing I had Irons to bring my complaints to.

Many similar incidents prompted my final resignation from the Portsmouth Police Department in January of 2001. Most importantly, my emotional health was taking a dramatic downward turn that I seemed unable to control. I didn't have the strength to pull my wagon back up the hill anymore, and at the same time contend with the never ending onslaught of grief from the agency.

By this time my ability to concentrate had declined to just about nil. Previously an avid reader, I couldn't read a book anymore because I couldn't stay focused long enough to read more than a sentence; and then I couldn't remember what the sentence said. I was plagued with headaches every day. My nights were void of sleep; when I did sleep I had night mares about the Police Department. I'd lost interest in all the things I loved; no more reading, running, playing the saxophone, or spending time with family and friends. When I wasn't at work I was usually watching television or in bed. When I was watching television, I had no idea what was on; I was just staring at the box. I suffered panic attacks. I trusted no one and believed everyone lied to me about everything. I was lost in the ugly cesspool of depression.

It was time to take care of myself and let the agency go, but, to be honest, I didn't know how. My upbringing told me that I'd be quitting, and quitting wasn't good. Remember? Practice makes perfect; never do just half a job; don't start something unless you plan to finish it. These rituals, to my detriment, had been my automatic generator for so long, I wasn't able to discern when enough was enough. They had become Idols of worship, rather than principles to live by.

I even brought these Idols into other facets of my life, including my rigid exercise program. One day, in August of 2000, in a futile attempt to loose myself from the bonds of my deepening depression, I suited up for a casual three mile run along the back roads of my neighborhood. This was a route I'd taken countless times before and, though the roads were narrow, hilly, and windy, I felt a need to sweat out some of my demons. Admittedly, my running skills weren't the best, but in the years since my indoctrination at the police academy, I had learned how to complete a run without throwing up, and this was definitely a plus.

As I completed my first mile and a half I reached a hill that bent downward and to the right. The pavement at the bend in the road dipped abruptly, and my left ankle turned under, and me with it. I rolled to the ground scraping my entire left leg and arm; and, amazingly, though I don't remember how, my right side also became bruised and scraped. I must have done a complete tumble of some sort; a rolly-polly-pell-mell-kind-of-thing. I was a bit dazed, but I stood and brushed the debris from around the bloody scratches, and removed the grass and leaves that had embedded my scalp. I timidly placed some weight onto my left foot and astutely assessed that I had done some damage to the ankle, but figured it would survive the walk home. It didn't occur to me that it might be best to ask one of the neighbors for a ride, or even for use of their phone so that I could call for a ride.

The walk home wasn't necessarily pain free; when I arrived and sat to take a breath I couldn't help but notice that my ankle was the size of a grapefruit and medical attention was a must.

To make a very long story short, after I broke my ankle I was never able to return to work. The longer I stayed out, the more depressed and anxious I became about returning to work. It was as though being away allowed every hurtful memory to rise to the surface and taunt me. The memories and feelings caused extreme panic attacks, nightmares, migraines, constant high anxiety, fear of people, and difficulty concentrating.

The most significant event occurred when I was home attempting to make dinner one evening. As I stood in the middle of the kitchen I suddenly became overcome with fear that I didn't know how to cook a meal. If I was going to cook, what order should I make each item in? Should I make the salad first or the potatoes? What should I put in the salad? What order should I cut those things in? Where was the knife? Where was the cutting board? What if I did it wrong? For each question, I felt a fear and panic that felt like I was spinning out of control, up and into a dark and whirling tunnel with no end. In order to make dinner that night I had to firmly focus on each minute detail and promise myself over and over again that nothing bad would happen to me if I did it wrong.

Many similar tasks became burdened with the same weight. Packing a gym bag. Getting dressed in the morning. Taking the dog for a walk. Taking a shower. More complicated jobs like doing the laundry or grocery shopping became nearly impossible, but doable if I gave myself the entire day to work into it and get it done. I became increasingly frustrated as I knew that I would get worse before I got better and there was no way I could return to work in this condition. Funny thing though. For the first time in my life, I was wanting less and less to return to work. I knew these phobias were the result of years of abuse in my workplace, and I began to realize I didn't want those things, or those people, in my life anymore. I no longer valued that institution. It repulsed me.

Between August and December of 2000 I struggled with my future. I was still receiving a paycheck from the Department, and they were expecting my return to duty by January 2001. I was afraid to let go; I had grown up in that Department, but there is no doubt I suffered emotional harm by being there.

I wanted to survive. I wanted to be well. I resigned effective January 1,of 2001.

The lawsuit loomed, causing some anxiety; but, for the most part, once I resigned, I felt free to start getting well again.

The City, still angry beyond words because I had filed the suit, was refusing to negotiate with me on any kind of settlement. They even filed a particular motion called a "Summary Judgment" which was a request by the City, backed up with pages upon pages of lopsided justification, as to why the Judge should throw the whole case out of Court. By June of 2001, the Judge hadn't yet ruled on the motion, but we did have a pretrial meeting scheduled. These meetings are intended to bring both sides together in one room, in front of the Judge, to present facts, evidence, and information that will give the Judge a good idea of what direction the case is going, whether both sides are fully prepared, and how many days the case will take to present to the Jury.

On that day, myself, Slawsky, Joyce Smithy (another attorney representing me), waited in a small but elegant, Federal Court, waiting room as the City's wolf-pack entered, teeth sharpened and polished to gleaming. They always traveled in a pack. The City Attorney, Bob Sullivan, the case attorney, Bill Scott, Chief Craig Brasso, Brasso's personal attorney (whose name I never did get), Deputy Chief Irons, and two of the three Commissioners, sat around the room and awkwardly stared at one another while sitting with perfect posture, in attire meant to impress a Federal Court Judge.

The air was heavy with resentment, anxiety, and fear; so palpable it left an acidic taste in my mouth that begged for the relief of a candy mint, and created a noticeable sour odor.

A professionally dressed woman opened the lobby door and beckoned us into the Judge's conference room; we filed through the narrow door like recently unearthed mummies, speechless and robotic in our movements. Neither side wanted a group member caught in the tangle of the other group's filing in process, so we clung together like globs, making the division of our teams clear.

Now we stood before a conference table meant to bring adversaries together. Idle chit chat over who should sit where created soft, insecure vibrations through the dense air; and in the end, our teams still divided, they sat along one side and we faced them from the other. Slawsky leaned toward my right ear and whispered something meant to calm my nerves just before the Judge walked in. We all stood to give the Judge his deserved respect, then sat and waited.

"Good afternoon," the Judge said.

"Good afternoon," we all replied in unison.

"Has there been any success with regard to settling either of these cases?" he asked.

Don't forget. Karen Johnson had joined with me in filing the suit about a year or so after I had already filed.

"Not yet," said Scott, "but we have been negotiating a settlement with Johnson."

"Johnson?" The Judge asked, looking confused. "Why not the Truax case?"

"Well," Scott lied, "to tell you the truth we thought the Johnson case might settle quicker, and we haven't had time to work on the Truax issue."

What Scott wasn't saying was that they had refused to negotiate with me because they were sure my case would be thrown out at Summary Judgment. Why give me anything if they didn't have to? I can't say I disagree with that view; but, what was about to happen was the last thing they ever imagined could or would happen to their case.

I could tell that something significant was about to happen because Scott suddenly became defensive in his tone of voice, and he physically pulled away from the table and the Judge as though he no longer wanted to be in the room.

The Judge, on the other hand, was glaring at Scott, obviously angry with his response.

"Why not?" The Judge boomed, "Why haven't you made the time?"

We all looked at Scott waiting for an answer. Nothing.

"Would it help if I told you what my ruling will be on the Summary Judgment?" the Judge asked.

"Sure," Scott squeaked.

"I have reviewed the entire package," he began, "and we all know how long and detailed it is. My Summary Judgment is nearly as lengthy as your case file, and a lot more boring, but in short, I have thrown out the Johnson case because none of the incidents about which she is complaining took place within the year prior to filing. I will explain that further in a minute. With regard to the Truax case, it stands in full, with all charges against the City of Portsmouth in tact. Any claims, however, that fall before that 365 day limit cannot be brought forward. That does not mean that those incidents from years previous cannot be discussed at trial, just that they will not stand as claims against the City. If there were discriminatory incidents from years past that shed light on a current incident, I will allow that evidence to be heard by the jury."

I watched as the group across from me turned pasty white and dropped their jaws. They were obviously shocked by the ruling as they considered Johnson's case the stronger of the two. As a matter of fact, they considered my case to be totally frivolous and without merit.

"Does that help you in your efforts to find the time to negotiate a settlement in the Truax Matter?" the Judge asked.

"Yes, Your Honor," Scott said.

And that was the beginning of my settlement process, which didn't culminate until mid October of 2001. The process involved a lot of bumping and banging of heads and egos, but we got the job done. Lots of people have asked me how much I settled for, but I won't say simply because that wasn't the point. Neither was revenge the objective. Education, empathy, understanding, leveling the playing field, breaking the glass ceiling. Mostly it was about doing the right thing. So simple! If we, the human race, could make more of our decisions based on a theme of "right-ness", it seems to me that life would be a lot easier.

I believe that the true measure of success is changed lives; yet, I now know that you can't change what you don't acknowledge. So, very simply, life is a process, and the quality of that process depends wholly on each individual's ability to evaluate their personal successes and failures, and then act appropriately on that evaluation.

A failure can be turned into a success; thank God!, because if they couldn't we would be a miserable bunch of homosapiens.

So, if we understand that the only lives we have a right to dissect and evaluate is our own (provided you haven't been summoned to jury duty or you don't have offspring under the age of 18), then you must be wondering about my personal critique.

I learned an awful lot about myself along the way, some good, some bad, but all helpful. I am a different person today than I was in 1981; I'm a different person today in comparison to the person who started writing this book. Do I regret any of the decisions I made along the way? I would have to say no. I learned enough from those decisions to be the person I am today, and I like that person.

When I first came "on the job" I tried to fit in to remain unnoticed even though I stuck out like a sore thumb. Rather than speaking out when I felt threatened, hurt, or used, I clamed up thinking the harassment would end. That was the mistake. Today I speak out. I make my boundaries clear, gently and politely, if possible. But, Clear. Maybe Portsmouth Police Department was the fire I needed to walk through to understand the value of respect toward others.

My marriage to Vinny seemed like a good idea at the time, otherwise I wouldn't have done it. Today I realize, even knowing my past, I would go through the exact same torment and MORE if that's what needed to happen for me to have the same two, most beautiful and talented children that I have today. Maybe that is the test I needed to pass to realize that children are the most priceless of all gifts. So you see, God did bless my marriage.

And finally, the lawsuit. The best thing I can say about that is, "It is done. Let it remain there because Done is a good place for things that were difficult to endure." I just am not as tough as I thought.

Life is about learning and growing, and learning and growing some more. It is a process. It is a commitment to yourself. So, as you go through life, treasure these experiences as gifts. Otherwise when you reach mid-life, you just might find yourself topless at the bus stop, munching from your freshly opened bag of Gravy Train, wondering why Gray Hound won't let you board.

Printed in the United States
5887

9 780972 070539